REAL BAD, REAL SOON

REAL BAD, REAL SOON

A CARTER McCOY NOVEL

ERIC BEETNER

Praise for Real Bad, Real Soon

"Honestly, I didn't think anything would be better than Book 1 of this series, boy was I wrong. This novel shines with its unflinching exploration of the choices that define us. *Real Bad, Real Soon* is a thrilling, hard-hitting crime novel that doesn't pull punches. Do not miss this."—Best Thriller Books

"Right at the beginning of Eric Beetner's *Real Bad, Real Soon*, the follow up to his first Carter McCoy book, you know you're in the hands of a craftsman. Beetner as always, delivers twists, turns, and (more lately) pathos than the book's compact length would make you think."—The Hard Word

Praise for the First Carter McCoy Thriller,
The Last Few Miles Of Road

"Beetner breaks out with *The Last Few Miles of Road*, a perfectly crafted crime story. Terminally-ill vigilante Carter McCoy is the hero we've been waiting for, finding purpose and connection in his waning days as he weighs the moral burden of taking justice into his own hands. I absolutely loved it."—Laura McHugh, award-winning author of *What's Done in Darkness*

"Beetner has spun another notable tale here. Noir at its best."—David Swinson, author of *The Second Girl* and *Sweet Thing*

"Featuring an anti-hero straight out of an Elmore Leonard novel, *The Last Few Miles of Road* is a twisty-turny country noir with a heart of gold. Beetner conjures up a cast of memorably heartbreaking characters, featuring an angel of death killer trying to make the world better, one hit at a time, and a femme fatale in the guise of a desperate teenager, eager to live a better life than the one she was dealt. Carter and Bree are the 21st century Bonnie and Clyde, and I can't wait to see what's next for them!"—Halley Sutton, *USA Today* bestselling author of *The Hurricane Blonde*

"*The Last Few Miles Of Road* is a scintillating tale of sorrow and salvation. In aging, tortured Carter McCoy, Eric Beetner has crafted one of the least likely thriller heroes you've read about, but I dare you not to root for him!"—Joseph Reid, bestselling author of the Seth Walker series

"In *The Last Few Miles of Road*, Eric Beetner puts a welcome new spin on the revenge thriller by giving his elderly avenger an extra motivation: He only has months to live. Beetner also digs deeper into the unexpected consequences of going vigilante, resulting in a thriller that leavens the suspense with nuance and humanity."—Steve Hockensmith, author of the Holmes On The Range series

1

On his way to kill a man, Carter McCoy saved a life. His red pickup truck rolled over low rises in the road while a stiff wind blew to the East, occasionally rocking the truck to one side. While most of the rest of the country were still admiring fall foliage, Minnesotans were already planning for another long slog through winter.

Carter wasn't even supposed to be here. His diagnosis had called for him to be dead before fall, but here he was carrying on almost to Halloween. He still hadn't learned the name of the rare disorder destined to kill him before long, and he attributed some of his unexpected longevity to avoiding the name of his killer. Like his immune system was playing dumb. What you can't pronounce can't kill you.

His time through summer had been mostly peaceful. He enjoyed his reprieve and tried his best to make every day count. He lavished affection and too much ground chuck on his dog, Chester, also living well beyond his sell-by date. He ate well himself, bought some very expensive coffee beans, started watching some TV shows he'd meant to get to, and finally saw all of the James Bond films he'd missed over the years.

The brief detours from his simple happiness had come from his new avocation. After he'd proven that he could kill another man if it meant doing it for what he felt were the right reasons, he'd gotten some assignments from a local detective. Carter knew his loose association with the law might be the only thing keeping him out of jail, though he also figured Detective DeFore didn't have the evidence to put him behind bars for the murder of Justin Fields or of Eddie Durrand, or the killings he didn't even know

Carter had been involved in. But Carter had taken the jobs figuring if he could mete out a little justice in his final days, he could help some very bad people from going unpunished.

It didn't sit well on him.

There was a lot of self-convincing he had to do the first time he killed anyone, and that was for deeply personal reasons. Retribution for his daughter. A missing gap in the justice system. He'd only done it once for the detective on a case he had no connection to at all. This new assignment would make his second, and he didn't feel good about it. Couldn't make himself feel right no matter how hard he tried.

It had taken a few weeks to work up the courage to make the drive out to see a man who, according to DeFore, had killed his wife and gotten away with it. "Without remorse," DeFore had said.

Finally, he convinced himself this was worth doing. Although it was harder to justify killing a man who had gotten away with murder when that very description fit Carter perfectly. He felt as certain as he was going to, so he left Chester at home and climbed into his truck.

Overnight it had dipped below zero for the first time that year. Anyone native to Minnesota adjusted to winter driving easily, but transplants didn't know the signs for hidden ice, the way to make a turn without spinning out, and when to switch to winter tires. It wasn't quite new tire weather yet, but Carter sat at a stop light and watched as the SUV in the lane crossing his came in too fast, didn't see the patch of fresh ice, and tried to over compensate, which led to him driving off the road and into a ditch, flipping the SUV over on its roof.

Carter shifted into PARK and got out, not bothering with a jacket or gloves. A lifetime in the upper Midwest had turned his blood thick and his skin impervious to a little late fall wind. He reached the SUV and found the driver alone, hung upside down and dangling from his seatbelt. A wide gash had opened on the bridge of his nose, and he bled into his eyes as the cut ran red across his forehead and into his hairline.

Carter leaned into the broken driver's side window. "Hey, buddy?"

The man didn't answer beyond a choked grunt. His face had gone dark red from the blood rushing to his upside-down head, but Carter could see another form of distress there as well.

"Hey, you doing okay?"

The deflated airbag hung limply draped across the dashboard. The driver's side window had broken inward, and tiny hexagons of safety glass were scattered around the inside of the SUV like loose diamonds after a heist. Carter tugged at the door, but it was jammed against the side of the ditch and would not open. He reached in and felt the man's pulse at his neck. He was so stiff and tense, Carter could barely get a feel for it.

"I'm gonna let you down, okay buddy?"

He leaned in farther and unclipped the seatbelt. The man tumbled down on top of Carter. He was a good-sized adult, six foot one or two, probably over two hundred pounds. He pinned Carter to the roof of the SUV, and Carter could not push him off.

"Little help there, pal," Carter squeezed out. The man only squirmed and turned over on his stomach, but still held Carter down like a wrestler going for the win.

Carter pulled and managed to slide himself almost free, lifting his shirt and thermal undershirt up to expose most of his torso to the wind and the sharp edges of the glass scattered everywhere. The man muttered what Carter thought was a swear word, but he couldn't make it out cleanly. With a final pull, he slid out from under, fixed his shirt to cover himself again, and took a closer look at the man who was clearly in distress.

Heart attack, Carter figured. It might have been that which took him off the road rather than any hidden ice. The man couldn't speak, so Carter had no idea if he was a native Minnesotan. But he did know the man needed help.

He was no longer thinking about the man he had been planning to kill as he got the driver over on his back and started giving CPR. He gave twenty pushes on the man's chest and then sat back for a short break. He pulled out his phone and set it on the ceiling of the SUV. He dialed 911, set it to speaker, then resumed pushing on the man's chest, even as his own chest started aching with the effort.

"Nine-one-one, what's your emergency?"

"Car crash with a rollover. I think the guy's having a heart attack. I'm doing CPR."

Carter gave the dispatcher the intersection and then had to take another breather. He didn't like to wait too long between chest compressions, but unless the ambulance had room for two heart attacks, he needed to rest.

The man was still breathing, at least, so Carter knew he was doing some good. Carter's artificial pumping made the blood flow from the wound on the man's nose, so Carter knew blood was moving. Blood had found tiny rivers and creases in the man's face and spread across in every direction, so his face looked like he'd walked through a blood-red spider web.

By the time the ambulance arrived, Carter was worn out. He slid out of the SUV and laid down on the banks of the ditch while two paramedics took over and worked the man out of the SUV.

A paramedic gave Carter a quick once-over and offered to take him to the hospital as well, but Carter declined. He'd had enough of hospitals. They offered nothing but bad news to him.

He rested for a while after the ambiance had left, then gave a short statement to the police, got back in his truck, and drove home. Both the driver of the SUV and another man would live for a little longer.

The truck made a new rattling sound that hadn't been there before as Carter pulled up in front of his isolated farmhouse. He'd deal with the truck later. He got out, arms sore and ribs aching after his CPR, and walked tentatively to the porch. When his feet hit the steps, he heard Chester inside give a single bark. His home security system. Something had changed with his age, he noticed. Soreness used to live in his muscles. If he'd done a full day of yard work, played ice hockey, climbed too many stairs—he felt it in his calves, his arms, his abdomen. Now, he felt it in his bones. The pain ran deeper, and it held on longer, rooted inside him.

Carter went inside, and Chester's tail thumped twice on the floor. He hadn't even gotten up to bark at the possible intruder. Carter dropped the keys onto the side table just inside the door, went to the back door, and opened it for Chester. He knew he didn't have the energy to take the old dog out for a proper walk, but all Chester wanted to do, really, was to have the run of the back yard and its symphony of smells. Carter moved back to the couch, landed there in a heap, and let out a long breath.

In addition to the aches from his exertion in saving the SUV driver's life, he felt a grip of pain in his stomach. His illness had no pattern to when it reared its head, but when it did, it came at him like a knife-wielding mugger in a dark alley. He'd resisted the urge to rely on pain pills, even when the doctors seemed all too eager to get him dosed on a steady stream of opioids and sedatives. He breathed deep and shut his eyes.

Chester gave a short glance to the open back door, but could sense Carter's distress. He pushed up off the floor and took a moment to set himself before he climbed awkwardly onto the couch and laid his head on Carter's leg. Carter scratched the old boy's ear and it helped drain away some of the pain.

"Don't even ask," he said to the dog. "You wouldn't believe me anyway."

Carter pushed out a long, slow breath between pursed lips. Chester made a low whine deep in his throat.

He thought of Ava, his wife. A heart attack had taken her. He hadn't been able to do anything about it at the time. He'd have kept up until his own heart gave out if that's what it would have taken back then. There had to be something to it that made the killing okay. His desperate need to be *doing* something. To save someone or to even a score. None of it made much sense if he thought about it too long, but he knew there was something to it, some explanation.

The more cynical side of him worried that his empathy died with her and his daughter, Audrey. That he could now do these things because of an emptiness carved out.

The pain in his gut faded slowly away; the killer retreated to the shadows again. He stood and tapped his leg.

"C'mon, boy."

Chester got up even more slowly and followed Carter to the back door. Carter sat in a chair looking out over the long green stretch of back yard. The cold would come soon and knock all the green to brown, cover it in snow, and send the critters Chester loved to chase underground. He hadn't spent a winter with Chester yet. Neither one of them was supposed to make it this long. Carter watched Chester put his nose to the ground and start his detailed exploration of the yard and thought about how much he looked forward to sitting inside by a fire with Chester and a good record on the stereo.

SUMMER

The piece of paper with a name and address sat on his kitchen table for a week. Carter tried not to look at it, but it drew his eye every time he walked into the room. He knew he should throw it away, to ignore the request from the detective. Something made him keep the paper where it was. A bad man, Detective DeFore had said. A bad man who got away with it and was walking free. An injustice.

Carter had just been through more violence than he thought he'd ever endure in his lifetime, all crammed into a couple weeks. He wanted nothing more than to leave it behind. He also knew the truth of it. He had rid the world of some bad people. Men not worth the dirt it would take to bury them. Predators of the innocent. The people left behind, they were better off without these monsters breathing the same air. Carter believed this to his core.

And the detective seemed to know what he had done and now asked for his help. The asking came with a clenched fist of motivation behind it. DeFore would ignore what he knew about the killings Carter had already been involved in. He'd trade his silence for this help, for Carter to act where the justice system had failed. But this was far beyond what Carter expected when he launched his plan to kill Justin Lyons. That was to be a one-time, personal score he needed to settle. This was murder for hire.

But wasn't it the same thing?

DeFore had danced around the request. "If you have the time," he'd said. It almost made Carter laugh. He had no idea how much time he had left.

The detective had made himself clear, but without saying anything, really.

He knew Carter could step in where justice had failed. Technicalities, mistakes, greedy lawyers plea bargaining killers out onto the street. It happened. On TV, in big cities, right here where Carter lived and DeFore worked.

Just a couple of pals talking. Musing about what ifs. Like, what if this guy didn't get away with it after all?

Carter set down a plate for Chester and listened to the room fill with his sloppy, jowly feeding ritual. He finally touched the paper, lifted it, and looked at the name. A man who should be in prison. A man who did not deserve to be walking free.

Chester looked up from his now empty plate, a line of drool hanging from his lip. Carter tipped back his bottle of Coke and finished it off. He'd go out for dinner and think about it. Maybe burgers tonight. Get a shake with it, onion rings. He'd think about it and come to the decision that this man, too, had to pay for his sins.

Chester sat shotgun. The piece of paper now sat on the dashboard of the truck, guiding Carter to his first look at the man he intended to kill. He knew he needed to do some reconnaissance. It had worked with Justin Lyons. He didn't like that he had developed an M.O., a way of going about a murder, but the facts were irrefutable. He didn't want to simply show up at the man's house and kill him. He needed to know what he was walking into and a little of who this person was. DeFore had said rape. Somehow uglier in Carter's mind than murder. There's little else a man can do to a woman to take more from her. Men like that needed to be locked up. Or buried.

Carter held no vengeance in his heart, or so he thought. He didn't burn with hate the way some men do. He didn't see the need to strike out at another man, had never been in a fight. Now that he had short time on his hands, this was a service he felt he could provide.

"Let's check it out," he said to Chester.

He stopped across the street and a few doors down from the address he'd been given. The house was a small home with a high-peaked roof in a faded red that needed repainting. He read the name again, Wayne

Hedstrom. A sedan sat in the driveway. The yard was simple. No flowers or border-defining bushes. Carter guessed Wayne lived alone.

He gave Chester a scratch on the ears. "What do you think?" Chester snorted. "I know you want me to go get us some dinner, huh, boy? You don't understand any of this. Be grateful. I wish I had your untarnished view of the world."

He wasn't sure what he would learn from watching the house, but it also put off the task itself. His stakeout was procrastination, and he knew it.

The front door opened, and Wayne stepped out. He was a portly man, carrying all his extra weight in his gut, which hung out over his belt. His hairline had receded back to the crown of his head and he walked with a stiffness that said to Carter he wasn't much for physical activity. He wore a plaid flannel shirt and tan corduroys with a simple light jacket. He shuffled to the sedan and got in.

"Looks like we got some following to do," Carter said to Chester. "You're a hunting dog, right?"

Carter followed him to a diner. Wayne hauled himself out of the car and made his way inside. Carter could see him through the glass as he sat himself at the counter and didn't even open a menu.

"Well, I haven't eaten yet." Chester gave him a crooked look. "I'll bring you something. I promise."

Inside, Carter found the seat next to Wayne. He could have sat with one seat between them, might have been smarter, but his hearing wasn't what it used to be. Again, he wasn't sure what all he could learn from sitting next to the man, but he needed dinner anyhow.

A waitress who Carter could tell had been on the job too many years set down a cup of coffee in front of Wayne and handed Carter a menu.

"What's good?" he asked.

"The Italian place down the road."

He smiled at her, but she kept a stoic expression. "Make it a burger and fries. Chocolate shake on the side."

She wrote it down and went away.

"Smart choice," Wayne said.

Carter turned on his stool. "Oh yeah?"

"They keep adding things to the menu like short ribs or chicken teriyaki, but about all they do well is a burger and fries. The fried chicken isn't too bad."

Carter nodded, and Wayne went back to the paperback book in his hand. Some military thriller with a picture of a fighter jet over the Capitol on the front and a well-worn spine as if he'd read and re-read this book many times. Up close, Wayne seemed to Carter to be about in his mid-fifties. He looked around, and everyone else in the diner was on their phones, even those not eating alone. A couple of old geezers, him and Wayne, content on their off-ramp of the information superhighway.

The waitress brought Wayne's food, his burger piled high with bacon. When she turned around, Wayne caught Carter's eye and thrust his chin out at the waitress.

"Not the best, but she'll get you where you want to go."

Carter didn't know what to say to that. Wayne didn't seem to care about a response. He regarded his plate.

"That's the way it ought to be, am I right? The natural order of things. Women serving men. It's how it was in the old days, am I right? You were there, old timer. Nowadays, who knows what you're gonna get? Hard to find one that'll be happy cooking and cleaning like she's supposed to."

Carter was stunned. He thought hard about what to say, but again, Wayne didn't seem to care for a dialogue. He seemed satisfied to run his mouth as if the thoughts had found a way to spill out past his teeth without his realizing it.

Through a mouth full of half-chewed beef and bacon, Wayne said, "These days, it's hard to tell if you even get a real woman with all these he/shes running around. Never used to be like that, am I right? And they want to use our bathrooms? I don't think so." He let out a sort of laugh, and a wad of chewed burger and bacon sailed across the counter.

Times had indeed changed in Carter's lifetime, but he never thought of women that way. As servants to men. As objects to be owned or bossed around. His mother had a job working in a hair salon, and he saw not only the extra money it brought in, but the enjoyment and satisfaction she got from her work. He liked to think he never tried to put Ava into that box and that they raised Audrey with an eye toward more than merely a husband. He came here wanting to know about Wayne, but he already learned enough, so he tuned him out.

An industrial coffee maker and a poster of how to administer the Heimlich maneuver had never been more interesting to Carter. He studied them intently while listening to his seat-mate chew louder than Chester. When the waitress returned with his cheeseburger, he said, "Can I get another one to go, add bacon, and lose the lettuce, tomato, and the bun?"

She blinked twice at him.

"It's for my dog."

This satisfied her, and she went away. Carter ate and kept his focus on the plate. He'd heard enough from the portly man to his left. It wouldn't hold up in court as reasons for justifiable homicide, but if he was looking for corroboration of the accusations DeFore had leveled against the man, he got them.

Wayne ate like a starved man and finished in no time. He snapped his fingers twice to call the waitress back. He put down a twenty-dollar bill and let her take it away.

"They got a younger one here too. I try to come when it's her shift, but I never know for sure."

Again, Carter didn't know if he was trying to have a conversation or if these thoughts merely slid out unconsciously. What he did know was that he feared for the younger waitress. If this man had urges, he could not control, and if he now felt like he'd gotten away with it and could not be touched by the law, then he may become bold about his crimes. That meant this young waitress could be a target.

Carter had done his scouting. He'd made up his mind. Wayne Hedstrom had to go.

The public library had three computer terminals set up in a far-off corner that anyone could use for free. Nobody did anymore since they all had more powerful computers in their pockets, but they kept any sketchy internet searches off your phone or home computer. Carter sat alone in the corner on a computer still attached to a chunky CRT monitor. No flat screens for the public library in Bellington. No ergonomic chairs for the patrons. Not even new carpeting since the Clinton administration. His research turned up a solution to an idea he had but wasn't sure he could implement. He needed very few supplies, and he could do the job on Wayne.

The two types of fuse he found burned at thirty seconds per foot or thirty-eight seconds. He chose the faster fuse. He bought one fifty-foot spool in bright green, and the sales clerk never asked what he intended to use it for. So many things in the farm supply store could have been used for killing purposes. Carter didn't like that he saw the aisles that way now. Sharpened tools and poison pellets now had a different meaning to him with his new line of work.

He fought the instinct to be pleased with his idea for how to dispose of Wayne. He didn't want to be proud or to get good at this, but he couldn't deny a feeling of self-satisfaction in figuring out the solution to his wild idea.

In the three days it took him to source the fuse and to make his plans, he drove by the diner each day and looked through the window, once at breakfast, once at lunch, and once at dinner. On his third attempt, he saw the younger waitress. Still there, safe for now.

On the third day, Carter loaded Chester in the truck after sundown and drove to Wayne's house. He sat and waited until the lights went out inside and then stepped out. All that sitting made his muscles stiff. He groaned as he unfolded his body from the front seat and tried to straighten out. After a moment of shaking his arms and legs out to get the blood flowing, he walked to Wayne's driveway.

Carter had printouts of the areas of the engine he needed. He bent down and slowly lowered himself to the cold concrete of the driveway and then shimmied himself under the car. Using the flashlight on his phone, he checked his paper with the view from under the engine.

It took some doing, several scraped knuckles, and a full minute to clean some debris from his eye, which left it red and irritated. He tried not to use any tape if he didn't have to, instead wrapping and looping the fuse around metal bits. He wasn't sure how much investigation this would get, but the less evidence he left, the better. Tape held fingerprints better than anything else in the world.

He ran the fuse from the engine back along the underside of the car and to the gas tank. He used an awl he found in his garage to poke a tiny hole in the top of the tank and pushed the fuse through. The fit was tight, and he had confidence in his design.

It took Carter a while to stand back up. He ached all over, and the cold of the concrete had gone through him, soaking up into his bones like a sponge drinking from the cold, hard ground. He brushed off, checked around to see that nobody saw him, then made it back to the truck.

At first, he thought about maybe staying the night, seeing the fruits of his handiwork in the morning, but then Chester let loose with some of his famously lethal gas, and the idea of being trapped in a small space with the old coon hound lost its appeal.

Carter drove home, lit a fire, poured a whiskey, and slept with Chester on the couch.

At four a.m. Carter jerked awake. Chester lifted his head up off the couch and a line of drool flung off his jowls and landed on a cushion. When the pain gripped Carter, he always expected to look down at his gut and see a hole bored straight through. He tried to sit up, but bending in the middle made the pain worse, so he shut his eyes and grit his teeth through the pain. He knew it wouldn't last long, but nothing about his disease was predictable so far. But it wasn't only his illness. He'd come from a fitful dream. Alongside the sharp stab of pain, he felt guilt and regret for what he'd done to Wayne. The new Carter didn't sit well yet. The man capable of such things.

After ten minutes, he was able to sit up. He went to the kitchen and found his bottle of pain pills. He took one, bending down to drink straight from the faucet. Three left. He would have to call in for more if the pains were going to be this bad.

Chester wandered in and stood beside him.

"I guess we're up now, huh?" He scratched at the long ears of his best friend. "Course, you're never more than a few seconds away from sleep."

He pulled on a coat and held the door open for Chester. A thick dew clung to the grass. Chester barked once, low and musical. A trio of deer at the tree line jumped and ducked into the woods. Years ago, Chester might have followed, but not now. Not at four-thirty in the morning.

Carter held open the door to the truck and lifted Chester inside. They drove to the address on the piece of paper.

Wayne was still asleep, the car still parked in the driveway. Carter watched as the sun crept up and birds began to wake up and call out morning greetings. He thought of disconnecting the fuse. Giving Wayne a second chance. He thought of the waitress. He thought of the other women DeFore said had been Wayne's victims. What was their morning like? What thoughts vaulted them from sleep at four a.m.?

He sat and watched.

Around five-thirty, Chester's snores lulled Carter to sleep. When he woke, it was past eight. The car was still in the driveway. He opened the door and lifted Chester down, let him roam a bit and do his business, delighting in the fresh and unfamiliar smells of a new neighborhood. Other cars pulled away from their homes, trips to the office or out for errands had begun.

Chester latched onto the scent of a cat and followed it along a fence line. Carter heard a car start behind him. He turned to see brake lights on Wayne's sedan.

"Chester. C'mere, boy."

Chester had no intention of giving up the scent of the cat. He remained focused, nose down, turning his head side to side to follow the last known whereabouts of his prey.

A coffee mug sat on the roof of Wayne's car, forgotten there. Reverse lights came on, then went out. The door opened, and Wayne leaned out, his hand reaching up blindly for the mug.

"Chester, let's go."

Chester turned to look at Carter, then dipped his head again and picked up the scent.

Wayne had to get out and stand up. He lifted the travel mug, then bent himself back into the car with a grunt Carter could hear from across the street. Brake lights came on again, then the reverse lights. The sedan backed out, and the white reverse lights winked off, and the car moved forward. He drove past where Carter stood doing math in his head—thirty seconds a foot. How long had it been?

Carter grabbed Chester by his collar. "We're going. Come on."

Chester reluctantly gave up the hunt and let Carter lead him back to the truck. Carter bent and lifted, letting out his own grunt with the effort. He set Chester down on the bench seat, wondering how many more times he could lift the old dog before his back gave out, when he heard the explosion.

At the end of the block, paused at a stop light, Wayne's sedan was in flames. His plan had worked. A bit of spycraft in suburban Minnesota.

Carter watched to see if Wayne would stumble out, perhaps coughing out smoke, perhaps on fire himself. But the car continued to burn aggressively. Black smoke obscured the windows, and Carter could not see in to tell if Wayne was alive and in agony or if the blast had killed him. Either way, once again, Carter McCoy was a killer.

Three days later, Detective Brian DeFore showed up at Carter's house. He stood on the porch in a loose tie and a sly grin.

"Clever, Mr. McCoy."

Chester barked twice and then sniffed DeFore's feet, deciding he was no threat. Carter didn't invite the detective inside.

"Part of me wants to see the file on this guy, see what all he did to deserve this. I'm taking a lot on faith with you."

"I can't remove files from the building. You'll have to trust me. A very bad man is off the streets."

Carter nodded and worked his tongue along his teeth to dislodge a raspberry seed.

"Probably should have been in jail."

"Definitely should have. But this gets the job done, too. I came by to say thank you."

"No fruit basket? No bouquet of flowers? Not even a cigar or a bottle of nice whiskey?"

"That would constitute payment, and that would make this a whole different transaction."

Carter folded his arms across his chest. "And what is it now? Just two old friends doing favors for each other?"

"Something like that."

"I see what I did for you. What is it I'm getting out of this?"

DeFore turned and regarded the wide open space around Carter's home. "You're here, instead of in jail."

Carter nodded slowly, finally got the seed free from its trap. "I see how it is."

"I'm saying thanks. I'm trying to be nice here."

"Just so long as I understand the nature of this quid pro quo."

DeFore gave a dry laugh. "You using Latin on me?"

"I'm from a generation who learned it in school."

"We don't have to be antagonistic, Mr. McCoy. There are real-world benefits to this arrangement."

Carter leaned against the door jamb. "I don't like it, detective. I don't like the way it feels. I don't care for planning another man's death."

"You sure seem good at it."

"An accident, I'm sure. But I take no pleasure in it."

"That's what makes you good. I don't want some psycho running around with a taste for blood. All I wanted was a few bad apples taken off the table. I know you feel the same way. Nobody has missed Justin Lyons, right? Well, nobody's gonna miss Wayne Hedstrom."

"I suppose not. That all you came out here for?"

DeFore smiled and took a step back. "Just a friendly visit to say thanks. You're right, though. Next time, I'll bring the whiskey."

"No offense, detective, but I hope there isn't a next time."

"I hope so, too. And you can call me Brian. Should I call you Carter? Seems like we earned it."

Carter put a hand on the door, ready to close. "I think we're doing fine as is. Goodbye, detective." The door closed. DeFore stood for another moment, then, with a shake of his head, turned and walked away.

At the beginning of October, he returned with another name and address on a piece of paper. And a gun.

FALL

Dew on the grass turned to crystals and nearly all the leaves had fallen from the trees. Carter was up before the sun again and held a coffee mug in both hands for the warmth. Steam rose from the cup as he stood on the back porch, waiting for Chester to descend the stairs and begin his sniffing ritual. But today, Chester hesitated. "Too cold for you, bud?" He patted Chester's ribs a few times. "I hear you."

Carter turned and went back inside. Chester followed. A slow morning followed where Carter read a little, piled laundry but stopped short of running the washer, and then around ten, fell back asleep for a bit on the couch. He woke hungry, coffee the only thing he'd ingested so far that day, and decided he needed a good meal. He let Chester out to handle his business and sniff around now that the sun had warmed the grass enough for the dog, then he got in his truck and headed to Mesa Grande.

He hadn't been in as regularly as he used to. Seeing Ivana gave a stark reminder of the violent spring Carter had tried to forget. The melancholy but pleasant memories Mesa Grande held before, dinners with Ava and time quietly spent, were now blood-stained.

Still, he enjoyed seeing Ivana. He stepped inside and she looked up from the small kitchen pass-through window and brightened at seeing him. She seemed happy since her husband was out of her life, though behind the thin smile, he could see a longing for her daughter. Katy and Bree made their escape to California and had no plans to return. Carter knew what it was like to lose a daughter, and though Ivana had only lost Katy to a thousand miles or so and not forever, he empathized.

Ivana came out from the kitchen, the sweep of the door bringing smells of spices and seared meat with her. Lunchtime always did well at Mesa Grande. Nobody who ate there only came once. She had a regular stream of familiar faces and usual orders. Carter took a small table and grinned at the full house of people enjoying Ivana's cooking. She waved off the full-time waitress who had come on over the summer and lightened the load for Ivana immeasurably. A young woman recommended by Carter. A woman who used to work at a diner on the other side of town.

"Carter. So good to see you."

"Always good to see you, Ivana. Any word from Katy?"

"Doing well, last I heard. Both had jobs, a small apartment. They go to the beach every weekend."

"Must be nice."

She put a hand on his shoulder and squeezed, an unspoken thank you between them every time he came. He appreciated it, but wanted her to move on. To stop the reminders of the violence he caused.

"I'll get you the usual," she said and rushed off to tend to her kitchen.

Aileen, the waitress, passed by and gave Carter a smile. She didn't know what Ivana had told her about her best regular customer, but he knew it wasn't all she had to tell. Would she smile if she knew what he had done?

Carter ate his enchiladas until past being full, finished his horchata, and then, when he paid the bill with a twenty left behind on the table, held the folded piece of paper with a name and address in it in his hand. He had another stop to make.

The gun came from an evidence locker, so DeFore told him. It was a revolver and looked like it belonged on the hip of an old west sheriff. When DeFore had delivered it, Carter refused to take it at first. "I don't want it."

"You might need it. And it's clean. At least there's no connection to you."

Carter gave the detective a squint-eyed stare. "You can just do this? It's breaking the law."

DeFore sighed. He set the gun on Carter's kitchen table.

"You know as well as I do, McCoy, that this is a parking ticket compared to what this guy did. And let me tell you something, if a creep like him can get away with it, the law *is* broken."

Carter went to the fridge for a beer. He didn't offer DeFore one.

"What does it say about me that I can do this?"

"It says you believe in justice. In fixing something and making it right."

"Is that why you got into law enforcement? To make it right?"

DeFore lifted his chin. He knew Carter was trying to goad him, but he felt confident in this new arrangement. "It is. And this is part of it, even if it's a little outside the regulations. This is sometimes the way justice gets served." DeFore went to the fridge on his own, got a beer for himself, twisted off the top. "Not too long ago, the law would go and string up a man like this. No trial, no judge. Solve the problem at the end of a rope. If you ask me, we've come a little too far from that."

"Jesus, that's—"

"Tell me I'm wrong, Carter." He sipped on his beer. Foam overflowed from the neck when he took it down. He swallowed, watching Carter with fixed eyes, neither one blinking. "Tell me I'm wrong."

Carter said nothing.

The man in question had been accused of the abduction and murder of at least three young women. The case had been thrown out due to some discrepancy in testimony and some minor infraction by the police when they were gathering evidence. Carter remembered the case from the news. Most everyone seemed to think the man had done it and there was outrage that he wasn't convicted.

Since the trial went bust, even more cases had been linked to him, at least through gossip and hearsay. These were the families Carter thought of on his way to the address. The ones left behind.

He knew the feeling, living long after someone you love has been taken from you. The unnatural order of a child going before their parents. He knew it too well.

Maybe it was the coming cold, but he felt hardened. This time, he didn't hesitate, or at least hesitated less. He didn't stalk and scout. He didn't want to think about it too much, to feel as if he were hunting this man. Just do it. Take the gun and do it.

Vernon Holliman, originally from Canada. Fifty-eight years old. A Midwestern sales chief for a vinyl siding company. Bland as a bowl of bran flakes and exactly the kind of man the news loves to pin a crime like this on. Unsuspected. Unremarkable. The kind of guy who could live next to you right now. Proof that you never can tell what monsters lurk in plain sight.

When Carter parked, he couldn't help but notice the siding on Vernon's house looked a little tired and worn. Guess he wasn't using his employee discount on his own home.

He wished he had a holster for the revolver, but instead tucked it into the waistband of his jeans and pulled his coat down over it. The metal was cold against his skin. Not exactly fit for a quick draw, but if Vernon wasn't expecting him, then the element of surprise was still on Carter's side.

He moved quickly up the walk, intently not thinking about what he was about to do. He thought of getting back home to Chester with the plate of ground beef and tortillas Ivana had prepared for him. She loved feeding that dog as much as she loved feeding Carter.

A million tiny decisions. Ring the bell or knock? What should be the last sound he hears?

Carter knocked. He looked over both shoulders at the empty street. Nobody out and about to see. He moved his hand up under his coat. The gun had warmed to his body temperature.

The door opened, and a woman stood there.

Carter let his mouth drop open, but didn't make a sound.

"May I help you?"

"Sorry," he said. "Wrong address. I was looking for Vernon."

Her expression darkened. "I'm his wife. He's not here."

A wife. Would have been nice of DeFore to mention that.

"Sorry, then."

"We're separated," she said. There was a lot packed into her two words. She seemed to want Carter to know she was no longer with a man accused of his crimes. To know she was no accomplice. "After the trial." She left no doubt.

"Sorry to bother you." Carter turned to leave.

"He doesn't live here anymore. In case you were thinking of coming back." Carter stopped and turned to face her. "I kicked him out."

She was tall and thin with silver hair that ran past her shoulders. She had a stately appearance. A matriarch. All bones and sinew and a tough exterior from all she'd been through in life, yet still feminine and light.

"I'll look for him somewhere else, then."

"Are you from one of the victim's families?"

He didn't know what to say.

"I figured you right away for one of the dads." She evaluated him again. "Or a grandfather."

"No," he said. "I'm not."

"I keep expecting them to come. Someone who wants to face him. You're the first, though."

She seemed suddenly fragile. Carter shook his head.

"I'm not from one of the families."

"Are you with the police?"

He didn't quite know how to answer that.

"No, ma'am."

"You're not a friend. I'd have seen you. You're not the press; they don't give up that easily. You did come here to confront him, didn't you?" The way she asked didn't seem to need an answer. Carter wondered if the gun was showing.

"I've already bothered you enough."

He turned to walk away again.

"I wish someone would."

Carter stopped. A chill breeze kicked up and crept in under his collar.

"I keep waiting," she said, "for someone to come here looking for revenge or blood or some sort of justice. I wish maybe I'd done something when I had the chance."

Carter let her talk.

"I can see it in your eyes, y'know?" she said. "The loss."

"I don't think you understand."

She took a step out of the door, wrapped her arms around herself against the cold.

"My mistake then. I thought you were here about what my husband did."

He could see quite a bit in her eyes, too. The hurt. The humiliation. The guilt.

"You think he did it?"

"Yes, I do. Mr...?"

He hesitated, not sure if it was a good idea. "McCoy. Carter McCoy."

"Mr. McCoy, I didn't want to believe it. I tried for a very long time not to. But through the start of the trial, I could see it in him. He was afraid in a way no innocent man would be. And then he was freed, when it all fell apart, the relief and the joy weren't of a man who avoided being wrongly accused. I don't know how to describe the difference, but he was a man who knew he'd gotten away with it."

She gave a slight shiver, and Carter thought about offering her his coat.

"That's when I kicked him out. I haven't seen him since. I wish I'd never met him. And I wish to God I had noticed something and could have helped those girls. I can't believe I was so blind. So if you're here to exact your pound of flesh, Mr. McCoy…I want you to get it."

"Well, ma'am—"

"Veronica."

"Do you happen to know where he is now, Veronica?"

She shook her head. "He's retired, so he doesn't have to go to an office. He hasn't called because I told him not to. If you're working with the police, maybe there are credit card records or something. If you're not…" She gave another shiver. Her own body heat wasn't enough to beat back the chill. Her silver hair and thin frame made her look brittle in the cold, as if she might crack like thin ice. Her eyes wanted something from Carter. A resolution. An answer to who her husband truly was.

"Thanks for your help."

Carter turned again and walked down the path.

"I've been waiting for someone to come," she called after him. "Someone must want justice for those girls."

Carter didn't turn around.

The hospital loomed before him like a thick shelf of snow threatening to tumble into an avalanche at any second. He hated being here, but he hadn't stopped by for himself. The reception desk was as calm and generic as any office building. Two women sat behind a pane of Plexiglas in civilian clothes. Not nurses.

"I'm wondering if you can help me. A man was checked in the other day. He had a heart attack while driving. An ambulance came and got him."

The woman closest to him in a bright blue top poised her hands over her keyboard.

"His name?"

"I'm not sure."

She gave him a skeptical look.

"I helped him on the scene. I didn't get his name."

"What do you mean?"

"I saw his car go off the road, and I stopped to give him CPR. All I really want to know is if he lived or not."

The other woman chimed in. "I remember that one, Sheila."

Sheila in the bright blue gladly turned over the problem to her coworker in a sweater with red hearts.

"You're the good Samaritan," said the woman in the sweater.

Carter could disabuse her of that notion real quick if he wanted to, but he said, "I guess so."

"He's alive," she said and she tapped a few keystrokes. "Second floor. Room two-oh-six."

"I don't need to visit. I just wanted to make sure he's all right."

She scowled at him. "Oh, you have to go see him. His wife's been crazy about wanting to meet you."

"No, no. That's okay."

She stood, her head almost clearing the Plexiglass. "You have to go." She pointed to the elevator bank. "Ruben Barnes. Second floor. When you get off the elevator, turn left. See the desk up there."

Carter felt her stare and was sure that if he turned and walked out the sliding doors up front that she would chase him down in the parking lot and drag him back inside like a child who doesn't want to go to school.

The elevator let him off on two; he turned left and approached the desk. This was a working floor, and nurses manned the desk. They looked busy, even though they were sitting. Both wore tight ponytails and purple scrubs. No makeup, just a square look on their faces that gave you comfort that if something went wrong, they'd fix it, whether that was your appendix or your transmission.

"Hi, um, I'm looking for Ruben Barnes."

"Family?"

"Uh, no, I just…kinda met him the other day."

The hum of machinery and low murmur of people in other rooms hung in the air as thick as the smell of antiseptic. A phone rang and one of the women snatched it up before it could ring twice. The woman focused on Carter never took her eyes off him.

"You don't have a visitor pass."

"The lady downstairs sent me up here. She didn't give me anything."

"You need a visitor pass." She picked up a phone and pressed a single button. "This is Rita on two. You sent a guy up here without a pass?" She waited for an answer. "Okay, I'm sending him back down." She listened for a moment, then looked at Carter, studying him closer now. "He is?" After a brief explanation from the other end, she hung up. She waved a hand.

"Go ahead, two-oh-six. Nice work, by the way."

Carter moved down the hall, careful not to look to either side and see inside one of the rooms. Even though his time in the hospital had been for tests, he always noticed the lack of privacy. He could be in a gown or laid out on a table waiting for someone to come and take blood, and doors would be open, people milling around, private conversations broadcast for the entire ward to hear. Plus, he didn't want to see anyone sick. He knew that was absurd inside a hospital, but the more he avoided the trappings of illness, the more he could deny his own.

The door to two-zero-six was ajar. He knocked lightly.

A woman's voice. "Come in."

He pushed inside and stopped, barely past the door.

"Hello." He recognized Ruben in the bed. He'd been up close to him long enough he doubted he'd ever forget the face. It was clear Ruben did not recognize him, though.

"I'm Carter. I, uh…I was with Ruben after his accident."

The woman, his wife Carter assumed, broke into a wide grin and let out a gasp like she'd just been given a diamond ring. "Are you the man who saved him?"

"Well, the paramedics did that. I just kept him hanging on a bit until they got there."

"Oh!" She ran to him and wrapped her arms around him. She was a short woman with dark hair, a dark complexion for Minnesota, and, Carter discovered, a strong grip. Over her shoulder he could see Ruben in bed was also smiling at him, though less enthusiastically due to the EKG monitor and oxygen tubes.

"Thank you, thank you, thank you, thank you," she said. "You saved his life."

Carter wanted out. He'd wanted to avoid this, but he let himself be guilted into it.

"No, no. I did what anyone would have done."

"No, you saved him. You saved my husband."

She hadn't let go, her face buried in his chest and her hair tickling under his chin. He wanted to tell her his insides were a disease-ridden mess and to stop squeezing him, but he let her get it all out. He felt like a fraud. He may have helped keep Ruben alive, but he was no lifesaver. The opposite.

He didn't deserve praise.

"I'm so glad you came." She released him, looked into his face through tear-stained eyes, then grabbed him again.

"I just wanted to make sure you were doing okay."

"He's alive. That's all that matters." She released him again and looked him in the eye. "Because of you."

"It's really no big deal."

"No big deal? Most people wouldn't have stopped. Most people wouldn't have kept giving him CPR for so long. The paramedics said you must have done it for ten minutes."

"I don't know. It was kind of a blur."

"That's what they said. You saved him. You really saved him."

He needed to escape. He couldn't stand to hear her any longer.

"I should go. Like I said, I just wanted to see that he was okay."

Ruben held out a hand. An IV line was taped to him, and a plastic bracelet with his name and blood type. Carter didn't want to shake it, but he knew if he did, he could leave. He stepped closer and took Ruben's hand. Ruben had a grip as tight as his wife's.

"Thank you." Tears came to Ruben's eyes. It made Carter look away like he'd been pepper sprayed. "Thank you, sir."

"I don't even know your name!" his wife said, suddenly realizing.

"Carter McCoy. Glad to see you're doing all right."

"Thank you," Ruben said again, weak and choked by tears.

"I need to get running now. I'm late with my dog's dinner."

She clamped a hand on his arm. "You're a saint, Mr. McCoy. A saint!"

"No, no." He pulled, but she held firm.

"Come by again. Any time. And when he's out, you're coming to dinner."

"Oh, that's not necessary."

"It is. You will. Bless you, Carter. Bless your heart."

He extracted his arm and made for the door while he could. He didn't want to say anything else for fear of prolonging the conversation. He turned right in the hallway, moved quickly past the desk, and got on the elevator. A sharp pain seized his gut.

She came to the hospital to visit her husband, who had nearly sheared off two fingers using a handheld jigsaw. He'd been in three days while they waited to see if the reattachment surgery had worked or if he'd have only a thumb, pinkie, and ring finger on his left hand. She tried to be supportive and brave, but inside, she kept thinking what a dumbass he was. The elevator door opened to take her up to the ICU, and she saw an old man crumpled in the corner, clutching his gut and looking like he might be dead, or at least close to it.

"Oh, jeez." She turned back to the lobby. "Nurse!"

The two women behind the counter, neither of them nurses, looked at her, confused.

"He needs help," she said.

She knelt next to Carter and felt his wrist for a pulse. He grunted and moved, so she knew he was alive. Sweat beaded on his forehead.

A minute later, two porters arrived. The woman stepped out and let the men tend to the old man. She checked her watch, wondering how long it would be before she could get upstairs. No way she was taking the stairs for that idiot of a husband, though.

They gave Carter water in a paper cup.

"I'm all right now," he said.

A nurse finally showed up and quizzed him on how he felt. He brushed it off. He couldn't tell her the name of the disease he had, but he tried to reassure her that these were temporary spells and this one had been brought on by stress.

She didn't look convinced.

"I really think you should come with me for a real workup."

"Nah, nah. I'll be okay. You can reach out to my doctor if you want all the details."

What he wasn't saying was that he would be damned if he'd spend his last days in a hospital. And if checking in meant the start of all new rounds of tests only to come to the same conclusion—that he was dying—then no, thank you. He knew if he checked in, he may never check out.

The one thing he could count on with a nurse is that she would be busy. And if he didn't consent to being admitted, the law was on his side.

"Okay, Mr. McCoy. I can only advise you, but I do advise you to see your doctor." She listened to his heart one more time, shined a light in his eyes. His pulse came back strong; pupils reacted as they should to her pen light.

"I think that was more like a panic attack than anything."

"Stubborn old fart, aren't you?"

"I've been called worse."

"Do you have a ride home?"

"I'm all set, thank you."

Reluctantly, she stood. Other duties called, and with one last furrowed-brow look, the nurse moved on.

Carter stood, took a moment to get his balance, then left the hospital.

Carter went home and slept. When he woke, he stayed groggy for a while. Didn't feel like reading, didn't want to play his guitar. He put on the TV and watched re-runs of shows he didn't think were funny the first time.

He called Detective DeFore.

"He left home. His wife doesn't know where he is."

"Well, shit."

"Yeah, look, I'm not a bounty hunter or anything. If he's in the wind, then that's it for me."

"Yeah, no, I get it. You don't have to go traipsing around creation looking for the man."

"I wouldn't know him if he bit me."

DeFore sighed. A little too upset that a man wasn't killed today, for Carter's money.

"Thanks anyway, McCoy. How are you feeling?"

Carter felt like the question meant more like *how long do I have your services before you croak?*

"Not dead yet. About the best I can say."

"Yeah, isn't that about all of us?"

An awkward silence followed. Light static on the line the only indication DeFore hadn't hung up already.

"Y'know, McCoy, you never ask me about my life at all."

"We're not friends."

"Yeah, but I just asked how you were. Showed an interest. No reciprocation?"

"You're not the one who might die any day."

DeFore exhaled, and it was loud in Carter's ear. "Fine, be that way. I met a woman, though. It's going pretty good."

"Congratulations."

"Save your sarcasm. Jesus…"

The line went dead. Carter started to think DeFore was a lonely man. He didn't have anyone else in his life to tell his good news to? It would be a sad state of affairs if Carter McCoy was this man's best friend.

Two days later, DeFore showed up on his porch again.

"Let me guess? You found him."

Carter stood in the doorway again, not inviting DeFore in. They weren't friends, and Carter wanted him to know that.

"Who? Holliman? Nah. I got a new one for you."

"Don't you catch anybody over there?"

"It's not the catching them that's the problem, is convicting them."

Carter crossed his arms over his chest. "I don't recall signing up to be a black ops department of the force. This is getting to be a little too regular for me."

"Last one, I swear."

Carter had to scoff at that one.

"This guy killed his wife. Everyone knows it. Had some cock and bull story about the gardener, but any jury would have convicted. Goddamn DA found some irregularity with the arrest or the lawyers. Something, I don't know. Short story, the guy got off, and his wife is still dead."

"Hell of a lot of sloppy police work going on over there."

"It wasn't us. This was over near Saint Cloud. But a killer is walking free."

Carter got tired of letting in the cold air. He waved DeFore inside.

"Tell me the whole story."

Carter served him a bottle of Coke and listened to the details of the case. Having a little more connection made him feel more invested. It was the thing that made his first killings easier decisions. They weren't just strangers. If he knew something about the victim, the void left behind, then he could talk himself into it.

"So what do you think?" DeFore asked.

"I think before I came along, a whole hell of a lot of killers were just out there walking around."

"Yeah, maybe so. But you're here now. You're doing a hell of a thing for us, McCoy. Righting wrongs. You're like the friggin' Batman."

"Jesus Christ, DeFore, don't look so goddamn pleased about it all."

"Why shouldn't I be? The biggest frustration of my job is when bad men walk free. And I can't do a friggin' thing about it. Then you come along with this superpower...I wish people could know about it. They'd make a movie about you."

"Paul Newman's dead, so there's nobody to play me."

DeFore rolled the empty Coke bottle around in his hands. "So you'll do it?"

"Last one?"

"Yeah. Last one."

"Bullshit, and you know it."

DeFore looked away, caught out and he knew it. "Come on, McCoy. You know this is the right thing to do."

Carter pouted a little, then gave in. "An angel of death is still an angel."

He took the information from DeFore.

"You've already got the gun."

"Yeah," Carter said. "I got the gun."

Chester walked into the kitchen and nosed around the table, sniffing the two men.

"Next time," Carter said, "have the decency to bring some hamburgers with you at least."

DeFore made it to the bottom of the porch steps.

"So, how's things with the new woman?"

DeFore stopped. Carter spotted a small grin on his face when he turned.

"Real good, yeah. Her name's Margot. Been a real long time since I had a good relationship."

"Don't screw it up."

DeFore took the small gesture with him and didn't argue Carter's sarcasm. He got in his car and drove away.

Carter wasn't sure why he asked him anything about his personal life. Pity, he supposed. If he really let him go after this one, then Carter wouldn't have to fake an interest any longer.

Halloween arrived. Carter watched old monster movies on TV. The Universal Studios classics with the mummy and the wolf man. Silly films it was hard to believe ever scared anyone. Sure were pretty to look at, though. He remembered programming horror films each year at the movie theaters he ran. He'd always pick a few classics. His favorite were zombies. *Night Of The Living Dead* could still scare them. A lot of the kids, even in the 1980s, didn't go for black and white, though. For them, he brought in Italian films like *Zombi* and *Suspiria*. Those sent them screaming out into the night. He always held that one screen open for revivals at the holidays. *Miracle On 34th Street* at Christmas. *What's Up Doc?* or *The Way We Were* at Valentine's Day.

Chester snored through *Cat People,* and by the end, even Carter was dozing.

He was too far out to ever get any kids knocking at his door. Didn't even buy any candy. He used to love taking Audrey around to houses in his truck. She liked dressing in elaborate gowns to be princesses and Cleopatra and the Queen of England. She always saved her candy like it would earn her interest and multiply into more and more by Thanksgiving. By New Year's, it was stale and going moldy, but she didn't seem to mind.

Days like this a loneliness gripped him. Knowing other people were gathered, celebrating, always caused a melancholy to drop over him. He missed seeing the kids smiling through the macabre.

Cat People faded out and *Invasion Of The Body Snatchers* started up. He sat up straighter and opened another bottle of Coke and stayed up for the whole thing.

In the morning, he shaved. He'd let his beard grow, but it had gotten itchy and too long. It took him a while to hack through the thick whiskers and it left a pile of short, white hairs in the sink. The skin under it all was pink, and he looked younger, which made him look less sick, but his sunken cheeks made him look more sick at the same time.

He looked at himself for a long time and then decided to let it grow out again.

A few stalwart flowers hung on. They were wilted, color drained, but they hadn't fallen yet, stubbornly clinging to stems that no longer could hold them. One more good overnight freeze, and they would be gone. Fitting for the landscape outside a nursing home. Carter parked in his usual spot and walked through the automatic doors. A sign on the wall stated that masks were required, but nobody had worn one in some time, even the staff, so Carter didn't bother. What damage the virus had done to this place had already happened.

Cardboard cutout Halloween decorations still hung on the walls. Headstones, skeletons, warning signs not to pass any farther, for this way forward lies madness. Carter thought it cruel to hang this stuff around all these people who probably saw skeletons dancing in their dreams.

He didn't need to ask directions, and the woman at the reception desk hardly looked up. He wasn't sure if they recognized him or were just indifferent. Certainly, nobody ever greeted him here. Nobody acknowledged that he was a regular visitor to his friend, Ken.

Carter wandered down to the activity room. Heat pumped from the vents overhead and the whole building felt like an oven on preheat. Four residents sat in the open room. One woman at one of the puzzle tables, two in their wheelchairs and asleep, and one sitting in an armchair with a book open on her lap, but she ignored the book, giving a flat stare off to some unseen memory. No Ken.

Carter turned down the hall toward his room. The loneliness from Halloween hadn't dissipated, and Carter needed to talk to someone.

He passed by an open door. The name card next to the door had been removed, and the room was nearly empty. A hospital-style bed stripped of linens, a TV console without a TV, and a bored-looking man in coveralls disinterestedly swiping a putty knife and filling in small holes in the wall where picture frames once hung. Memories of the prior tenant. Pictures they liked, family photos, frozen moments in time from a life lived now in the past tense. It made Carter wonder who would clean out his place once he was gone. He needed to start downsizing some. Arrange to donate the furniture, his old clothes.

Ivana would inherit the house; he'd made arrangements already. What she did with it was up to her, but he felt sure she didn't want his old junk. The only thing worth bequeathing to anyone was Chester, and he knew she'd take good care of him. Probably turn him fat as a tick within weeks.

Ken was asleep, sitting up in a chair. Carter knocked on the open door frame. Ken stirred.

"Am I bugging you?" Carter asked.

Ken opened his eyes, but there was little recognition there. The fog of sleep fought the other thick fog banks in Ken's mind.

"Mind if I sit and stay?"

Ken worked his tongue around the inside of his mouth like he was chasing a marble. He shifted in his chair and coughed, unclogging a plug of phlegm before he spoke.

"Have a seat."

There were no other chairs in the room, so Carter sat on the edge of the bed. He heard the rubber underlayer creak.

"I'm back on my nonsense again," Carter said. "That detective. He gave me another name."

"Mmm."

Really, it didn't matter much if Ken could comprehend the things Carter told him. In many ways it was better that way. Carter told him too much. But there were times when he needed to say things out loud, and Chester wouldn't cut it.

"Guy who killed his wife. Tried to blame it on the gardener. Even did her in with garden shears. Got off on some technicality."

Ken started to come around. "Was she pretty?"

"Don't know. Haven't seen a picture or anything."

"A nag."

"Maybe. Still, doesn't deserve killing, does she?"

Ken shook his head, continued to work his tongue around. "Nope. No one does."

Not what Carter wanted to hear. He wanted Ken to agree with him that this man needed Carter's special services. This every-life-is-sacred was a new attitude for Ken.

"'Cept some," he added.

Carter nodded along to that. There have always been the outliers. Criminals and ones who don't seem to respect the lives of others. And like DeFore had said, for a long time, they would have been strung up to a nearby tree, gunned down in a dusty street. For centuries, the fastest advances in human technology were ways to torture and kill those who committed crimes. Only recently did people start thinking everyone deserved a second chance. Public executions used to be a grand day out for the whole family. Carter would have made a good hangman.

"I'm gonna do it," Carter said. "Because there's no other way for this guy to get what's coming to him. But for all the ways it becomes a little easier each time, it also becomes harder in different ways, you know?"

Carter smiled a little. "No, you don't know," he said. "I just said that because, y'know? There, I said it again. Jeez, I'm as bad as a teenager."

"Carter?"

It was the first time he'd heard Ken use his name in quite a while. He could see a different look in Ken's eyes. A little glassy, maybe wet from tears that hadn't fallen yet. But there was a look there like he wanted so badly to be right. To put the name and the face together in his mind.

Carter didn't hold him in suspense. "Yeah, bud. It's me."

Ken smiled, his teeth yellow and two more missing on the top row that Carter noticed.

"The killer."

Carter felt as if the wind had been knocked out of him. He and Ken were friends. That's what he wanted Ken to remember about him. The past, not the last few months which barely counted as past yet.

They used to go to the movies, to Mesa Grande, fishing in the summers and ice fishing in winter. There lived a vast catalog of memories inside Ken's head, if he could only access them. Carter was a lot of things, but a killer was only a small part. But once you add that to your list, it can't help but live near the top in bold letters. Above husband, father, friend.

Carter McCoy—killer.

"Only ones who deserve it."

"That's a whole lot," Ken said. "A whole hell of a lot."

Ken turned to the window. The sun hadn't quite broken through yet. The plants outside his window were mostly bare. They had bird feeders set up on stands throughout the property, but the birds were smart and had all headed South already. It meant there wasn't much to see out there, but Ken studied it intently.

"Sure could use you around here," he said.

Carter contemplated that. Could he use his skills not for criminals, but for people whose time had run out? How many families would be better off if their parent or grandparent would just let go? How many people would welcome him to their bedside and get to say goodnight on their own terms, not in some hospital or struggling for breath? Not when their memories had gone, and their laugh had faded away. When songs stopped meaning anything and pictures of the past were only shapes.

He could walk the halls and visit the sitting rooms and quietly offer his services for a long good night. Carter bet he'd have many of the residents jumping at the chance.

Only ones who deserve it. Maybe there were people here who deserved it in a different way. Deserved to decide for themselves. Deserved to set their own timetable.

But that was for another time.

Carter stood. He set a hand on Ken's shoulder. Ken didn't turn away from the window.

"I'll see you, bud. Got a job to do."

"No birds," Ken said.

"Nope. Not today."

Carter unwrapped the gun which he'd swaddled in a dishtowel and placed in a kitchen drawer. He set it on the table, then filled a bottle with water. The drive was longer out of town than he usually went, and he wanted to be prepared. He didn't want to stop for food or gas out of a paranoid fear someone would recognize a stranger in town and comment to the cops about it if they came around asking questions. A quiet approach and a clean getaway were important.

He set the water bottle down next to the gun and paused there a moment. Chester came in to see what Carter had for him.

"Y'know what? Fuck it. This guy is a scumbag and needs to get gone. I'm doing the world a favor here." He glanced down to Chester for some backup. "I'm sick and tired of worrying about this. I don't need the guilt or the stress. I'm gonna do the fucking thing, and that's that. One more asshole off the street. Right?"

Chester licked his lips, wondering where the food was.

"I mean, if I gotta go, then why should this guy get to be here?"

Yeah, so maybe Newman wouldn't get to play him in the movie. He saw himself as more of a Clint Eastwood type these days anyway.

He looked up directions to the address for Ronald Landrum. He found a photo of the guy in a news article about his wife's killing. Typical story, a well-liked man, quiet according to his neighbors. Friends called him Ronnie. All the coverage seemed pretty convinced he had done it, and the trial was a mere formality. Then, when the judge threw out the verdict, the story in the press wasn't that an unfair conviction had been overturned, but that a killer had walked free. This guy's life was already ruined, Carter thought. What more damage could a bullet do?

He went to the fridge and dug out a packet of lunch meat, a squeeze bottle of mayonnaise, and some bread. No greens. He made a quick sandwich, then got out an old takeout container he used as storage and emptied a can of dog food into it.

"And you're going with me," he said to Chester. He'd be gone several hours and didn't want Chester to be alone that long. And he knew the truth was he also didn't want to be alone that long. He tossed the dog a slice of turkey, and Chester caught it in midair.

He walked to the truck with Chester following. He set the bag with food in between the seats, then put the gun in the glove box and lifted Chester inside. Carter felt his back twinge and almost dropped Chester before he was settled. He didn't want to lose his ability to lift Chester into the truck. That would mean the old dog would never get to come with him again. He'd be housebound, a fear Carter had about himself since his diagnosis. As long as he could still get around, he felt less like he had one foot in the grave. Really, all Chester needed was the yard and the smells he followed, but Carter didn't want his own limitations to hold back his dog. Carter leaned against the side of the truck and took several deep breaths, balling his fist and pressing it into the small of his back. When the muscle pain passed, he stood straight and straightened his spine. He seemed to have avoided any lasting injury, but made a mental note to be more careful when he lifted.

He realized with all the stuff in his hands he had forgotten his cell phone. Not a problem. He couldn't remember the last time someone called him on it. He hadn't locked the door either, but that mattered even less. On Carter's way around to the driver's side, Chester took the opportunity to pass gas, and when Carter got in, he immediately had to roll down the window.

He stopped to fill up the truck with unleaded at his usual spot. Nothing out of the ordinary, nothing noteworthy for the police. He turned the truck West and drove on, confident in his task.

Out on the highway, a wind picked up, and Carter could feel the gusts shake the truck. It had been a while since he took any sort of long drive. Nowhere to go, really. He certainly wasn't going down to Iowa for the sightseeing, and Wisconsin was more of the same as what he had in Minnesota, so, no point there.

The highway was narrow, and the lines faded from sun in summer and being frozen in winter. Then, the plows would come along and scrape a layer of paint off every season. He always admired those jobs. The simple tasks that went unseen by most people. Wake up in the morning, get your assignment, do the job. Paint the lines on a street, change the bulb in a traffic light, hang a new stop sign. He could have done those jobs.

Carter tried to see this job the same way. He got his task, now do the work. Treat it the same. You're cleaning up. You're a garbage man, that's all.

He drove a half hour, and a pain gripped his gut. It came on suddenly and stabbed through him dead center, just below his belt line. His eyes went out of focus for a second, and he wanted to bend at the middle and shut his eyes through the pain, but he couldn't. He checked the rearview quickly. No one behind him. He slowed, easing over to the shoulder, what there was of it. A low field of some crop that had been harvested already sat dormant to his right. A drainage ditch dipped between the highway and the field. He tried to pull over as far as he could without slipping a tire into the ditch.

Chester sat up in his seat. He could tell something was wrong.

The pain stabbed again, another thrust of the knife into him. He let out a grunt. Chester leaned over and licked his face.

The tires hit the soft gravel on the shoulder and the wheel jerked to the right, but he pulled it back to center, pressing the brake a little harder. He got it over and stopped, pulled the knob on the emergency flashers, and put it in park. He let go of the wheel and bent forward until his head pressed against the horn. He let out a bellow that frightened Chester in the tiny cab of the truck.

The pains left him with nothing to do but hold on and bear it. They came from inside him, sharp and cold, like being stabbed with an icicle. He could only wait it out.

Outside, the wind blew and battered the truck. When a car would pass it rocked the pickup on its shocks. Nobody stopped to check on the old man and his dog.

Detective Brian DeFore missed having a partner. His time earlier in the year with help from another detective, Nava, from the robbery squad had been a reminder of how much he liked working with someone when he was a beat cop. Now Nava was back to robbery full-time since the spate of murders had died down. Since Carter McCoy had finished his business.

But being a one-man homicide division still left DeFore with too much time on his hands. And with cases like this Ronnie Landrum getting tossed out, his batting average was low. But he had started to take a real satisfaction in his extra-judicial handling of these killers who got away with it.

Really, Carter McCoy was just another tool in his arsenal against criminals.

But Carter wasn't a partner, and the old man seemed determined to keep DeFore at arm's length.

DeFore had worked with a guy his first six-and-a-half years on the force in St. Paul. Doug Heyes had been a cop for three years, and to DeFore, he was an elder statesman. In truth, they both learned on the job. A bigger city meant more action, and they saw their share. The meth trade was in full swing; cheap pot came down from Canada before anyone started legalizing it. And anywhere they went, people didn't seem to like the police, so they were enemies from the moment they pulled up.

Heyes had saved DeFore from a knife in the back once. As DeFore was putting cuffs on a fifteen-year-old kid, his older brother came out of the shadows and tried to stop the proceedings with a kitchen knife. Heyes ran forward and rammed him with a shoulder like the ex-high school defensive back he was. Took the kid right off his feet.

DeFore had the opportunity to return the favor a year later when Heyes took the lead in breaking up a brawl at a late-night drift and drag race session. The days were gone when people heard sirens and scattered. Now, everyone took out their cell phones and tried to get a clip that would make CNN. Backup had arrived, and two men were already in custody when Heyes had a third up against his cruiser. He had one cuff on, and half of Miranda read to the guy when one of the drifters gunned his engine and slid the back end of his Toyota Supra with purple underlights directly toward the car. DeFore didn't know if the guy was aiming for Heyes or the guy he was cuffing because they still had beef, but DeFore sprinted forward and knocked Heyes out of the way. The back end of the Supra pinned the half-cuffed guy between the bumper and the door of the cruiser. He had to be taken away in an ambulance, and the driver of the Supra got away, but was caught two days later when the crunched back end of his car made him easy to identify.

Those sorts of got-your-back moments are what DeFore missed most. That and the conversation. The meals together.

As he sat waiting for his coffee in a shop that made killer danishes he could never resist, he stood there awkwardly talking to no one and eating his danish while standing like some divorced dad before a support group meeting.

Nava had mentioned the possibility of divorce last time they talked, and right now, DeFore could be helping him with that. Lending an ear, offering advice, commiserating on how much of a bitch his wife was being. Without a partner, you had no one to cry to, complain to, come to for help. And he was woefully out of touch on the latest dirty jokes.

He could be telling a partner about Margot and how great she was. How he thought she could be *the one*. How, after his long dry spell, the rains had opened up and flooded him with the best women he'd ever dated.

The bored girl behind the counter called out his coffee. He picked it up and noticed the side of the cup said *BRAIN*. He would have laughed about that with a partner for a long time. Might have been the latest in-joke between them.

Instead, he carried his coffee out and walked back to his office alone.

The coffee and the danish were gone by the time he got back to his desk. With no homicides to work, DeFore had a stack of municipal complaints to sort through and see if any needed following up or if they could be filed, and by filed they really meant thrown away.

Within ten minutes, he'd grown bored and searched reports on the latest injuries to the Vikings from the week before. Two more offensive linemen down. Another disappointing season ahead. Such is the lot in life for a Vikings fan.

A knock at the door. DeFore looked up to see Chief Winters pushing through without hearing a "Come in", but it was his station so the chief did what he wanted.

"How's it going there, Brian?"

"Good, chief. Just looking over those municipal jobs."

"Ugh, yeah. Not a lot there, I suppose."

"Not a lot, no."

"Well, thought you'd want to know your wife killer got a bit of good news today."

Wife killer? He meant Ronnie Landrum, the man set free on a Fourth Amendment technicality.

"Yeah?"

"Yeah. Court got it right. He ain't the guy."

Mr. Landrum, whose name DeFore had given to Carter McCoy.

"What do you mean he ain't the guy?"

"Nope. Gardener confessed. Just like he said. A crime of passion. She'd slept with the kid once and then tried to ice him out. I guess he didn't take to that and killed her. That was the guy's whole defense, right? The gardener did it. Man, nobody believed that for a hot second, did they?"

Mr. Ronald Landrum. An innocent man.

"A real confession? Not coerced? Not a prank phone call or something?"

"Nope. Gardener walked into a station and laid the whole thing out. Said the guilt was killing him, and he thought he was going to hell because he's

Catholic. I mean, he's going to hell for the murder. Why would the lying be the thing that made him break?" Winters shook his head at the disconnect in the kid's confession. "Damn good thing they tossed the case, though, huh?"

"Yeah. Yeah, good thing. Could have been a real mess. Real messy."

"Yeah."

"Yeah." DeFore shut his laptop a little too hard. "Hey, I gotta go check on a thing. I'll get on those files as soon as I'm back."

"No rush on those. Busy work, I know. But hey, fingers crossed you'll catch a murder soon, right?"

Winters grinned and held up crossed fingers. DeFore thought it grotesque, but laughed along as he pulled on his coat and rushed out the door.

2

The pain subsided gradually like a sound fading away, but leaving your ears ringing in the aftermath. He was able to lean back, but kept his eyes shut. He could feel Chester's hot breath against his cheek. "It's okay, boy. I'll be okay."

Carter reached out a hand and scratched at Chester's ears. Outside, another car passed by at sixty miles an hour and shook the truck.

Carter was sweating. He wiped a hand across his forehead and then ran the palm across his jeans. He let out several deep breaths through pursed lips and almost made a whistling sound, but he thought the irony of whistling while he felt like his insides were being torn out was a little too much.

He took a drink of water. It stayed down, which he didn't think would have happened ten minutes prior. A good sign he was returning to normal. But how long before stabbing pain was his normal, and the moments of calm were the exceptions?

A trio of crows were picking at the empty field, too stubborn to fly south away from the coming cold. A gray shroud covered the sky and drained all color from the landscape.

Chester yawned and then chuffed. Carter knew he probably needed to go out and pee. He tried shifting in his seat. It went okay. When the pain went, it didn't leave lasting scars. Even if it felt like his skin had been torn open, there was no healing to be done.

He checked behind them and no cars were coming. He got out and was hit by a bracing wind that chilled the sweat on his face. He walked around to the passenger side and had to walk a tightrope along the edge of the ditch there. He opened the door and barely had enough space to plant his feet firmly enough to lift Chester down from the cab. He set the dog down and pointed him toward the field. Chester put his nose to the ground and made short left and right turns as he scanned the area for whatever scent he could find. Carter shoved his hands down into the pockets of his jeans and waited. The cold took his mind off the pain attack. And watching Chester always gave his mind something else to focus on. The dog had been the best decision he'd made in years. A companion, a distraction, a second chance for an old hound nobody else wanted.

Not a bad way to live out your days being fed cheeseburgers and sniffing the ground like it held all the secrets of the universe. Farting whenever you wanted, drooling when you slept. Not too far of from a lot of men Carter's age.

Chester finally lifted his leg and did his business. Carter gave him a quick call and Chester looked up, then dropped his head down to the ground again, but started sniffing his way back toward the truck.

When he got close, the gap of the drainage ditch was suddenly too far for him to jump. He looked up at Carter expectantly.

"Are you serious?"

Chester dipped his head and began sniffing again.

"Okay, hold on. Don't get distracted. I'm goddamn freezing out here."

Carter eased his way down the ditch. With the fields shorn down to the dirt, no irrigation was needed, so the ditch was dry. He crossed the gap and lifted Chester, the old dog, about all he could handle in weight. Carter turned, and the incline on the far side of the ditch seemed insurmountable. He stepped across with one leg, straddling the ditch with the old dog cradled in his arms. He had to work to push off and get both feet on the highway side of the ditch.

"C'mon, help me out here."

He set Chester down and, with a hand on his collar, led him up the short slope of the ditch until they were standing next to the truck again. Carter bent again and lifted Chester onto the seat. He had to lean against the side of the truck to catch his breath.

Carter was exhausted. He was mad. The pain made him irritable. He was in the perfect mood to go kill a man.

61

The cell phone rang in an empty room. Carter had kept the ringtone an old-school telephone. No beeps or buzzes. A phone should sound like a phone. It vibrated at the same time and did a small shimmy on the kitchen table. It rang five times and then went to voicemail, which was still set to the default automated message because Carter never figured out how to record his own.

"God dammit, McCoy, pick up your phone. Listen, call it off. Landrum isn't your man. Don't do it, you hear me? Don't do it. He's innocent."

DeFore thumbed the phone call dead and opened the door to his car. He whacked his head getting in, and dropped his phone onto the floor on the passenger side.

"Fuck, fuck. Dammit, fuck."

Where the hell was McCoy? He hadn't heard a report that Landrum was dead, but maybe nobody found him yet. Maybe McCoy hadn't left his house to do it. DeFore had no idea what the old man had planned for Landrum, or when. All he knew now was that he had sentenced an innocent man to death.

He cranked the engine and pulled out of the lot. He hit redial on his phone and listened through five more rings and the start of the robotic voice greeting. He didn't leave a second message.

DeFore made a new call. He had plans with Margot, his girlfriend. He'd wanted to tell her he loved her tonight, to make it official. Now, he had to cancel.

She answered, "Hi there."

"Hey. Uh, so sorry, but I have a work thing. I can't make dinner tonight." He hoped the revving of his engine didn't come through as he raced to beat a traffic light.

"Oh, okay. Everything good?"

It was about as much as she ever asked about his work. She wasn't interested in the details of a homicide case. DeFore had hoped she would be more disappointed at the canceled plans.

"Just something I gotta take care of. But I don't know how late it'll go. I'm so sorry."

"It's okay. It's just dinner. We'll do it this weekend."

He thought about saying "I love you" now, but he wanted to see her face. To have her smile and dip her chin shyly the way she did. He wanted her to say it back and then embrace and then make love filled with the words.

"Okay, I'll call you tomorrow."

"Sounds good."

"Bye." It almost slipped out anyway.

"Bye."

The call ended, and he refocused on his task.

Now is when he missed rolling in a cruiser with flashing lights and sirens. He could get anywhere he needed to much faster than in this unmarked civilian car. But he needed to be careful. He couldn't get a police escort without explaining why he needed one, which would be difficult, to say the least.

Likewise, he couldn't blow any stop signs or go too far over the limit. Normally, a flash of his badge would get him out of a situation like that, but with no good excuse and no desire for a paper trail of his whereabouts, he couldn't risk getting stopped.

His first question was whether to head to McCoy's place or to Landrum directly. Hell, maybe it was Carter lying dead on the floor. That day was coming soon, so why not today? It would solve this dilemma succinctly.

The light ahead of him turned red. He pounded the steering wheel seven times in a row.

"Shit, shit, shit, shit, shit, shit, shit."

A woman walking a French bulldog crossed the street in front of him. Midway through the crosswalk, the dog squatted and began trying to poop. The dog was old, nearly as old as his owner. The woman stopped and watched him. The old dog was struggling, his back arched and a pained look on his graying muzzle.

The light turned green.

The dog turned ninety degrees, still couldn't start his business. DeFore's hand hovered over the horn. The old woman kept focus on the dog, and when he finally starting going, she clapped her hands and praised him.

He was a well fed dog from the amount of excrement he let loose. Only when the dog had finished did she reach for the plastic container of bags on his leash. She unspooled a single bag and tried to get it open. She had to lick her fingers to start the plastic separating.

DeFore could feel his blood pressure mounting.

The light turned red again.

The woman tied a knot in the very full bag, and she continued on her way. DeFore checked the time on his phone, debated called McCoy again.

The light turned green, and he decided to head toward Landrum' place—at a reasonable pace.

A sudden tiredness fell over him like heavy chains had been draped across his shoulders. It might have been the steady rise and fall of Chester's snoring beside him on the seat, but Carter rubbed at his eyes, afraid he might fall asleep at the wheel. He didn't want to, but he pulled over at a gas station with a small shop attached. He didn't need to fill up the truck, so he bypassed the pumps and parked in the far corner of the lot. He left Chester in the cab while he went inside to buy a Coke. To be safe, he bought a second one to have for the ride back.

He doubted the regular consumption of Cokes helped his condition at all, but he didn't care much about what he ate these days.

He spotted the cameras above the cashier, facing the entrance, under the eaves outside pointing toward the pumps. No way to stop here and not be recorded. If anything went wrong, his anonymity and his alibi were gone now. But he needed the energy boost.

Any detective on the case would have to be on top of their game to search for cameras this far out, but he didn't know what kind of AI search systems they had now to spot his license plate or to match his face to some database somewhere. Truth was, there weren't many places he could go anymore where he wasn't being watched.

He finished off the first Coke before getting back into the truck. He let out a long belch and set the second can in the cup holder. Chester looked up, checked that Carter hadn't gotten anything he was interested in, then lay back down.

Back on the highway, and according to the signs, he had thirty-eight miles to go. He checked his watch. Ronnie Landrum had about an hour left to live. Carter knew the feeling.

What a goddamn idiot. DeFore cursed himself as he drove, wishing the lane lines would pass by faster. Wishing he could flip on lights and sirens and call ahead to have highway patrol stop Carter's beat-up old truck. Maybe the thing would break down. Hell, DeFore didn't even know if Carter had gone to do the job yet, but the fact he wasn't answering his phone made the detective nervous.

Would Carter think ahead enough to turn off his phone before he went to shoot Landrum?

Yeah, the old man was smart. He couldn't be lying in wait only to have his cell phone start ringing. He'd already gotten away with multiple killings and not been caught, so he had to know what he was doing at least a little. One is good luck, Carter's record spoke of a certain skill.

Ahead of him, an SUV cruised along at the speed limit. Did anyone stick to the actual speed limit anymore? Even as desperate as he was not to get pulled over, DeFore had been cruising at five miles above. He'd met the guys who sit with a radar gun aimed at a two-lane highway all shift and these weren't the most motivated crackerjack squad of troopers. You'd have to be going fast enough to make it worth their while to put their patrol cars in drive. Five miles over wasn't going to do that.

DeFore waited while the car rolled over a long, slow rise. When the road opened up, and he could see ahead and tell that no one was coming from the opposite direction, he gunned the engine and passed the SUV.

Once he was clear, he moved the needle to seven miles over.

Without his phone, Carter had to rely on old fashioned techniques for getting directions. With paper maps in short supply these days, he needed to ask. He knew the perfect place. He parked the truck, got Chester down for a bathroom break, then stowed the dog in the cab again and went inside a pizza place called TASTE OF ROMA. If anyone knew addresses, it's these guys.

It smelled like burnt crust. There were four small tables, all empty since he was between the lunch and dinner rushes. But this place probably did ninety percent of its business in takeout. Good for Carter.

The guy behind the counter had that defeated look like he'd taken the job in high school as a part-time way to make a few bucks, and when he looked up twenty years later, he was the manager, and this was his career.

"Help you?" he said.

"I'm looking for Waverly Street?"

The guy blinked. It wasn't an order or a list of toppings, so his mind temporarily short-circuited.

"Waverly?"

"Yeah. Do you know where it is?"

"Um, yeah. I think."

He turned to a map on the wall behind the counter. It was yellowed with age and pitted with pushpin holes. Packing tape held up the edges, and tomato sauce stains speckled the brittle paper. He scanned the street names, almost nothing in a straight line. Whoever had laid out this part of town had done it free-form and with no regard for easy navigation.

"Waverly?" he asked again.

"Yes," Carter said.

"Uhhh…here."

His finger landed on a spot about three o'clock.

"And where are we now?" Carter asked.

"Here."

The finger on his left hand landed about six inches away.

"So, close?" Carter asked.

"Yeah. Real close."

"Okay, thanks." No need to ask for the specific address. Too easy to remember someone asking about something that specific. Again, it would be a reach for the cops to ever come investigate a mom-and-pop pizza joint, but he never knew. Once Carter found Waverly, he could follow the street numbers.

"You want anything?"

Carter thought about the food in his truck. Pizza did smell damn good now that he was inside, but he didn't want to wait for it to be cooked.

Then again, could arriving as a pizza delivery guy act as a good cover?

No. Why did he need one? Knock on the door, he answers, shoot him. No need to bring role-playing into this.

"No, I'm good. Thanks."

Carter went back to the truck, got in, and turned right out of the parking lot. It wouldn't take long to get there. The clock ticked down further for Ronnie Landrum.

The voice on the GPS was supposed to be calming and neutral, but to DeFore, her flat, robotic voice grated on him like a squealing pig before the slaughter. He was close now, at least. He tried Carter one more time. Voicemail picked up. Where was that old man?

He'd have to camp out at Landrum's place until Carter showed up, or he called him back. He couldn't exactly tell Landrum the story and warn him to watch out for an old guy to show up on his doorstep looking to kill him. Jesus, what a mess he'd gotten into just because he was impatient. If he admitted it, he also had developed a taste for this extra-judicial justice he had going with McCoy. No paperwork. No delays. No lawyers, that was a big one. Only right and wrong, black and white, alive and dead. Simple.

And what if McCoy had finally died? It could happen any time, he said.

He took his eyes off the road for far too long to look at his phone and dial up the coroner's office. When he looked up, he had to swerve back across the yellow line he'd drifted over.

"Coroner's office." The man's voice filled the car through the speakers.

"This is Detective Brian DeFore. I wanted to see if there was a death report on a Carter McCoy. Aged seventy plus, white male."

DeFore could hear keyboard clicks as the man searched. "White male, seventies, you said?"

"Yeah. McCoy, Carter. Wouldn't have been a homicide or suspicious in any way. He's got some disease."

He waited.

"Yeah, no, I got nothing like that. Had a female aged fifty-five, a black man aged eighty-eight, and a female aged thirty-nine. No white males."

"Okay, thanks."

He pressed the END CALL button on his steering wheel. The call had muted the GPS lady, and he'd missed a turn. His screen reset with a new map.

"In six hundred feet, turn left at the stop sign."

How far was six hundred feet? He slowed and turned left at the next stop sign and started to backtrack.

Mr. Landrum lived across the street from a cemetery. Death didn't follow Carter so much as he dragged it along with him wherever he went these days.

Carter had turned onto Waverly Street and searched the houses for numbers. The first two either didn't have any displayed or were too obscured or small for his eyes. The third house on the row had a chunky 348 on a porch post. The house next door a 352. Right direction.

Three blocks down and he pulled to the curb.

He sat in the truck and looked out over the field of headstones. It reminded him that he hadn't been to see Ava and Audrey in too long. A black iron gate surrounded a flat, featureless rectangle of land. It seemed the perfect plot for a graveyard. The grass had turned a yellowish green, dying slowly in the creeping cold.

It seemed every plot was filled. No people passed the gate. Nobody visited these former fathers and mothers and spouses and grandparents. Bodies lain to rest alone, not caring if the ground got cold.

He turned to look at the address he'd been given. A red house with white shutters. A second story on one half over the garage. Modest-sized lawn neatly kept, even after Carter assumed Mr. Landrum would have fired the gardener he tried to accuse of killing his wife.

A navy blue SUV sat in the driveway. He may have owned two cars and he could be out in his. The SUV could have been his wife's, but there was a good chance he was home.

Carter reached into his bag and pulled out a sandwich. He wasn't sure if he could eat, but he wanted to take a moment. He pulled the sandwich in half and gave it to Chester while Carter drank his second Coke.

He watched the house while Chester made obscene chewing noises.

He finished the can and set the empty back in the cup holder. He belched and held a fist to his mouth to keep it in. Chester had taken the half sandwich in three big chomps. Carter leaned over and opened the glove box. He waited, hand hovering. A sandwich, a gun. What's the difference? Do the damn thing.

He lifted the gun and sat upright in his seat. He pulled on a sweat-stained and sun-faded Twins baseball cap he had sitting on the dashboard.

"Be right back," he told Chester.

Carter got out, and the cold hit him. Not winter cold yet, but a kind of cold that told stories of what's to come. A warning cold. Be prepared.

He tucked the gun into his pocket and walked along the iron fence by the graveyard for a half a block. Nobody was out on the street, nobody tending to their yards or walking dogs. Nothing. Perfect conditions. The chill had driven everyone inside. How did anybody murder anyone in California?

Carter crossed the street. He had to double back now to make it to the red house. He pulled his hat down low over his face. He turned into the driveway and moved past the blue SUV. He glanced inside. Nothing to see there.

He walked up the pathway to the front. No cameras, no smart doorbell with a fisheye lens on it. He was justice. He was right over wrong.

A high-pitched squeal of tires sounded from far off. Carter looked behind him and tucked back against the side of the house, trying not to be seen. A car came around the corner and pulled to a stop behind his truck.

Detective DeFore got out. He ran up the window of Carter's truck and peered in, then recoiled as Chester barked at him. His head whipped around the street, left to right, then landed on the red house. Carter leaned out, and their eyes met.

He could see a combination of relief and panic on DeFore's face as he started to sprint across the street.

"Wait!"

Carter stepped out and away from the house. They met on the sidewalk.

DeFore was almost breathless from the short sprint. "You didn't do it yet, did you?"

"No."

"Oh, thank God. Don't. Go home. Get away from here."

"What the hell is going on?"

"He's innocent. He didn't do it."

The muscles in Carter's legs went soft. He nearly crumbled. DeFore put a hand under his arm and held him up.

"What the fuck?" Carter said.

"Just go. Now. Go home."

"You said…"

"I know. I was wrong. Let's…" He tugged at Carter and pulled him across the street, away from the house. "Let's go."

They reached Carter's truck, and he pressed his back to the door. Inside, Chester began barking and flinging drool onto the window.

"What did you do to me?" Carter asked.

"Nothing. It's fine. You didn't do it."

DeFore bent at the waist and let out a massive exhale.

"But I could have! I almost did."

DeFore straightened up. "Look, it was a mistake. Okay? It's over now." He ran a hand across his face, then to himself, "Thank God it's over."

"I can't believe this. You almost had me kill an innocent man."

"I'm sorry. Look, this shit is complicated. This one…this wasn't supposed to happen."

Carter spun on him, forcing DeFore up against the truck. Chester barked again, muted by the windows.

"I don't kill innocent men. If I had, I…" Carter didn't know what he would have done. Turned the gun on himself?

"Carter—"

"I'm done. Don't ever ask me for this again." He pulled the gun from his pocket and pushed it at DeFore, grip first. DeFore covered it quickly, keeping it out of sight. "Never again. I don't want to see you, hear from you, ever. You fucking irresponsible asshole."

Carter let go of the gun. A head rush came over him, like the missing weight of the gun had made him lightheaded. Most likely, it was the two Cokes, the lack of food, and the adrenaline dump.

Carter went down to one knee. He tried to get his breath, but didn't feel like he could fill his lungs. He sat and leaned back against the front tire.

"Hey, McCoy, you okay?" DeFore pocketed the gun and bent down to him. "Shit. You okay?"

Carter brushed him away. He shut his eyes, fighting a dizzy spell.

DeFore put a hand on his shoulder and shook it. "God dammit, don't die on me here, will ya?"

"Just go away."

The door on the red house opened. Ronnie Landrum stepped out, straining to see the commotion across the street. DeFore clocked him and lowered his voice.

"You gotta get up, McCoy. Get up right now."

Carter kept his eyes shut and leaned his head forward into his hands.

"Now, dammit," DeFore said. "Get up, we gotta go."

Landrum stepped out and shut the door. He started walking down the path.

DeFore put a hand under Carter's armpit and lifted. Carter was dead-weight and didn't move. Inside the truck, Chester got more agitated.

"McCoy, I swear to God…"

He tried lifting again, but it was no use. He turned, and Landrum was at the curb. DeFore stood straight and held out a hand.

"It's okay. No problem. I'm a cop."

He reached around for his wallet and shield, but his back pocket was empty. He could feel his face fall, exposing a guilty look to Landrum, the innocent man. More innocent than either DeFore or Carter.

DeFore jogged back to his car. "It's okay. I'm just gonna get my badge."

"Is he all right?" Landrum asked.

"He's fine. Just an anxiety attack."

DeFore bent into his car and got his wallet from the center console. An old habit. He hated sitting on his wallet while driving, one ass cheek riding higher than the other.

He came out with the wallet open and his badge showing.

"I'm a police officer. I got this under control."

Landrum stopped on the dashed white lines in the middle of the street.

Carter was cold now, a chill seeping up from the concrete into his legs, his backside, his spine. He tried to push up to his feet, but he faltered. DeFore pocketed the wallet and went to help him. With both hands under his arms, he got Carter to his feet.

"All good now," he said over his shoulder to Landrum. "I got it from here."

"You need any help?"

"No, all good."

"Want me to call an ambulance?"

DeFore couldn't hide the frustration in his voice. "I got it. I'm okay. Just go back inside, sir."

Landrum started to walk backward, still eyeing the strange scene in front of him.

DeFore leaned close to Carter. "Get in the goddamn truck and drive home."

"Look at him," Carter said. "Look."

DeFore turned.

"You almost made me kill him. You did. Well, that's the last goddamn time, you hear me? No more. Stay away from me. Don't call. Don't come to my house. And when I die, don't come to my funeral."

Carter shoved DeFore away, wobbled a bit, then turned and opened the door. Chester greeted him with a lick to the face, which was wet and sloppy from all his barking.

In the cemetery, a single crow perched on a headstone and watched Carter drive away.

Chester had eaten the second half of the sandwich. In his excitement, he tore open the bag and chewed the meat, the bread, and most of the paper bag with it. Carter pulled over. He didn't know where he was exactly, but he spotted a small park, and he stopped to let Chester out to pee. Old men like them needed quite a few breaks. The two Cokes were pushing on him as well.

He lifted Chester down, his muscles tired and his bones achy. He breathed through his mouth with a slack jaw, but he didn't care how he looked. He led Chester around the park, and the dog peed twice. He brought Chester back to the truck, and the old dog looked ready for a nap.

Carter noticed a bar in the next block. He locked the door and walked as if drawn to the neon sign like a moth.

Outside it was dusk, but inside a mix of neon, yellowed lampshades and red EXIT signs lit the inside of a bar sunlight hadn't seen in decades. It was early enough there were only a few regulars there. He took a seat at the bar and ordered a beer from the bartender, whose gut said he liked to sample his own wares.

"Whatcha want?" The bartender wore a black t-shirt with a faded image of Jimi Hendrix and a black leather vest over it with black jeans.

"Something on tap. Whatever's your favorite."

In under a minute, the bartender set down a beer, and Carter took a drink. Whatever brand it was hit the spot exactly. He took another long sip.

The bartender caught his eye, looking for approval. Carter nodded.

"It's good. Let me have a shot, too. You pick it."

"Trust me already?"

Carter nodded, and this made the bartender smile. He poured from a bottle and set it next to the half-vanished beer, the left Carter to his drinking. Before he took the shot, Carter walked to the back of the bar and fund the bathroom. He relived himself with a great sigh and a slight shudder of his shoulders. When he washed his hands, he avoided looking at his reflection. He ran his hands, still wet, over his face and then toweled off with the brown paper hand towels that could have doubled as sandpaper.

Carter returned to his seat and downed his shot. He didn't brood, didn't order more drinks. Just sat and let the anxiety drain away. It was like he'd come close to a cliff edge and felt one tire go over before wrestling it back on the road. Too close of a call for his liking. Only he wasn't the only one in the car. If he'd gone over the edge, Ronnie Landrum would have gone with him.

"Son of a bitch," he mumbled to the beer.

He played out what he thought shooting Landrum would have been like. The dead man, flat on his back, and then DeFore running up with the news he'd just murdered an innocent man. He knew he'd be seeing the image of a shooting that nearly happened in his dreams from now until he went.

"Another?" the bartender asked.

"No, thanks. You can tell me how to get back to highway ninety-four."

He pointed a hand with a gnarled index finger. "Down this way about two miles, turn left at the Chevron, then that'll take you to highway fifteen in about ten miles. Take that south, and you'll meet up with ninety-four."

"Thanks."

Carter dropped a twenty dollar bill on the bar and stood. No jukebox could be seen, but music played. Probably off the barman's phone into hidden Bluetooth speakers. A song Carter didn't know faded out, and "Don't Fear The Reaper" came on. There he was, dragging death with him again.

He stepped outside into the chill air, tired and feeling the drinks move through him. A wooden bench sat out front under a large window that had been tinted dark so no sunlight accidentally crept into the bar. Carter sat down, gathering himself before the long drive home. He wondered if he'd have to wait a while as the alcohol worked on his empty stomach.

A guy stood on the sidewalk smoking. He was tall and skinny, his pants loose and his jacket ill-fitting over his narrow frame. He held out a pack of cigarettes to Carter.

"You want a smoke there, pal?" His voice sounded scratchy and pitted like an old 78 record.

Carter started to shake his head, then thought, *why the hell not? I'm going soon anyway*.

He started to reach for the pack, then stopped. Smoking had seemed so stupid to him his whole life he couldn't think any differently now, even when the health risks didn't matter much. Why the hell would you want to do something that smelled bad, made you cough, and cost a fortune? No, smokers he would never understand.

"No, thanks," he said. "Where can I get a quick sandwich around here?"

"There's a Hardee's about a mile and a half up the road." He got a smile on his face. "But there's a Portillo's 'bout three or four miles that way." He pointed the opposite direction Carter needed to go. "Got a frozen custard shop right next door, too."

"Thanks."

Carter tucked his hands in his pockets and walked back to the truck.

DeFore's hands still shook on the wheel. In his years as a beat cop, he'd never dodged a bullet, but he felt like he knew the feeling now. That could have been really bad. He wasn't going back to the office today. No way. He needed a friendly face. He needed to see Margot.

He called her, and the call went through on his Bluetooth, the ring loud over the car speakers. She answered. "Hello?"

"Hey there. What are you doing? I'm out early and figured we could meet for a coffee or an early dinner."

"Ooh, sorry. This isn't a great time. I'm really busy."

She worked as an interior designer, and she often said her clients made her crazy. Unreasonable demands, shifting timelines, unrealistic budgets.

"Oh, no worries. Just a hard day at work. And there's nobody else who makes me feel better when things are going bad."

He knew it sounded cheesy, but he wanted her to know how special she was to him.

"Aw, Brian, that's sweet. Maybe a late dinner. I'm on a deadline here, though."

"Yeah, yeah, I get it. I'll call you later."

"Okay. Sounds good."

She hung up. No *I love you*. She hadn't said it yet.

DeFore was trying to take it slow and casual. He'd been told before that he went too fast in relationships. Saying I love you on the third date, planning weekends away after a month. Meeting his parents way too soon.

And every woman he dated said some variation, usually right before they dumped him, of him oversharing about work. For some reason, he'd never dated another cop. There weren't that many to begin with, and he never found them attractive. The women he did date had no appetite for stories about homicides or violent drunks. They wanted to feel safe with a boyfriend, not get a list of all the ways a burglar could enter their home through its multiple points of weakness.

He had tried to give Margot her space. He stopped himself at least twice a day from calling when he had nothing really to discuss, but just wanted to hear her voice.

And he tried to watch what he said. His attempts at sweetness and movie-dialogue romance talk usually sounded like a stalker or a serial killer right before he plunged the knife. One girl, Katherine, his last serious relationship three years before Margot, he'd told that she made him feel more welcome than anyone ever had before and that all he wanted to do was crawl inside her and live in her skin. He could hear it as soon as he said it and saw the look of horror on her face, but in his mind, it was a sweet thing to say.

So, with no Margot to run to, DeFore stopped off at a liquor store and bought a pint of Jim Beam and a six-pack.

A hirsute man with thick glasses rang him up.

"One of those days, y'know?" DeFore said.

"They're all one of those days," he said, shoving the glasses back up his nose. "It's why my business is recession-proof. The more depressed people get, the more money I make. So forgive me if I don't tell you to have a nice day. I don't want you to have one. I want your shitty little life to get worse so you'll come back and see me again."

DeFore blinked at him twice.

"Maybe recession-proof, but statistically, you chose a job with the highest percentage chance of being robbed outside of taxi drivers, and now they don't get robbed anymore since nobody uses cash."

"That's why I got a double barrel sawed off back here."

He handed DeFore his change.

"Would it matter to you to know that I'm a cop?"

"Nope. I got permits. I know my rights. I shot a guy in eighty-nine. Never even went to court. I know my rights."

DeFore stuck his thumb and forefinger in between the cans of the six-pack and put the brown paper bag with his pint in his pocket. "Well, hope you don't have call to use it any time soon. Have a good one."

"You have a shitty one."

Chester knew where to go by now. He wound his way through the headstones, stopping to sniff here and there where squirrels had buried peanut shells. He got to Audrey and Ava's graves before Carter did. Everyone needs somebody to talk to. A girlfriend, a dog, your dead family. Some things you could only tell the dead.

"I'm sorry," Carter started. "Been too long, I know."

He brushed a dead leaf off of Audrey's stone.

"I can't even say I've been too busy. Time just sort of gets away from me, I guess."

Chester did a loop around the stones on either side of the McCoy family plot then settled in and lay down across Ava's grass.

"I had a hell of a thing yesterday. Almost a goddamn tragedy. Almost a mistake I couldn't take back."

He didn't need to explain it all to them. He didn't want to go through it again, anyhow. It had already plagued him the whole night before.

"But I'm done with that now. I made my choices, and I can live with them. But no more of this hired gun bullshit. That's over. Don't know why I did it in the first place."

He knew why. Because DeFore could send him to jail. Probably. If he really had enough evidence, Carter would already be behind bars. The threat was enough, though.

"The only thing is…"

He turned over a thought that came to him the night before when he couldn't sleep. If he was done now, with vigilante justice and working for the police department in the shadows, what would he do with the rest of his life?

Yeah, he could do puzzles and read books and watch movies, but what else?

The weird little missions, the help he provided, in addition to the justice, it had given this last act of his life a little purpose. He knew how messed up that sounded. He didn't know how to explain it to Ava other than it felt like *doing* something rather than doing stuff meant for in between doing the important stuff.

"You know me and my idle hands."

After he sold his theater chain, Carter did not settle easily into retirement. There were the birdhouses, all thirty-seven of them. Then the archery lessons. The attempt at writing a book, which stalled out on chapter three. The six shades of blue he painted and re-painted the dining room.

"The devil's playthings, you always said. Not that I took to drinking or shoplifting. But I do like to have something planned to do. Maybe I need to make that thing not dying. That's a full-time pursuit."

He put his hands in his pockets and stood there a while. Chester had fallen asleep and snored happily. That dog didn't have any problem easing along through his day aimlessly. Chester worked at leisure like a full-time job.

"Maybe I'll take some cooking lessons or something. That would make you laugh," he said to Ava. "Or maybe starting rolling over down there."

At the bottom of the hill, one of the caretakers started up a riding mower. Carter looked his way and the man threw him a wave, the old man and his dog familiar sights to everyone at the cemetery. Carter gave him a high wave and then turned back to the graves.

"Anyway…had a close call. Been having some more pains. I guess I need to have a follow-up with the doctor, but they aren't pushing for it at all. What are they gonna tell me at this point? They got better things to do. Hell, we both have better things to do with our time. I just need to figure out what mine is."

He tried playing a few songs. He'd recently discovered that the chords to pretty much any song were online. And somewhere, some guy had recorded himself showing the chord pattern on YouTube, so any song Carter wanted to learn could be found in a private lesson. Today's task was *Sunshine (Go away today)* by Johnathan Edwards. It wasn't going well. The strumming pattern was hard for him to get and Edwards' voice was too high for him. But he sure did love that line about a man who couldn't even run his own life, and *I'll be damned if he'll run mine*. That stuck with him since he first heard the song in seventy-one.

He set aside the guitar and decided he should eat. He fed Chester and then left him to fill up the house with farts alone.

Carter drove to Mesa Grande and got there around eight. Only one other table was occupied, and they were almost finished. Ivana was there alone, either not needing a waitress on a slow weeknight, or sending them home early when the dinner rush was over.

"Am I too late?"

"For you? Never."

Carter took a seat at the counter, and Ivana went to the kitchen. The couple in a booth left cash and headed out, pulling on coats as they left. Carter sat in the cloud of smells and the gentle lilt of the music Ivana played.

She came out a few minutes later and set a plate of enchiladas down and a glass of horchata, then she sat on a stool behind the counter. She let out a long exhale like the quitting time whistle at a factory.

"I know that feeling," he said.

"Hard day?" Ever since she learned of his diagnosis, she looked at him with pity in her eyes.

"Hard day. Hard week. Hasn't been easy since I was a kid."

Ivana nodded and sipped at a cup of water.

"That's not true," he said. "I had a lot of easy days with Ava. Those days when there's nothing to do, those are the best when you're with someone. When you're alone, those days can be the worst."

"I know."

Carter nearly kicked himself for bringing it up around the woman whose husband and daughter were gone from her life, one of them permanently.

"Don't you get dragged down by my moping."

"On bad days, one thing that always makes it a little better is good food. And good friends." She raised her glass and sipped. She looked at the cup, disappointed. "And maybe a good drink."

"Yeah, tonight might be the night for that."

"What do you say? A nightcap?"

He knew she wasn't flirting or anything. And yeah, why shouldn't two friends who are alone go get a drink together?

"Great idea."

He finished his meal and paid her, despite Ivana's protests. Carter would never take a meal on the house.

She locked up, and she followed in her car to a bar a few miles away. It was a loud place with pool tables, a punching bag game for measuring strength, but really, all it did was give guys and excuse to pump it full of quarters in a futile attempt to impress women or intimidate other men.

They sat at the far end of the bar, away from the jukebox.

"So what made your day and your week so bad?" she asked while they waited for their drinks.

"Long story. Just another reckoning with the choices I've made."

"You think too much."

"Probably."

The bartender set down two long-neck beer bottles and two whiskey shots. Carter raised his beer to her and she did the same before they drank.

"You think there's any difference between a big decision and a small decision?" she asked.

"There must be. I mean, they're different enough to qualify them, so yeah. I guess so."

"I don't know." She sipped her beer. "Significant things can come from small decisions. Like I turn left instead of right and I get hit by a car. Or I decide not to go the grocery store that day, and I miss when the store is held up, and they shoot everyone inside. Those are small choices that had big impacts."

"Yeah, but whether or not to turn left doesn't keep me up at night."

She lifted her shot glass and nodded for him to do the same. "Maybe that only happens when you make the wrong decision."

She tipped back her shot and downed it in one gulp. Carter got half of his down.

"Sometimes you don't know it's the wrong decision until the last fucking second before it turns tragic." He stared into the rest of his whiskey, picturing what would have happened if he'd arrived at Landrum's door five minutes earlier.

A young man, maybe early thirties, tapped Ivana on the shoulder.

"Can you help me and my friend settle a bet?"

"A bet?"

He wore a blue chambray shirt, open two buttons at the neck. Jeans and a carefully cultivated beard groomed to look like it was a few day's stubble and not the result of expensive trimmers and beard oil. Carter eyed him while Ivana was merely confused.

"I think I can get over six hundred on the punching bag. My friend thinks I can't break four hundred. Will you be the judge for us?"

"I don't know what you're saying."

"Ooh, what's that accent? I love it."

Carter leaned around her. "Hey, guy, she's not looking for a pickup tonight, okay?"

He gave Carter a tough guy stare mixed with a little fake confusion.

"Was I talking to you?"

"No, but you shouldn't be talking to her, either."

He pulled an exaggerated face like he was stumped by everything Carter had just said. He turned to Ivana, "I know you're not with him because he's old enough to be your father. But he's not good-looking enough to have you for a daughter."

Ivana tried to let him down easy. "We're just here to have a drink."

"C'mon, it'll only take a minute. You come watch me destroy this machine, and maybe I'll buy you a drink with my winnings."

Carter saw the young punk in a different light now than he would have in his younger days when he spent more time in bars. He'd killed men. He'd taken men who behaved badly and brought them down. He dealt out justice in secret. A guy like this? He could start this way, a tiny bit obnoxious and disrespectful, but who knows where he'd end up if nobody corrected him or taught him a lesson.

Carter got off his stool. The guy watched Carter as if he couldn't believe it.

"C'mon, man," Carter said. "Give the lady a break."

"As soon as she comes to judge the competition."

"Hey, asshole—"

"Woah. What?"

Ivana swiveled on her stool to Carter. "It's okay. I'll go watch them. I'll be right back."

"No," Carter said. "He won't let you leave once you go over there. He doesn't look like the kind of asshole who takes no for an answer."

Visions of his daughter hit him stronger than the shot of whiskey. The guy who wouldn't take the no. Who then put her in his car and then crashed that car and killed her. This was Justin Lyons all over again. This time, he could do something.

"Dude," the guy said. "You need to sit back on that stool right the fuck now."

"I'll sit down, and she'll stay with me, and you need to go back to your friend and pay your tab and go. Go home and give each other a reach-around for all I care, but you're not doing a goddamn thing with this woman here.

She's too fucking good for you."

"You're pissing me off, man."

"Good."

Carter thought about shooting him. He thought of other ways to kill him. Waiting in the lot until he left and then running him off the road. Or maybe running him over with the truck before he ever got to his car. A razor to the throat. A knife to the gut.

This was his mind now. And these weren't just fantasies.

"Just fuck off, okay?"

Carter pushed the guy near his shoulder. He never even saw the punch. A cymbal crash sounded in his head, and his world leaned to the left. The music never stopped, but the lights went out. He tipped and hit his head on the brass rail, then a stool before he landed on the floor, his muscles slack and with no attempt to break his fall.

He heard Ivana scream, and he thought, *damn, this guy would have won that bet.* Then he woke up in the hospital.

He'd fallen for his own myth. The disease had nothing to do with how easily he'd been beaten by a man fifty years his junior. The hubris Carter showed while trying to defend Ivana had been his downfall. Now, he had a fractured orbital bone and multiple bruises to show for it. Luckily, the brain scan showed no bleeding inside his skull. He opened his eyes into slits, the bright fluorescent light bore through him and made his eyeballs throb.

Ivana sat up straighter in her chair.

"You're up."

The way she said it made Carter think it was a sight she thought she'd never get a chance to see.

The slightly open eyes were one thing, but words were still far off. He felt the dull pain in his face, his shoulder, his ribs. Whatever they had him on had worn off, and it's probably what led to him waking up. He grunted at the pain.

"What's wrong? Are you hurting?"

Ivana stood and went to the door, leaned out in the hall. She looked left and then right and called, "Nurse? Nurse, he's awake."

In no rush, a nurse entered. She went to a machine by his bedside before turning her attention to Carter.

"Hello, Mr. McCoy. How do you feel?"

He grumbled again, then tried to clear the thick gum from his throat. "Pain," he whispered.

"I bet you are in pain," she said. With a quick glance at the chart, she reached into the pocket of her uniform and drew out a small bottle and a syringe. Always ready to deal out the pain meds. She drew up a small amount and injected it into the port of his IV. She made a note on the chart and before she could put the clipboard down a warm rush came over him.

He reached up and touched his face, flinched at the jolt of pain and the feeling of raised flesh around his left eye.

"It's fractured," Ivana said. "But they said it will heal."

"It's a small one, nothing major, but might take some time," the nurse said. "At your age."

She pressed a button on one of his machines, then turned for the door.

"I'll let the doctor know you're awake, but after what I gave you, I think you'll sleep a little longer."

She breezed out the door. Ivana came to his side.

"You don't need to stay," he said.

"Don't be silly. This is my fault."

"How? You didn't hit me."

"I shouldn't have asked you out for a drink."

He made a dismissive noise in his throat, then found it hard to swallow. He eyed the cup of water next to his bed. Ivana followed his eyes.

"You want water?"

Carter nodded. Ivana held the cup for him, the bendy straw angled into his mouth. He drank nearly the whole cup.

"Go on," he said. "She said I'll just sleep." He looked for a clock. "What time is it?"

"About eight-thirty."

He hadn't shown up at Mesa Grande until around eight. "Morning?"

"Yes."

"You been here all night?"

Ivana nodded.

"Go home, then."

"I feel bad leaving you."

"Don't be. I got a whole staff."

She smiled. "Okay. I'll be back this afternoon."

"No, no. Go to work."

She shook her head. "No. Restaurant is closed today."

He grunted a frustrated sound.

"I'm the boss," she said. "I can do that."

She stood and gathered her coat. "You need anything?"

He shook his head. Then he remembered and said, "Shit."

"What?"

"Chester."

"Oh." Her hand went to her mouth. "Poor baby."

"Do you mind?"

"Of course not."

"Door's unlocked. His food is above the stove."

"Don't worry. I'll take care of him." She set a hand on his.

"Thanks."

She turned to go. "Oh." She turned back. "Police came by. They arrested the man who hit you. Said they might come back to ask you questions."

"Don't know what I can tell them. It's all a blank. Plus, I think it was my fault."

"Don't say that. You didn't make him hit you."

"I should have minded my own business. Told the bartender to toss him out or something."

"No. You did the right thing, Carter. It's what you do. You help people. Protect them."

"And look what happens."

She gave him a sad smile. "I'll be back later."

Less than five minutes after she left, Carter was asleep again.

"Turns out he was telling the truth, it was the gardener." DeFore took the last sip of his second latte.

"Who knew, right? I mean, nine times out of ten, it's the husband. And using the garden tools to kill her like that, a brilliant misdirect. Only it wasn't."

Margot winced, her cup of tea halfway to her mouth.

"You know I don't like murder talk. Especially so early in the morning."

"Sorry." He'd been warned about this before, but it was on his mind. He cursed himself as he saw her start to pull away. Another one lost. Another civilian who didn't understand or appreciate his job. Of course, he didn't tell her the whole story of his role in almost killing an innocent man. He'd really lose her then.

"You must be suspicious of everyone in the world," she said.

"Not everyone. But when someone is killed, it's usually by someone they know. I mean, bad things happen. We can't ignore them or pretend they don't."

"I'm not saying that."

He knew he was too wired on coffee. He didn't want to come off as defensive, but the words tumbled out too quickly.

"It can get damn ugly out there. Usually, you're only one step away from something bad happening and your file ending up on my desk."

"That's a pleasant thought." She turned away from him and looked out the window, letting the sarcasm float between them. Her mind was already outside. Her body would follow soon.

"Well, tell me about your day."

"Oh," she said. "More with Mrs. Stivers. Probably another change to the wall color, if the last two weeks are any indication. And if she changes that—again—then the couch needs to change—again—and probably ten other things. It's like they have no concept of how these things ripple, y'know?"

He loved her, he did. But as interesting days go, murder would always win out over decorating. But DeFore nodded and smiled and thought about a third latte.

"Look, Brian," she said. "I don't think I'm going to be able to go away next weekend after all. There's a furniture show in Milwaukee, and I really should go."

"I could join you. It's no problem to cancel the cabin. We'll do the big city instead."

She made a clenched teeth grimace. "I'll be working the whole time. And at the conference hall. I won't really have time to spend doing anything fun."

"Oh. Okay. I get it."

Maybe a shot of whiskey instead of another latte. Probably not at nine in the morning. Then again…

"I'll let you know when I can reschedule."

"No problem. We'll just do it another time. The lake isn't going anywhere." He made a lame attempt at a laugh and she smiled, then sipped her tea.

"Okay, I'll call you later." She stood, smoothed her skirt, and headed for the door.

DeFore noticed there was no goodbye kiss, no I love you.

He was losing her. His second huge mistake in as many days.

She felt odd about turning up at his door uninvited, but then again, he had done the same to her. Veronica Holliman pulled off the main road and headed up the short drive to park in front of the old farmhouse. Seemed like a nice place. Out of the way. No longer a working farm, she could tell, but not in too much disrepair. She didn't see his truck, but there was a car there, so she got out and walked to the front door. A woman answered.

"Yes? May I help you?"

She had an accent. Something Spanish.

"I was looking for Carter McCoy?"

"He's not here right now."

"Oh." Veronica wasn't sure how much to tell to anyone but Carter. "Well, Mrs. McCoy, can you tell him to call me when he gets back?"

The woman blushed. "I'm not his wife. I'm just looking after his dog. Carter is in the hospital."

A dog padded up behind her and sniffed the air at the newcomer.

"Oh, forgive me. Is he ill?"

"He had an accident."

Veronica noticed she didn't add the usual, *he'll be fine* that most people do. Instead, she got a slightly sad look on her face.

"I'm sorry to hear that. Thank you."

"I can have him call you when he gets out."

Veronica was already turning back toward her car. "No, thank you. That won't be necessary."

Carter was awake, sitting up in bed, reading a book Ivana had brought him. He'd told her to go to his shelf and look for anything where the spine looked intact and that meant he probably hadn't read it yet. Trouble was, Carter was gentle with his books, and they all looked brand new to Ivana, so she picked a title she liked and brought him *Walkin' The Dog* by Walter Mosley and *A Simple Plan* by Scott Smith. Both were books he'd read before, but he didn't tell Ivana that.

"I thought this would remind you of Chester," she said when she handed over the Mosley book. "And this one…well, your life could maybe be more simple."

Carter had read through the Mosley book the first night, fighting with the swelling in his left eye to be able to read the words clearly. But on the second day, the swelling was down considerably, and he made it halfway through *A Simple Plan* when Veronica walked in.

"Mr. McCoy? May I speak with you?"

It took a moment to recognize her, but when he did, he was shocked to see her.

"Oh. Yeah. Hello there."

He closed the book around his finger to mark his place. Her silver hair was piled neatly in a bun on top of her head. She wore gold hoop earrings and a quilted vest over a dark sweater with floral knitting.

"I'm Veronica Holliman. You came to see me about my husband."

"Yes, I remember."

She looked him over, the dark purple bruise around his eye, the brace keeping his shoulder from moving. He was off any IV, but they still had him hooked to a heart monitor.

"First off, are you well?" she asked.

"Oh, this." He waved his free hand at his face. "This is the least of my worries. Just a trip and fall."

"Glad to hear."

"How did you know I was here?"

"Your housekeeper. She told me you were in the hospital, and there aren't many options out here."

"You mean Ivana?" He chuckled. "She's not my housekeeper. Just my friend. And she's a fan of my dog, I think."

"I'm sorry. I assumed."

"Don't worry about it. So why are you looking for me?"

She threw a look at the door, making sure they were alone. She stepped closer to the bed, her purse buckle chiming on the metal bedrail. "You wanted to find my husband."

"I did," Carter said. "Before."

"I think I know where he is."

A hospital room is never fully silent. It hums and clicks and beeps. They sat in this industrial noise for a long moment while Carter debated how much to tell her and how to let her down that he no longer wanted or needed to know where Vernon Holliman was.

Veronica broke the silence.

"I was packing up the rest of his things. When I threw him out, I only gave him a short time to pack the essentials. I got tired of looking at all his, pardon my language, his crap cluttering up my house and my life."

"And you found something that told you where he is?"

"It's more what I didn't find. He took most of his hunting gear with him. I wouldn't put that on a list of essentials, would you?"

Carter considered it.

"He's kept a small cabin for years," she said. "Before I met him, even. It's deep in the woods, away from anyone. Good for hunting. And I think, good for hiding."

Carter liked the idea. It made sense. But he didn't want to find him anymore. Yes, he more than likely did the things he was accused of. If his own wife felt this confident in his guilt, then Carter doubted he'd have another false accusation to deal with. But he was done with all of it. The weight of it had become too much to bear.

"You might be right," he said. "But I'm not looking for him anymore. You should tell someone else."

"Mr. McCoy, you're the only one who has come seeking him. Even the families of the victims, they haven't sought him out after the case got thrown out." She folded her hands in front of her. To Carter, she looked too proper to be discussing such things. "When you came to my door, I felt that you had…intentions, Mr. McCoy. Forgive me if I'm being presumptuous."

"You're not really saying much of anything specific, Mrs. Holliman. At my age, in my condition, I don't have time to beat around the bush."

Veronica turned and walked to the door. She shut it quietly, barely a sound except the click of the door handle. She came back to Carter and stood over him.

"I felt you were seeking retribution, Mr. McCoy. Am I wrong in that assumption?"

He paused a moment, then shook his head slowly.

She continued, "Again, you were the only one. The police let it go. The courts let it go. The families let it go. But I can't let it go."

"The police didn't fully let it go."

"So you are working with them?"

"Not formally, no." Carter tried to sit up straighter, adjust himself so he didn't seem too frail in bed. "Look, Mrs. Holliman—"

"Veronica, please. I've left that name behind. I filed for a formal name change back to my maiden name."

"Veronica, the less you know about my intentions, the better, okay? For your own sake, not mine or the police."

"Mr. McCoy, I don't care why you sought out my husband and what motivates your retribution. I only know that I share the desire to see justice done where it has failed. My role as a victim in this is minor. He lied to me. He betrayed my trust. That's an insignificant thing compared to what he took from the women, the girls, really, that he took so much from. In some cases, their lives. I did nothing for so many years. It doesn't even matter to me that I did it out of ignorance. I should have known. I should have seen the signs. My ignorance is no excuse for my inaction. Women were victimized. Girls were killed. I cannot simply do nothing, still. I did nothing for too long."

Carter saw a solid veneer about to crack. This woman was strong and hardened by bitterness, but about to break apart.

"Then why do you need me at all?"

"I know what I can and cannot do, Mr. McCoy. I know my desire for justice and to right my husband's wrongs will fall short in the face of what I am capable of doing."

Carter let out a dry laugh. He waved a hand over himself, the bed, the machines. "And you think I can do any better?"

"It's not about physical strength. Mr. McCoy. Dealing with my husband means being capable of something else entirely. Something beyond physical strength."

He knew exactly what she meant. That he seemed to wear it on his face bothered Carter. If she saw this in him when he came to her door, it meant he had changed fundamentally from the inside, and he didn't like that at all.

"It's not my business anymore. I have other issues I need to deal with."

"So you know the truth, but you'll turn a blind eye?"

Carter sighed. "I'm dying. Soon, so they tell me. I thought it gave me a special permission to do things, but as you can see, it's not a free pass to live without consequences."

"The woman at your house said you'd be okay. As did you when I came in. Has something changed? Maybe you just don't believe in justice."

He smiled at that. He itched around one of the heart monitor leads stuck to his chest.

"There's a lot you don't know. You don't need to know all of it, but trust me when I say I understand what you're feeling more than you give me credit for. But there's a lot more that comes with it. A heavier weight than I think you want to carry. And one that if I add to the burden I'm already toting around, it might break my back."

He met her eyes. She stood, stiff-backed and stern.

Carter sighed. "I can't help you. I'm sorry. You should contact the proper authorities about where you think he is. They can help you."

"I think maybe I was wrong about you. But then, I've been wrong about a lot of men."

"I'd appreciate it if you didn't lump me in with him just because I'm telling you something you don't want to hear. You have to consider that I have my reasons, and beyond not wanting to burden you with them, they're my own business."

The hard plaster look of her face softened. He waited for tears, but none came.

"You're right. I'm sorry to have bothered you."

"It's not a bother," he said. "I want justice, too. I'm just…not the guy for that anymore."

"Well, I hope you recover and get back to yourself soon."

"That's all I'm trying to do."

"Good day, Mr. McCoy."

She turned and walked out, leaving Carter feeling like he'd been scolded by a favorite teacher.

"You're free to go, Mr. McCoy." The doctor closed the folder with Carter's charts. "Nothing life-threatening at all."

Carter began to laugh. The doctor paused and thought, unsure what joke he made.

"It'll take a while to heal fully, but you shouldn't see any long-term effects. I'm sending you with a prescription for Gabapentin and Hydrocodone. You can get those in the lobby pharmacy."

They sure did love their pain pills.

There was an air of finality in the doctor's tone, the way a waiter hands you your change and implies they need your table for the next paying customer. Carter's clothes had been delivered in a plastic bag and on his way out, the doctor pulled the curtain closed to allow him privacy while changed.

He gave the pharmacist his name and stood next to a row of empty chairs to wait. He'd been laid out and sedentary for too long. He needed to move his legs.

Goddamn stupid, the fight he got into. He couldn't even blame it on the drinks. They hadn't had time to reach his bloodstream by the time he was face down on the floor. There might have been a time when Carter would have gone home and put up a heavy bag, started to learn how to fight properly. Those days were long gone.

A cop had come by and asked him questions about the fight. He declined to press charges. The cop acted indifferent, maybe even a little appreciative, since it meant less paperwork. He didn't say it, but Carter could tell he was the kind of guy who thought bar fights were a part of the natural order of things and should be exempt from prosecution. He couldn't tell if the cop had any respect for him picking a fight with a guy forty years younger than him with a much better right hook.

"Mr. McCoy?"

Carter looked up to see Dr. Geisz, the specialist who had given him the fatal diagnosis months earlier.

"Did you have an appointment today?"

"No," Carter said. He waved a hand at the dark purple bruise on his face. "Something else."

"I see, I see."

Carter couldn't help but notice how the man seemed surprised that he was still alive.

"How are you feeling otherwise?"

Carter shrugged a bit. "Pains now and then. Tired easy, but that's not really new. Still kicking, so…"

"Glad to hear it." Geisz smiled like maybe he'd done something to miraculously cure Carter, even though he'd sent him away with nothing but a bottle of pills to dull his senses. "You should come see me; let me check you out, see how things are functioning."

"Yeah, I will."

He would not.

Dr. Geisz put a hand on Carter's arm. "Are you making the most of your time?"

The abrupt change from rare disease expert to strip mall therapist shocked Carter.

"I'm doing things I never thought I'd do. Things I didn't have the courage for before."

"Good. That's good. Making the most of this time is the best medicine."

"I thought it was all the pills." He nodded toward the pharmacy counter.

Geisz smiled. "Oh, yes. Yes, that, too. Good to see you. Call my office and make an appointment, okay?"

"Will do."

They shook hands, and Dr. Geisz walked away. The pharmacist called

Carter's name, and he picked up his bottles of pills. The names were starting to become familiar.

"Got any time in a bottle back there?" he asked.

The pharmacist, too young to know Jim Croce and clearly not in the mood for jokes, gave him a blank stare so empty and cold he swore he could hear the second hand on the clock tick.

A chorus of Canada geese overhead greeted Carter when he got home. He looked up and watched the V formation move South until they were out of sight. Smart birds. Get out while the weather still held. Ivana opened the door and welcomed him home. He hadn't realized what a sanctuary his home was to him. He so seldom left these days that he took for granted how comforting the old place felt. Surrounded by his memories, the worn fabric and floors scuffed smooth by his feet after decades. His plot awaited him next to Ava and Audrey, but there was a part of him that wanted to be buried here, on this land. But he could never give up a chance to lay next to his wife for eternity, or at least until they plowed under the cemetery, and he wouldn't care by then anyhow.

"So good to see you," Ivana said.

Chester came to the door, wagging his tail and trying to do little bounces. It made Carter smile to see the old dog's version of excited. He bent down and let Chester lick his face. When he stood, he said to Ivana, "I think someone's been giving him something more than just his canned food."

"What?" she said with a smile. "He deserves it."

"Lord knows what kind of smells I'm in for."

"Yes, that I will leave you with."

"Thanks for looking out for him."

"My pleasure." She put a hand under his elbow and led him inside. "Let me help get you settled."

He pulled his arm away. "I'm not that decrepit yet. You go. You got stuff to do, and I've kept you from it long enough."

"Are you sure?"

"Yes, I'm fine. I broke my face, not my arms or legs."

Ivana kissed him on the cheek. "I'll bring you dinner tonight after I close."

"You don't have to do that."

"I'm going to bring him food," she petted Chester on the head. "So I might as well pack you some too."

Carter gave a scowling look to Chester. "Spoiled rotten."

His tail thumped against the couch.

"You sure you're okay?" she asked.

Carter lifted his paper bag of pills and shook it, rattling the bottles inside. "They got me all fixed up before they kicked me out."

"You rest, then."

Ivana left, and Carter set down his bag, determined not to open any of the pills unless he couldn't stand the pain. The dull throb he felt right then he could endure.

He walked to the record player, passed a finger over the spines of his collection, and came out with a Chet Baker album. Ava used to love him. His sad, sweet voice such a contrast to his tragic, self-destructive life. He dropped the needle, and a muted trumpet filled the room.

Carter opened the back door and let Chester roam. He walked slowly down the steps, dropped his nose to the grass, and started his rounds, sniffing the yard inch by inch. A few stubborn leaves clung to tree branches, but otherwise, the woods were ready for winter. Carter leaned against the door frame and felt the chill in the air, even when the breeze wasn't blowing. He wondered how long until he had to start lighting a fire. Now that they were in November, chimneys all across the lowlands would start spouting white smoke.

A small brown bird landed on the railing of the porch. A sparrow of some sort, he assumed, but Carter had never been able to identify birds beyond the obvious robin red breast or a cardinal. The bird took two hops, turning her body, then darted through the open door.

"Hey!" He turned and followed the bird inside. It landed on the floor lamp and looked around the room. Separated from her flock? Lost? Either way, she was alone, and the warmth of the house seemed a better option than the outside right then.

"Go on now. Shoo."

He waved a hand in the air, but the bird didn't react.

"Come on, this isn't your home."

Carter took a step forward, and the bird flew into the kitchen. He spent the next ten minutes following the bird from room to room, always getting close but never close enough to grab it, and he couldn't steer it toward the open door.

When Chester wandered back inside, the bird had perched on the stair railing about halfway toward the upstairs. Chester didn't seem to notice.

"Come on, bird. You have to get out."

He flapped his arms again, but the bird ignored him, happy to be safe inside. Carter gave up. Perhaps she missed her chance to fly south. Maybe she knew if she tried going this late, she would be caught in a storm and die. She seemed satisfied to stay the winter in Carter's home. It made a strange sense to him. If he felt the comfort of the old place, why shouldn't some other creature? Chester surely did. If he kept the doors open, he might have a menagerie waiting out the winter with him. Foxes under the couch, possums in the attic, deer in the hallways.

Carter looked down at Chester. "What are you gonna do about it?"

Chester licked his lips and snorted.

The bird chirped once. Carter sat down on the couch, and Chester climbed next to him to get two days worth of overdue head scratches. They sat and scratched and listened to Chet Baker croon until they both fell asleep.

"Maybe I can retire."

DeFore watched Margot walk from the bed to the bathroom, his eye traveling from her naked back on down. He loved the little show of her backside even though they'd just seen a whole lot more of each other. It still felt like a sneak peek at something he shouldn't be seeing.

"I'm close to at least a partial pension," he said. "I'd have to check. I don't keep up with these things."

"What?" she said from the other room, the door open. "You don't want to retire."

True, he didn't, but he was trying to make a gesture. If he wanted to keep her—which he did—then he might have to leave the cop life behind. No more talk about bodies or crime or how dangerous the world is outside the door. Sure, he'd be miserable to leave it behind, but if he had Margot, she could fill that void.

"I'm just saying. Maybe it's time to think about it before I burn out or something."

The toilet flushed. "You're not gonna burn out. You love it." Margot appeared in the doorway, wrapped in a robe now. "Besides, you said you barely get enough cases to stay busy. Doesn't sound like burnout to me."

He leaned up on one elbow. "True. I just wanted to float it out there."

She pulled a hairbrush through her hair. "Brian, don't go making any big life decisions, okay? Not without really thinking it through."

He could hear the annoyance in her voice. "Yeah, okay. Sure. I was just spitballing."

"And look, I have a really early morning, so…"

He reached for the floor and picked up his t-shirt. She looked at him, eyes hinting at him, waiting for him to finish the thought so she didn't have to. He didn't say it because he didn't want to hear it, from either of them. She stopped brushing and let out a slightly annoyed exhale.

"I think it's better if you don't stay over tonight."

DeFore's face fell like he was eight years old again, and he'd just been told there's no Santa Claus.

"Oh, yeah. Sure. Of course. I don't want to mess with your schedule."

He pulled on his shirt and started searching for the rest of his clothes. What did she want? He can't talk about work and then when he tries to quit and give her what she wants, that's no good either. He knew he was bad with women, but how many times did he have to learn the lesson? He already reached expert status on the topic. Maybe this was just one of those classic men-and-women-are-different moments that all the comedians talk about. They'd laugh about these miscommunications later, when they were old and married and looking back on their life or answering the question of how they met at some cocktail party.

She sat on the edge of the bed. He could see the sympathy on her face, like the way she would tell a stray dog he can't come home with her.

"But hey," she said. "This was great. You were great. Really."

She leaned in and kissed him. He took the compliment and smiled. He knew some things about women, anyway.

"Yeah. It's always great with you."

She stood and went back to the bathroom mirror while he continued to dress.

"Maybe a movie tomorrow?" he said.

"I'll see. Gonna be a busy day."

"Yeah. Me too, probably. Full moon, y'know. More murders happen under a full moon than at any other time. That's not a myth. In the summer, heat and a full moon are a deadly combo. But even now, when it's getting cold. And I saw it's supposed to really dip this weekend. Might even get snow."

He wanted to kick himself and make his mouth stop moving. But when she stayed quiet for so long, he couldn't handle it. Especially after she'd basically kicked him out. Jesus, he was going to go home and get drunk tonight.

"Okay, well, I'll leave you to it. Get some rest."

"Okay, bye," she called from the bathroom. He heard her electric toothbrush start-up.

"Love you."

Nothing back. He knew she could hear. That toothbrush wasn't *that* loud. DeFore slunk out her front door, passing by the framed photos of her and her ex-husband still on the wall.

"He's still a part of my life," she'd said when he first mentioned them. "He'll always be the father of my child."

Her daughter was currently a senior at Marquette. He hadn't met her yet. Last time she was home, Margot kept them apart. She said they needed some "girl time."

He shut the door behind him and stood there for a moment, feeling lost. It was barely after ten o'clock. He thought about going to a bar for a drink. He thought about trying to find a late movie. DeFore stuffed his hands in his pockets and walked to his car, knowing full well he was going to get his own drink at home and watch some stupid TV rerun he'd already seen.

He texted her before he got in the car: MISS YOU ALREADY.

He waited a moment for her to respond, but nothing came through. He drove home.

She never texted back.

Carter opened the back door and spread bread crumbs in the doorway and then out and down the back steps in a line. He whistled a few times, trying to call the bird and get her interested in the breadcrumbs. He'd spent the night on the couch again, a more frequent habit. Chester couldn't do the stairs, and most nights, Carter dozed off on the couch and didn't have the motivation to climb the stairs only to get right back in bed, so he shared an awkward mingling of limbs with the dog on the couch.

A few times in the night, he heard the bird fly overhead. He found he liked the sound. Her tiny wings in the small space made a soft rustling in the air. After the melancholy horns of the Chet Baker album, the wings sounded like some kind of hope.

He knew the bird couldn't stay the winter with him, though. People did keep birds in cages, and what was the house but an oversized cage? But those birds were domesticated. And the cages had newspaper down for the droppings. He hadn't seen anything on the floor yet, but he knew it was only a matter of time and that he had probably already missed some.

He whistled a few more times, but the bird didn't appear.

"Fine, then," he said. "Just don't invite any of your friends over."

He left the door open, and the breadcrumb trail in place in hopes would lure her outside eventually. He walked Chester out to the truck and took him along to see Ken.

Guest parking was completely empty. No visitors today.

Carter left Chester in the truck for now. He'd bring him around to the garden later and let Ken get some scratches in and maybe a face lick or two.

One woman sat alone in the rec room, asleep in her chair. The speakers played a Neil Diamond song so low it took Carter a second to realize it was there. He walked down the hall to Ken's room. The door was open, and he stepped in, knocking on the door frame as he did. The first thing that struck him was that things were too neat. The bed was made, no empty food wrappers on the side table. The lights were all on. A plastic bin held Ken's toiletries and a picture frame tucked in at an odd angle.

But no Ken.

A nurse in a white uniform, red hair tied back in a tight ponytail, came to the door.

"I thought I saw you walk in," she said.

He didn't ask. He saw it on her face.

"When?"

"Yesterday. Late afternoon. He went quietly."

"Meaning you didn't even know he was dead until when? This morning?"

"Last night." She didn't get defensive. She had been trained in dealing with the grief of loved ones and how often they lashed out.

Carter looked at the empty bed. Might only be a day before somebody else moved in.

"I have boxes," he said. "At my house. For his stuff."

"It's okay. We have boxes. We reached out to his daughter this morning. She said to donate everything."

Carter looked at the picture frame angled in the box. Ken and his daughter, probably twenty years ago.

"Where is he?"

"They came and got him this morning. Anzalone Brothers Funeral Home. He asked to be cremated."

Carter had heard him mention that before. He looked at the closet, the bedside table, the armchair: all empty. He felt helpless, wanted to do something.

"You okay?" she asked.

"Yeah. Just…a little lost."

"I understand. Listen, I was going to go for a smoke. Do you want to come with me?"

"Oh, I don't…"

"Just to sit and talk. You can tell me about him. I only knew him a short time. Seems like you were a good friend."

Carter nodded and followed her outside.

In one of the many garden areas with small benches and birdbaths, she sat and lit up a cigarette. Carter stood.

"So it's Mr. McCoy, isn't it?"

"Carter."

She pulled aside the heavy coat and pointed to the name tag on her uniform. "Deena."

She blew out smoke, aiming it away from him. She pointed at her own face, mirroring his. "Had a fall?"

The mention of it made his bruise pulse with a wave of dull pain. "Yeah. Sort of."

"We get a lot of that around here."

"Don't worry, you won't be seeing me check in any time soon."

She blew out a cloud of smoke. Young people who smoked still confused Carter.

"You were the only one I ever saw visit him."

"His daughter lives on the West Coast."

Deena nodded. She'd heard all the excuses before. Work, distance, kids, time. Once they arrived here, most were forgotten.

"You knew him a long time?"

"You don't have to do this," he said. "He knew it was coming. It's coming for all of us." He put his hands in his pockets. "I really thought it would be me first."

"Don't say that."

"I'm not the only one. If my doctor is a gambling man, he's losing money on me right now. The smart bet would have been me being gone before Labor Day."

She chugged smoke out in puffs as she laughed. "You're a funny one."

"I'm sure you get dull to it after a while, the dying."

"It's part of the territory. Like you say, we know it's coming."

Carter nodded. He zipped his jacket higher to the collar. "A bird got in my house."

She raised an eyebrow at him.

"I know some people would think that was his soul or something. I know it's just a bird getting out of the cold. But, I don't know, things kind of line up sometimes."

"Yeah, they do."

"Did he leave a book unfinished?"

She thought about it. "I don't think so. I didn't see one in his room. I haven't seen him read much for a while."

"Well, that's good, at least. I'd hate to think he left a story unfinished. I guess you gotta know when to stop so that doesn't happen."

Deena stubbed out her cigarette. "At the risk of sounding like a life coach or Oprah or something, I do think we all kind of leave our own stories unfinished. You know?"

Carter smiled at this. "Spoken like someone young. No, all our stories come to an end. It just might not be the most satisfying end. May leave a lot of questions. And sometimes, the end of one person's story is the start of another story."

The words had just fallen out, but when he listened back to them as they moved through the air between him and Deena, he knew that he had ended people, and those endings were definitely the start of new stories. Some people only earned a few chapters in life. Others, long epics with footnotes and appendixes. He shook his head, done with his own metaphor.

"Aw, what do we know anyway? People die. Stuff gets put in boxes. They get put in urns. That's just life."

She flicked ash off the tip of her cigarette. "Yeah. Sorry. Just trying to find a little meaning in it. Most families like that."

"Oh, Deena, I'm not like most."

The bird had eaten several of the bread crumbs, but sat happily perched on top of the refrigerator when Carter got home. The back door was still wide open. He worried that word had gotten out among bird channels and he could be walking into an aviary in his home, but the little brown bird was still on her own. He felt certain the others had already moved South. She peeped twice when he walked in, but didn't move. Carter noticed two spots of white droppings on the kitchen floor.

"If you plan on staying, I'm gonna have to get you a cage. Can't having you crapping all over the house."

The bird watched him, wary. He sighed and went to the cupboard and dug deep behind the peanut butter jar and the box of instant oatmeal. He came out with a half-eaten bag of sunflower seeds.

"I knew I had this somewhere. They might be kinda old."

He took out a handful and spread them on the counter. Chester moved next to him, and he reached down and scratched his head.

When he heard the knock, he assumed it was Ivana coming back to check on him. Chester moved with him to the door and sat by his feet.

Veronica Holliman stood on his porch. Carter reached up and pushed down his hair, which he knew must be a mess. His whiskers had started to grow in again, dusting his face in white but covering the hollow cheeks.

"Oh, hello."

She smiled at him. "Good to see you up and about."

"Yeah. Shoulder is still sore. Face hurts like hell if I sneeze. Other than that…"

Chester yawned in the awkward silence, disappointed the visitor wasn't Ivana, and he wasn't going to get any carnitas with his meal.

"I have a favor to ask," she said.

"Look, Veronica—"

"I know you said you'd made up your mind, but I want you to come with me for one thing, and then I'll leave you alone. I promise."

She always looked so put together, like she didn't even own one of those outfits of loose sweatpants and an oversized t-shirt with an embarrassing logo. She never threw her hair in a sloppy bun on top of her head just to run out to the store. She didn't own sandals.

"Go with you where?"

"Will you trust me?"

He thought about it. He didn't see any reason why he shouldn't. He also didn't see any reason for her to be vague. But he also didn't have any plans for the day.

"You're buying lunch," he said.

"They have food there."

"If you say so."

He closed the back door and left a small dish of water on the counter for the bird, knowing all he was doing was making it easier for it to stay, but he felt bad for the little gal. He left Chester behind and followed Veronica in his truck.

She drove a simple sedan, immaculately clean. It took about twenty minutes until they pulled up to an Episcopalian church.

He got out and walked to her car.

"Listen, this is not my thing. It's a little late for me to find God."

She shut her door, not too hard, not too soft, that it didn't latch. "It's not a religious thing. We just use the space."

"Okay, who's we?"

She exhaled and crossed her arms. "This is a support group for victims." She paused, working hard to maintain her composure. "Victims of my husband."

Carter looked away from her to the building, more to give her a break from the scrutiny than to take in the bland white box with the cross on top.

"Like, survivors?"

"A few. Family too, from the ones who didn't survive."

"Jesus…"

"Now, who's invoking religion?"

He raised one corner of his mouth slightly to acknowledge her humor in the face of darkness.

"Okay," he said. "Let's go."

She led the way.

"I assume this food you spoke of is awful," he said.

"Yes. Terrible."

In the basement, surrounded by murals of Bible stories obviously painted for children, was a circle of folding chairs. Against one wall was a table with a coffee urn, some trays of hot dishes, obviously homemade. Typical noodle hot dishes, potato hot dishes, tuna with a crust of crushed potato chips.

Six people stood around sipping drinks, but no one had filled a plate yet. Carter figured they saved it for after, or they knew better.

There was one time he and Ava went to a survivor's group for parents dealing with the grief of the loss of a child. It was a thoroughly depressing evening with performative tears, questions of why howled at the sky, and detailed retellings of stories nobody should have to hear. It also took place in a church. The food was store-bought.

He and Ava made it nearly the whole way home in silence before they both admitted the night had been a waste of time and they never wanted to attend another. They were dealing with Audrey's death in their own way, which didn't involve wailing and moaning and sharing their heartbreak with strangers.

An older man came over and shook hands with Veronica. She declined to introduce Carter to the group. When it was time to sit, she took a seat outside the circle and Carter sat beside her.

They listened in silence as two sets of parents and two girls, now in their early twenties, recounted their experiences. Carter listened intently.

He was struck by how nobody cried. They all held their trauma like stones in their chest. The first girl to recall how this man had used his role as an adult to make her do things she never would consent to or understand, made Carter's heart ache for how mechanically she told the story. The experience was somehow not her, a process that happened to a shadow next to her that she could report on. A feeling remembered from an all-too-real dream.

One of the fathers spoke. He could feel Veronica tighten next to him when he expressed doubts about the trial. Maybe the man was still out there, waiting for another victim. More young girls would be hurt, maybe more killed.

From what she'd said to him, Carter could tell she wanted this man to stand up and fight for his daughter. To seek vengeance against the man who took her away. The same man who hid who he was from Veronica all those years.

Carter listened for over an hour, slowly losing his appetite.

Most of the talk steered toward supporting each other. No graphic accounts of violence suffered or losses endured. Just people building their own raft against a storm.

When it ended, they drifted over to the tables, but no one ate. By the time they said goodnight, the coffee urn was empty.

"I hope you don't think I was trying to ambush you," she said.

"Isn't that exactly what you were doing?"

Veronica tilted her head as she thought about it. "I suppose so."

Carter stopped in between their two vehicles, his back to the passenger door of the truck, hers to her driver's side door. He kept his hands in the pockets of his jacket. The sun had gone down, and a faint glow clung to the Western sky. Overhead, a light on a tall stanchion turned on, washing the parking lot in a yellow glow.

He asked her, "You don't have any doubts?"

"Why else did he run away?"

"Kind of hard to keep living like normal when your wife thinks you're a monster."

"He is a monster." He could see the cold on her, but she kept herself from shivering. Standing straight. A proper lady.

"You really think he might be at this cabin?"

"I think it makes a whole lot of sense."

"And you don't want to tell that to the police?"

She gave him a penetrating stare. "You saw what happened last time."

He nodded and looked down at his feet. Did he have one more in him? The words of the fathers sounded so familiar to him. Speaking of an absence instead of a daughter. A void in your home, your life, your day where there used to be light. No man should be allowed to take that away.

He could help.

"Okay," Carter said, lifting his eyes to hers. "Let me see what I can do."

3

He thought about calling, but figured they probably keep records or trace every call that comes in. Especially calls to homicide. So Carter chose to drop by unannounced. He knew DeFore's car by now, from all the times he'd shown up at Carter's place by surprise. It wasn't exactly payback, but Carter felt no guilt about springing a visit on the detective.

He saw DeFore leave the building and walk toward his car. He pulled out of the parking space and let his truck drift in idle down the row. DeFore turned when the rumble of the engine caught his ear. Carter saw him react. He waved Carter on, sending him to the far end of the lot. Carter complied and waited there.

DeFore got in his car and drove to the exit, subtly hung his arm out the window, and pointed to the right. He turned that way, and Carter followed.

A mile and a half later, DeFore pulled into the cracked asphalt lot of a place called Lancaster's. He went in ahead of Carter.

Inside, he wasn't hard to find. The place was a long galley with a bar along the left side reaching to nearly the back wall. The bar top was tall with stools and a padded red leather bolster notched with divots from elbows resting for a long evening's drinking. DeFore was near the back in one of the five booths under lamps with stained glass advertisements for beer. The kind of lamps distributors give away for free.

Carter sat opposite DeFore, who had already dug into the small bowl of pretzels.

"What's up, McCoy? What's this about?"

"You seem edgy," Carter said. "What's the matter? Don't like people dropping by unannounced?"

"Get to the point."

There was no waitress. The barman came out from behind his fortress and stood by the table looking slightly annoyed the men hadn't stopped off to order on the way back here. There were only two men at the bar, and they looked happy enough to nurse their beers for another hour without requiring any attention. He asked for their order wordlessly, with only a lift of his chin.

"Gimmie a Goose Island," DeFore said.

Carter nodded his head. "Same."

The barman went away.

"So," DeFore said. "You just here to talk about old times over a beer?"

"I need the gun."

DeFore took a long moment to chew his pretzel. "What for?"

"What the hell do you think?"

"He was innocent."

"Not him. Holliman."

DeFore squinted at him. "You found him?"

"May have. In case I do, I need that gun."

DeFore shoveled another handful of pretzels into his mouth. "Can't do it."

"What do you mean?"

"What do you think I mean? I mean, I can't. It was a dumb idea in the first place. I put it back in evidence."

"What the hell am I supposed to do?"

"I don't know. Stay home. Leave him alone. The fuck do I care?"

The barman returned with two glasses of beer, set them down without a word, and went back behind the bar.

"You wanted this done not too long ago," Carter said.

"Yeah, well, maybe I was wrong."

"You know what the guy did."

DeFore drank. Carter went on.

"You know it was you guys who screwed up and let him go."

"It wasn't my screw-up. Blame that one on the arresting officers and the

DA. A real perfect storm of incompetence."

"Men with badges."

"I can't help you, McCoy. You want to do this. You're on your own." DeFore took another healthy sip. "I got my own problems."

Carter lifted his beer and laid on the sarcasm. "You don't say? Wonder what that's like." He drank. They sat in silence for several minutes, each one trying to outlast the other. Each man confident their problems were worse by comparison, and neither wanting to admit how much they had in common right then. They could be friends, if they wanted. They could talk about things they couldn't with anyone else in the world. But both were stubborn, prideful. Neither one wanted a new friend and wouldn't know what to do with one if they admitted they could be good for each other.

"I'm not saying don't do it," DeFore finally said. "God knows I want that scumbag wiped off the face of the earth. I just can't help you anymore."

"*You* help *me*? When was that ever the case?"

"I'm dealing with some personal stuff. Thinking of retiring, actually."

"Then what the hell do you care if someone finds a gun missing from evidence after you're gone?"

"It was too risky in the first place," DeFore said, raising his voice. "I need to do whatever I can to keep Margot happy, and getting caught in some I.A. investigation isn't going to help what I think is a pretty tenuous fucking relationship right now."

The barman gave the men a look. DeFore lowered his voice to a near whisper.

"I think she's gonna dump me."

"I don't remember asking."

"Have a heart, McCoy. You've lived through loss. You know what it's like."

Carter swallowed a mouthful of beer and set his glass down on a square coaster with yet another beer ad on it. "Are you comparing some girl you've been dating for a few months to my dead wife of over forty years?"

"I'm just saying, you know what it's like to have your heart broken."

Carter lifted his beer, took a long swallow, then set it down.

"Thanks for the beer. Other than that, thanks for nothing."

He stood, grabbed a few pretzels, and walked out.

Snow began to fall the next morning. Small, dry pellets, not the heavy flakes that made people feel romantic about snow and write songs about it. Nothing more than tiny ice crystals, a harbinger of deeper cold yet to come. Carter drove to Veronica's and watched the snow blow past the windshield and gather in the tall brown grasses on the side of the road. It would likely be gone by tomorrow. Overhead, a flying V of geese passed by. Late starters getting out while they still could.

His second unannounced visit in a row.

Veronica answered the door, looking entirely too put together for someone home alone, not expecting visitors.

"I wasn't sure when to expect you," she said.

"Let me ask you, did he take *all* of his hunting equipment with him?"

Five minutes later he was standing in front of a hall closet while she dug into the deep recesses behind the coats. She came out with a leather gun case and a small hardshell case as well as a camouflage hunter's cap with ear flaps and a high visibility neon orange band.

"I knew he had more in here."

Carter took the long gun case and laid it across the dining table. He unzipped it and pulled out a .30-.30 hunting rifle that had been in storage for a long time. Inside the hardshell case was a revolver and twelve shells.

"Do you have ammo for the rifle?"

"I didn't see any in there."

"I guess I'll have to stop on the way. I'll wait until I get up closer to the cabin. Out there in the wooded areas, it won't be suspicious for a man to buy a box of shells." He moved the hat aside. "Looks warm, but I don't want to be seen that easily."

"Oh, right. Of course."

"Okay," he said and zipped the leather case back up. "How close can your directions get me to the cabin?"

"It's easier if I just show you."

"Well, since you're not going, you'd better just write it down."

"What do you mean? I have to go."

"No, you don't. This is nothing you need to be involved in."

She folded her arms across her blouse. "I'm already involved. And I know the way."

"Veronica—"

"I want to see this through." She lifted the hard case from the table. "We're going to do what nobody else could seem to: get justice."

Carter took the gun case from her hands and set it back down.

"You need to understand, I take no pleasure in this. Doing this…job. It's not fun or exciting or satisfying in any way. It's ugly and mean and nasty, and you don't want any part of it."

"If I don't go along, if I don't see it with my own eyes, it will stay with me forever. I'll never be rid of him. I'll never live down what I could have done, what I could have said." Tears came to her eyes and threatened to fall. "I let those girls down. Don't you see? I failed them. I could have done something, and now I get a chance to. It might be too little, too late, but if I don't, I'll never be able to live with myself."

He took in her words and the look in her eye, like crystal, but cracked. The way a hairline fracture can split the middle of even the hardest stone. It will weaken it from within, and one day, it will split in two.

"You'll do what I say? Stay back when you need to?"

She nodded.

"And any time you want to leave, you can do so."

She nodded again.

"Okay. I'll pack this up. Grab a warm jacket, some boots. We'll stop for food on the way there. And before we go I need to stop off at my place." He lifted the leather rifle case, looped the strap over his shoulder. "I need to pick up my dog."

Chester rode between them, making the bench seat crowded. For the first few miles he didn't know where to sit with Veronica in his usual spot, but he soon let his tiredness take over and laid down with his chin on her leg. She absently stroked his head. Carter hadn't said much. He didn't want to talk about what was to come, but he also felt he should reassure her or explain some things. Truth was, he didn't know what to expect. There was a freedom in knowing if he walked into a situation he would not come out of alive, it was no big deal. That simple fact gave him the courage to do it. With another person in tow, it changed his approach. He would need to be less reckless.

Before heading out of town, Carter drove them to Mesa Grande. They got there before the lunch rush, around eleven a.m. Ivana was surprised to see him, but more surprised that he came with a woman.

Carter saw her raised eyebrow look while Veronica scanned the menu.

Carter kept his voice down. "She's a friend."

"I see."

"I'm not sure you do."

"*Que bonita.*"

"I don't know what that means, but I'm doing her a favor. That's all, okay?"

"Okay."

They ordered burritos. Easier to eat in the car. Carter didn't know if it would be a bad omen to stray from his usual order. He didn't need any more dark clouds following him.

"It smells so good in here," Veronica said.

"Thank you," Ivana said, then went to the kitchen.

"You said about two hours?" Carter asked.

"About that. Maybe a little more. Not sure how fast that truck of yours can go. Maybe we should have taken my car."

"You'll forget you offered that once you see how much Chester drools and when he lets off some of his gas bombs, which he can't help, by the way."

"Maybe you're right, then."

Carter didn't tell her he also wanted less to connect her, should things go badly. If her car was seen in the area, she could be linked to her husband's death. In cases where wives are murdered, the search usually starts with the husband. Nobody talks about the wives who are statistically just as likely to kill their husbands.

Without asking, Ivana had included a bowl of meat, beans and cheese for Chester. Carter decided he would wait until they got there to feed it to him.

Ivana held on to the sack with the food when Carter went to grab it. He looked up at her and met her eye.

"Be careful," she said.

She knows what kind of favor I'm doing for Victoria, he thought.

"I will."

"And bring her back. She's very…elegant."

He turned and looked where Victoria was studying some photos on the wall of Ivana's home country.

"I know what you mean."

"Maybe this is not the right word," she said.

"No. I get it. Too nice for me is what it really means."

Ivana let the bag go and scoffed at him. "Stop it."

Victoria waved and said, "Thank you," as they left.

In the truck, Chester went wild with the smells.

"Might be hard to eat with him in your lap."

"It's okay," she said. "I'll save mine. I'm not that hungry right now."

"I know what you mean."

He stashed the bag in the narrow gap behind his seat and the door, then turned the truck North. Snow kept falling in icy pellets, starting to gather in the corners and against the walls.

Chester rode between them, making the bench seat crowded. For the first few miles he didn't know where to sit with Veronica in his usual spot, but he soon let his tiredness take over and laid down with his chin on her leg. She absently stroked his head. Carter hadn't said much. He didn't want to talk about what was to come, but he also felt he should reassure her or explain some things. Truth was, he didn't know what to expect. There was a freedom in knowing if he walked into a situation he would not come out of alive, it was no big deal. That simple fact gave him the courage to do it. With another person in tow, it changed his approach. He would need to be less reckless.

Before heading out of town, Carter drove them to Mesa Grande. They got there before the lunch rush, around eleven a.m. Ivana was surprised to see him, but more surprised that he came with a woman.

Carter saw her raised eyebrow look while Veronica scanned the menu.

Carter kept his voice down. "She's a friend."

"I see."

"I'm not sure you do."

"*Que bonita.*"

"I don't know what that means, but I'm doing her a favor. That's all, okay?"

"Okay."

They ordered burritos. Easier to eat in the car. Carter didn't know if it would be a bad omen to stray from his usual order. He didn't need any more dark clouds following him.

"It smells so good in here," Veronica said.

"Thank you," Ivana said, then went to the kitchen.

"You said about two hours?" Carter asked.

"About that. Maybe a little more. Not sure how fast that truck of yours can go. Maybe we should have taken my car."

"You'll forget you offered that once you see how much Chester drools and when he lets off some of his gas bombs, which he can't help, by the way."

"Maybe you're right, then."

Carter didn't tell her he also wanted less to connect her, should things go badly. If her car was seen in the area, she could be linked to her husband's death. In cases where wives are murdered, the search usually starts with the husband. Nobody talks about the wives who are statistically just as likely to kill their husbands.

Without asking, Ivana had included a bowl of meat, beans and cheese for Chester. Carter decided he would wait until they got there to feed it to him.

Ivana held on to the sack with the food when Carter went to grab it. He looked up at her and met her eye.

"Be careful," she said.

She knows what kind of favor I'm doing for Victoria, he thought.

"I will."

"And bring her back. She's very…elegant."

He turned and looked where Victoria was studying some photos on the wall of Ivana's home country.

"I know what you mean."

"Maybe this is not the right word," she said.

"No. I get it. Too nice for me is what it really means."

Ivana let the bag go and scoffed at him. "Stop it."

Victoria waved and said, "Thank you," as they left.

In the truck, Chester went wild with the smells.

"Might be hard to eat with him in your lap."

"It's okay," she said. "I'll save mine. I'm not that hungry right now."

"I know what you mean."

He stashed the bag in the narrow gap behind his seat and the door, then turned the truck North. Snow kept falling in icy pellets, starting to gather in the corners and against the walls.

The snow started falling with purpose. Carter thought of the window he'd left open for the bird. His house would be freezing when he made it home; possibly a snow drift would have built up under the window. He bet the bird would still be inside. He felt awkward about the silence. He'd gotten in the habit of not listening to music in the truck ever since he stopped buying cassette tapes. The few he had all wore out years ago and he never upgraded the stereo to a CD player. He rarely listened to the radio because he hated the ads. It never bothered him when he was alone, but the presence of another person seemed to amplify the sounds of the road, the creak and moan of the bodywork, and the low grumble of the engine into an industrial noise that could have been used to torture prisoners of war.

"Did you want me to put on the radio?" he asked.

"I don't mind the quiet," she said. "It's been a while since I drove anywhere of any distance."

Carter scratched his chin. He hadn't shaved in several days, and the whiskers were thick now, if not yet long. His chin had gathered a coat of white to match the ground outside.

"Snow's picking up," he said. The last bastion of small talk—the weather.

"Yes. Looks like it will stick a bit."

They moved West on 14 before turning North following signs to St. Cloud and Brainerd. The farmland was flat and cut close like a military haircut. Patchy trees stood in clumps as if they were huddled together against the cold. Carter turned up the heat.

"So," Veronica said. "You've done…this before? This sort of thing?"

"Yes. When it helped people. Or when I felt it could, anyway."

"And you're deputized, is that it?"

"Not formally. It's uh…complicated like that."

She shifted in her seat, turning her attention out the side window. "I shouldn't ask so many questions, I suppose."

"No, no. It's fine. I just don't have great answers. This is still new to me."

"Is it?"

"I don't want you thinking I've made a life out of this sort of thing."

They passed a turnoff to a lake and a campground. Still a long way from their destination, though. Snow moved in waves across the two-lane highway, snaking with the wind.

"I suppose it's not something we should talk about much at all if we can't even come out and say what it is we're talking about," she said.

"Actually," Carter said. "I'm of a mind to get it out there so there isn't any confusion. Can you talk about it?"

"I think so."

"I'm going to kill your husband."

Chester shifted between them. The wind outside and the blowing of the heater blended into one tone.

"Yes. That's right."

"Just so we know exactly what we're talking about here."

"The others that you've…" Veronica stopped herself. "They deserved it, you felt?"

"I did. No way I would do it if I didn't feel that with all my conviction. It's not an easy task. I need to know for sure."

"I'm sure," she said, a hardness in her voice. "Very sure."

"It's the only way this works."

He stopped for gas at a place that sold chainsaw sculptures. Life-size grizzly bears and oversized trout leaping in the air lined the side of the parking lot. There was artistry there, but a crude one, as only a chainsaw would allow.

Carter lifted Chester down from the cab and led him to the edge of the lot for a place to pee. He hadn't brought a leash, but Chester never strayed far.

He sniffed the new bouquet of smells, but didn't linger in the cold. When they got back to the truck, Veronica was eating.

"This is good," she said.

"Yeah. Ivana has the touch."

He opened the plate she had fixed for Chester and led him to the back, lifted him into the bed of the truck, and let him make his mess there. Carter ate half his burrito, then went inside to buy two bottles of Coke. Next to the register was a photocopied flyer for a missing child. A boy, eight years old. Last seen over three months ago. The edges of the flyer were curled and stained. Carter stared at it, and a helpless feeling came over him. There were more monsters out there. More men who needed to find justice, but he could never get to them all. He could never rid the world of the evil that lived in dark corners and under masks of genial kindness. Why do it at all if he had to pick and choose which evil to vanquish?

The cashier handed him his change. He walked out, leaving the boy behind.

He lifted Chester back inside, trying to brush off the snow that had accumulated on his coat.

They continued North.

"I'd say about two and a half more hours," she said.

"Okay. Puts us in around dusk. We'll scout it out and maybe wait until first light."

"You're in charge."

"Looks like you got one." Chief Winters slapped a file folder on DeFore's desk. "Single victim in a house fire," he explained.

"Arson?" DeFore asked.

"Not clear, but the medical examiner said his lungs were clean and pink. No smoke."

"Which means he was dead before the fire."

"A-yep. He's taking a closer look, but you should get started. Guy had an ex-wife and an ex-business partner."

"One more x, and he gets tic-tac-toe."

"One more, and he gets to be tagged as a homicide." Winters tilted his head at DeFore. "I thought you'd be more excited than this. You got a hot one. Literally."

"Sorry. No, great. I'll get right on it."

"You don't sound enthused."

DeFore swiveled in his chair. "Chief, you've been married how long?"

"Twenty-nine years."

DeFore nodded and grunted. "And she doesn't mind what you do? She doesn't mind hearing about your day or knowing the kind of stuff you see on the job?"

"Beth's father was a cop. She knew what she was getting."

"Ah. I see."

"Women troubles?" Winters asked.

"You could say that."

"My father used to say if you have a woman, you have woman trouble. I wouldn't worry about it, though. Most of the time, it blows over. They like being angry sometimes. It's entertainment for them."

"Yeah. Maybe."

"Well," he tapped a finger on the file folder. "Nothing will take your mind off it like a fresh homicide."

"Yeah. I'll dig in."

DeFore read over the file. Not much to go on, but the ex-wife and ex-partner did raise some red flags. He'd have to look at the usual stuff there, like insurance payouts to the wife. Business debts with the partner. Money. It was usually about money.

Except when it was about betrayal. Jealousy. Hatred.

He'd resisted all morning, but he finally relented and called Margot. He played it dumb, or cool. He wasn't sure which.

"Hey there," he said.

"Oh, hi."

"I was hoping to see you tonight."

"Oooh." She made a long grunt like she was going over complicated numbers. "I don't think tonight is good."

"Got another hot date?" He tried to put some laughter in his voice.

"No, just busy. Deadlines looming, you know."

"Yeah, I get it."

If she hated hearing about his work, she would not like to know what he felt about listening to stories of her job. A job that didn't help people the way his did. Redecorating a room was fine and made one person feel good for a while, but DeFore was out there saving lives and putting criminals behind bars. Making a difference in his community, not just someone's living room. But she treated her job like open heart surgery sometimes.

"This weekend, then."

"Yeah, I'll see. Should be good."

Why didn't she just break it off with him? What use was the lying? Was she that cruel or that timid?

"And hey, dinner on me, okay?"

"Okay. Let's talk on Friday."

"Okay. See you."

He didn't want to give her an I love you, mostly because he knew he wouldn't get one back. And if he did, it would be a lie.

137

They turned off into lush green trees dappled with white. The storm hadn't slowed and seemed determined to announce winter had arrived. They hadn't seen the sun in the entire time they'd been driving. Light but steady snow fell, swirled into spirals by the wind like the weather was trying to remember how it was done after the long summer off. "There's a lake up here," Veronica said, "but he didn't build on the water. He wanted a hunting lodge, not a fishing lodge. Most people build on the lake, so the cabin is at least a mile from anyone else."

A secluded spot away from prying eyes, Carter thought.

"He get much up here?"

"Deer. Wild turkeys. That's about it. He'll take a deer into a place not far from here where they butcher and section the meat. Then it ends up in our freezer for a year, getting freezer-burned until you can't eat it. Neither one of us even likes venison that much."

Carter had lived with a lifelong distaste for hunting. The desire to shoot a wild creature simply wasn't in him. He fished, but always catch-and-release, and never with the passion of so many men he knew. He'd never have a mounted trophy on his wall with glass eyes staring at him, filling him with guilt in his own home.

Now, he'd taken the lives of men. He needed no stuffed and mounted heads on the wall for their eyes to still follow him around. They chased him in his dreams, spoke to him in whispers, and haunted him with their names and their last expression burned into his memory.

They reached a turnoff, and Veronica seemed relieved that she had remembered the way.

"It's up here a little way."

Tall trees flanked the unpaved drive. Carter slowed the truck and resisted turning on the lights even though, with the fading light and tree cover, the route grew dark. He saw three vehicles parked—two SUVs and a sedan. Carter turned to Veronica.

"It must be Dave and Keith."

"Who are they?" he asked.

"Hunting buddies. They came up here and always drank way too much beer. I always worried someone would shoot somebody when they were drunk and acting foolish, which was most of the time." She gave a slight snort of a laugh at this.

"I thought he would be alone."

"So did I."

"This changes things."

"I'm sorry."

Carter pulled to the side and turned off the truck. He watched the cabin. It was a sturdy structure built of thick pine planks. A wide porch ran along the full front with three steps up. The roof was clean and free of holes or patches. A brick chimney stood on the far right side. Vern kept the cabin in good repair. Not easy to do when you leave it vacant for months at a time.

Carter saw no lights on. No smoke curling from the chimney.

"One of those cars his?"

"That one." She pointed to the dark blue SUV.

There were no tire tracks in the snow, so the cars had gotten there before the snow started to fall. No footprints, either, so the men had been out on the hunt all day. Carter sat and waited for ten minutes, watching for activity or any signs of life. Nobody was in the cabin.

He thought about getting out and having a look around, but he would leave footprints. Vernon would know he was among the hunted now.

A pain gripped his stomach. It blindsided him, his attention outside the windshield. It felt like an arrow had been shot through his gut. He let out a quick grunt and gripped the wheel with one hand, his stomach with the other. Chester lifted his head, and his ears went up.

"What's the matter?" Veronica asked.

Carter couldn't speak. The pain was sharp this time. It was localized to a small space, like a thin hole had been drilled through him. He lifted his hand off the wheel and held it out to her, asking for a moment of her patience.

Often times the pain would rise and fall, crash and recede like a tide. Now, it kept a constant fire. A hot metal wire strung through him and unspooled from a never-ending supply.

"What can I do?" she asked.

He shook his head, eyes clamped shut. "Nothing," he managed.

Chester sat up with a whine. He licked at Carter's hand, and Carter stroked his ears to calm him.

He tried to breathe deep through it. He squirmed in his seat to try to find a comfortable position, but nothing helped. For five minutes, he fought off the grip of pain until it subsided, fading out like a spring rain running its course.

Carter sat back in his seat, let go of his gut, and ran his hands down across his face, slick with sweat.

She could see the worst of it had passed. "Are you all right?" she asked.

"Sorry about that. It happens sometimes."

"Have you seen a doctor?"

"Yeah." He let out a big breath and with it a laugh, his muscles starting to unclench. "Even better, they saw me. Nothing they can do for me, though."

"What do you mean nothing?"

"Just that," he said. "Nothing can be done. One of these days, I'll get an attack, and it won't stop. Not until I do."

"My God, Carter. I had no idea."

"It keeps things interesting, at least."

He smiled, but the effort made him close his eyes. He thought for a moment he might drift off. He could use a nap, for sure. But now wasn't the time.

"We'll come back," he said and started up the truck.

"Come back when? Tonight?"

"Morning. I need to think about this and about those other men. Where can we eat around here?"

"If we get back on the highway and go another fifteen miles, there's a town. Decent enough size."

Carter backed down the unpaved path to the highway, driving deeper into unfamiliar territory.

Neither one ate much. Carter wasn't surprised about Veronica. To stay that thin in your old age took either discipline or a disease. Carter simply wasn't that hungry.

"So these other men," Carter said. "Do you think they know what he was up to?"

"I'm not sure. I can't imagine. But I don't know how blind I was anymore." She swirled ice in her tea. "If I missed as much as I did, who knows what went on under my nose."

"If they're all involved…"

He trailed off, thoughts taking over that he didn't want to say out loud. Killing three men amounted to a massacre. He didn't think he was up for it.

She let the silence pass until it became uncomfortable.

"So I guess it's poor judgment on my part to go off into the woods with a relative stranger. You said this wasn't always what you did."

"No, not hardly."

"Well? Tell me some about yourself."

Carter shifted in his seat. He wasn't sure how much to tell. What was relevant. In many ways, he'd lost track of who he was before.

"I was married. She passed. I had a daughter. She passed. I ran a chain of movie theaters until I got bought out by a bigger chain. And I'm dying soon. That about covers it."

She nodded slowly. "When you get to our age, it's odd to condense your whole life into a list. Feels like there should be more chapters in that book. Footnotes and appendices. But you look back, and it feels both long and short at the same time."

"I know what you mean. I see all these clear dividing lines. When my daughter died. When my wife died. When I first…when I started doing this."

"What were their names?"

"My wife was Ava, and my daughter was Audrey."

"Pretty."

He nodded with a smile and looked down into his glass.

Veronica went on. "I guess this is a dividing line for me. Finding out who Vernon was. That my life had been a ruse. And now this."

"Yeah, well, old dogs and new tricks, I guess."

Carter lifted his hand to signal the waitress they were ready for the check.

"Will his friends stay over the night?"

"They usually would go off for a long weekend, or even a week. Now that they're all retired, who knows? Go until the beer runs out, I guess."

"I think we should get a hotel. Go back out when it's light. Maybe I'll go out in the morning alone."

Carter still wanted to spare her the killing. And now, with three, he wasn't sure how complicated it could get. Or what his chances of coming back would be.

"I told you I need to see this through."

"I don't think you know exactly what you're in for."

"With more of them, isn't it better if there's more of us?"

"You ever fire a gun?"

"I've been hunting."

He met her stare. No more side-stepping what they were about.

"You ever fire at a man?"

Veronica's eyes darted away. The very thought made her flinch. Carter let out a breath.

"It's not easy," he said. "No matter how vile of a thing he did. You think hate can get you through it. You think you can get it done before you have time to think about it. You can't. If you're there to see it, that's one thing. I'm not putting a gun in your hand. I'm not giving you the burden I carry.

Not because you're weak, not because you're a woman. Because nobody should have to carry it. I only have to carry it a short way. It's why I took it on. But the weight of each man I've killed sits on my shoulders, and that, not the disease, is what's gonna push me into the grave."

She dry swallowed, then took a sip of her tea. He could see the truth of it land on her.

The waitress arrived and dropped the bill. She looked at the half-eaten plates.

"Everything okay? You need a box for anything?"

Carter shook his head. "I think we're okay." He set down his debit card. "Thank you."

She walked away. The interruption had given Veronica a welcome moment to collect herself.

"I know you're right. I also know whatever it was that made you do it the first time is what I feel right now. I'm not eager to pull a trigger, even at Vernon. I don't want to kill anyone. Just asking you to do this for me is hard enough. I don't take it lightly. I also don't take what those girls went through lightly. For me, it's the suffering of them that I carry with me. I don't know if it's as heavy as the burden you bear, but I know it's all the weight I can stand. And the only way to lift that load, is if he pays what he owes."

Carter studied her and tried to show her that he understood. Soft eyes, a slight nod. His hands brought together in front of him. They were a team now.

"Let's get some rest, see what's there in the morning. I'll have a plan then. I need to find out if these other men are involved. If not, then we need to wait until he's alone. We can't be impatient about it."

"I agree."

The waitress returned.

"Is there a good hotel nearby?" Carter asked. "I think it's too late to keep driving tonight."

"The Starlight is nice. You go down about three miles that way." She pointed over Carter's head. "Not a lot of choices around here. Some bigger places a little further out."

"No, that'll be fine. Thank you."

He filled in a large tip.

"You know what?" he said. "I will take a box."

She took the signed check with a nod and went to get his takeout box.

"For Chester," Carter explained. "I didn't bring his cans of food, and he's not picky."

He had to gamble. Would they go to her place or his? The classic line. He wondered if that's how they met. Some sleazy bar, a bad pickup line, a few too many drinks. Or was he a work friend? Someone who didn't talk about murders and assaults, but decorating and pretty things. How could he expect someone to love him? Certainly not a woman whose whole life was devoted to adding beauty to the world. All DeFore did was try to take away some of the ugliness. Even in that, he failed.

He'd added to it. Caused death, hired it out, and used an old man to pull the trigger. What's uglier than that?

But the men who were gone made the world a better place without them, right?

While he waited, he went over the murder file again. The victim's name was Jeremy Henault. Age thirty-four. Clean record, no health issues, suddenly drops dead in a house fire. Mysterious circumstances, arson to cover their tracks. This case had the goods, but he knew he couldn't discuss it with Margot. A bar-b-qued body wasn't her speed.

He guessed right. The Mercedes pulled up out front of Margot's place. The tall man got out, holding a bag of takeout food. He double-timed it to the door. DeFore understood why they chose her place. As you'd expect, it was decorated exquisitely. Homey, but elegant. The right mix of chairs you wanted to nap in and decor you'd be reluctant to touch.

So she canceled on him and then invited the tall man over. The dinner DeFore wanted to buy her was now being unpacked on her kitchen counter. The room filling with the smells.

Or maybe they'd let it wait. Get right to the sex. Then use the takeout to fuel up for a second go-round.

She was a liar. A cheater. He tried to recall if they'd ever said anything about being exclusive, but it should be implied. He told her he loved her. She could at least be honest with him. It was the bare minimum in a relationship, even a non-exclusive one.

He sat in the car, watching the windows, thinking of his options. He could go knock on the door, confront her, and have it out on the front step. He could call her tomorrow and break up over the phone, never see her again. He could ghost her and stop calling, not return her calls. He could write a letter detailing his heartbreak and make her feel guilty, as she should.

DeFore had options. But either way, something had to be done.

Carter had to pay an extra thirty dollars for having a pet. He tried to pay for Veronica's room, but she insisted on paying for her own. The clerk at the front desk checked them in with disinterested efficiency and gave them rooms next to each other.

Veronica checked a thin gold watch on her wrist.

"Probably too late to go out shopping for a change of clothes."

"At the finer establishments, yes. But Walmart is open late."

He saw the debate happening behind her eyes. She didn't look like she'd shopped in a Walmart her entire life.

"Well, beggars can't be choosers."

Carter used the restroom, splashed a little water on his face, and then went back into the hall. She was already waiting for him. Chester followed behind as they went back to his truck.

"I'm afraid this is turning into quite the excursion," she said.

"It's okay."

"I did want to thank you, though."

"Don't thank me until it's over."

They found the Walmart twenty miles away. Chester stayed in the truck, and they split up once inside, him heading for the men's department, her to the women's.

"I'm gonna go ahead and get camouflage," he said. "I know that's probably not your style, but at least nothing too bright."

She nodded her agreement, and they separated.

What kind of clothes are best to kill a man? So far, he'd only worn his regular clothes. Whatever he happened to have on that day. Now he was dressing the part, like some militia member. Or a hunter stalking the most dangerous game.

He filled his basket with toiletries, a small bowl for Chester to use for his food and water, and a few cans of dog food for him. He stopped in the sporting goods section and found a box of shells for the rifle. Thirty rounds. More than enough, he hoped.

When he met up with Veronica he was surprised to see her with a full camouflage outfit draped over her arm.

"Did you get layers? It'll be cold."

"How long do you think we'll be out there?"

"Good point. You're probably fine." He hoped she would stay in the truck anyhow.

They drove back to the hotel and stood beside each other at their doors, Walmart bags in hand.

"Good night," Carter said.

"Good night."

He pressed the key card against the pad, and it beeped. He opened the door and used a knee to guide Chester inside.

"May I ask you a question?" she said.

"Sure."

"How long were you married?"

He felt the familiar sting of missing Ava. No matter how many years it had been, when the thought intruded, it always came with a sharp edge.

"A long time."

"And you can adjust?" she asked. "To being alone?"

He saw the fear in her. She'd kicked out the man she'd made memories with, had plans with, told her secrets to. With him gone, it was like trying to keep a roof from caving in when you remove a load-bearing wall.

"Eventually," he said. "I won't say it's easy."

"You survived."

"In my way."

"It must be harder for you. You didn't want her to go."

"She didn't suffer. I'm grateful for that. It wasn't a long, slow decline or anything. She went quick. Hit me like a bullet, but better that than death by a thousand cuts, you know?"

Like what he was living through right then. He was grateful Ava didn't have to live through seeing his long slide down or have to wait for him to drop dead, knowing it was coming but unable to stop it. She didn't have to see the shadow fall across his face.

"I suppose so," she said. "I still don't know what to do with myself some days. I start talking and forget there's no one there."

"Get a dog." He raised one half of his mouth in a subtle smile.

"I've been thinking of a cat."

She did seem like more of a cat person to Carter. Made perfect sense.

"Look, it's like anything else. You one-day-at-a-time it. You learn to fill your days. You learn to be comfortable by yourself. You learn to cook for one person."

Her eyes went down to her feet. He knew she had still been cooking too much and dealing with leftovers. The only reason the transition was easy for Carter was he never cooked much while Ava was alive.

"I go out a lot," he said. "to solve that problem. But then you're stuck staring at an empty chair, and that's not easy."

"No. It's not at all, is it?"

"If you want to call this off, I understand."

"I'm not going to let that man off the hook and back into my life just because I'm lonely."

"I'm just saying live and let live."

"It's what those people have to live *with*. No, I haven't changed my mind. I just wanted to know it gets easier."

"Easier. Not easy. But easier, yeah."

Veronica reached out and set her hand on his. "Thank you."

"Good night."

They went into their rooms, and the doors closed in unison.

Carter filled a bowl of water for Chester who drank in sloppy gulps. He laid out his new camo gear on a chair, saving the bag to use as luggage for tomorrow. He brushed his teeth and got in bed. The curtains didn't close properly and the bright lights from the parking lot slashed through the room in a yellow line like someone had strung caution tape across the center of the room.

He thought about his approach for the next day, unsure how to do it. Chester stayed on the floor and was snoring within a minute. Carter stared at the ceiling, wide awake.

They both had coffee, black. No cream, no conversation.

The mood in the truck was somber. They'd fed Chester, but had each skipped breakfast. Checkout was easy, drop they key cards at the desk and carry their Walmart bags out to the truck. The snow had stopped falling and the air was crystalline clear with a sharp chill carried on a steady southward breeze. A fine coating of white covered everything, but let signs poke through of what was underneath. Part of a stone wall, the black smudge of a used tire, chipped blue paint on an empty newspaper stand.

They crossed out of the small town and onto two-lane highway sur-rounded by dark pine forests. It felt more appropriate. Nearly naked trunks of quaking aspen, black walnut, and white oak filled in gaps where sunlight could be reached for, but a flat coat of gray hung low over the sky like a ceiling of poured concrete.

Carter wore his new camouflage outfit, his heavy tan coat wedged behind the seat would obliterate most of the cao from his top half at least, but he'd need the warmth today.

Veronica looked quite different in her Walmart clothes. She'd taken out her earrings and removed her necklace, her hair pinned up in a silver ponytail like water spilling from a mountain spring.

Her makeup-free face showed a little more of her age, but did nothing to diminish her stately beauty, Carter noticed. She would have photographed well in black and white. Maybe could have been a big movie star in the 1950s.

Vern's rifle was wedged behind his seat, under Carter's coat.

Carter quietly hoped Vern's two friends had gone. Collateral damage was a risk, but he never wanted to hurt innocent people. If they had anything to do with Vernon's activities, though…

He took the turn-off and stopped when he felt he was out of sight from the highway, although no cars had passed in the last fifteen minutes. He saw no tire tracks in the snow on the driveway road leading to the cabin.

"Can I get you to stay here while I go reconnoiter the area?" he asked.

Veronica looked up the lane, then to him. "I guess so."

"Okay, good. I'll leave the keys. If you get cold, run the heater."

"Come back and tell me what you find."

"I will. Don't rush me, though. I want to take things slow and not make any mistakes."

You get near a dangerous animal, it's always the sudden moves that doom you.

Carter pat Chester on the head and got out. He didn't know if he did it for luck or out of habit, but it always made him feel a little better. He reached behind the seat and got his coat and the rifle case. He zipped the coat to his neck, the bitter chill already cutting into him. He unzipped the case, drew out the weapon, and dropped the case in the bed of the truck. He added his newly purchased box of shells to the pocket of his coat.

He stayed off the dirt lane and kept to the trees. Most were probably thirty feet overhead, never more than six feet apart. A dense forest probably thousands of years old, burned and regrown, traveled by countless deer, birds, small mammals, and at one point Native Americans before being given over to weekend hunters who felt "connected" to the wilderness two weekends a year when they broke free of the cubicle.

He moved slowly, but the walk was a longer distance than he remembered. After a half mile, he spotted the cabin and waited behind a tree. No smoke from the chimney. No sounds of laughter or conversation. Still three cars. He could see footprints in the snow leading to and from the porch and aimed off into the trees.

Carter waited, listening, watching. He was hunting, in his own way. Trying not to be seen or noticed, rifle in his arms, his reason for coming into these woods to take a life.

He moved closer to the cabin. Still no activity. He approached a window and peered in. No lights. A few empty beer cans on a table, three empty plates. He tested the door. Unlocked. No need for security. Who was going to come by here this far from anyone?

Carter thought about going back for Veronica, but he wanted to look around first. He stepped inside, bringing a footprint of snow with him. He closed the door.

The men were slobs, as he'd expect any three grown men to be on their own. The bones of a roast chicken were scattered over the counter, picked nearly clean. He looked closer and thought maybe it had been a quail or a ptarmigan the men had shot and cooked for themselves.

The main room was open with a kitchen on the back wall, a couch facing the fireplace, then two doors to bedrooms and a bathroom, door ajar, on the other side of the kitchen. At least they had indoor plumbing and a septic tank. A deeply stained oval rug sat in front of the couch covered in years of bootprints. A small dining table with four chairs made a token separation between kitchen and living area. The sink had a hand pump to draw water from a well. He wondered if they survived on cold showers, or perhaps no showers.

Inside the refrigerator was a half-eaten pack of hot dogs, some condiments, several six packs of beer, sliced American cheese, a jar of pickles, and a few pre-made containers of potato salad and cole slaw.

The freezer was filled with bagged cuts of meat with dates written on them, along with a few Hungry Man microwave dinners.

Floorboards gave off a chorus of different creaks from high to low, long to short. Each step brought a new tone, like a flock of exotic birds. He opened the first bedroom door. A queen bed, unmade, and a small closet door open to a rack of hanging flannel shirts and jackets. An extra pair of boots and two more rifles. He knew the men would each have one with them while they were out.

The second bedroom had two twin beds and the same style outfits in the closet. Two more rifles leaned against the wall, and a handgun sat on the dresser. Carter lifted it and checked it was loaded. It was. He opened the top drawer and found a box of ammunition for the handgun. He stuffed the gun and the box of ammo in his pocket.

He went to the bathroom and found three razors, three toothbrushes, and three sticks of deodorant. At least they were making an effort. As he suspected, the shower stall looked unused. A roll of toilet paper sat on top of the toilet, one end hanging down loose like Chester's tongue when he got hot.

A small rectangular rug was the only color in the room and the only surface not wood-grained. He stepped over to look inside the medicine cabinet. The thing that struck him wasn't a sound, but a lack of sound. He'd been giving off a steady song of creaks and moans from the floor joists since he entered the cabin and now there was nothing. The bathroom seemed to be fitted tightly. He stepped back, retracing his steps. His foot came down not with a creak, but a hollow thump.

Carter ignored it and checked the cabinet. Some first aid supplies, a jar of antacid, some Vick's, Tylenol, replacement razor cartridges. He shut the mirrored door and stepped back.

The lack of sound again.

Carter kicked aside the rug with his foot. He could see a seam along the edge where the floorboards met the shower stall. It would make sense, if not for the small notch cut-out. Enough for Carter to fit the four fingers of his right hand. He pulled, and nothing happened. He fit his fingers in a little deeper, felt something metal. A clasp of some sort. He pressed his fingers, and a latch released. He lifted again and the floorboards raised, five boards across and about two feet long. The trapdoor slid on a well-oiled hinge, and Carter found himself staring into a hole with wooden ladder steps leading down.

He thought again about calling Veronica, but he wanted to look first.

It was too dark to see without a light. He set the rifle down, leaning it against the sink, and went back to the kitchen, and under the sink, next to a fire extinguisher, he found a flashlight. Carter thumbed the power switch to make sure it worked, and it gave off a weak yellow light. Good enough.

Back in the bathroom, he laid down on his stomach and looked inside. A low-ceilinged room, dirt floor. A crawlspace. Not unusual at all. Maybe an old fruit cellar.

He tried to get a good look around, but the light would barely penetrate the black void of the space. Dark dirt made the walls and floor. No light got in other than from the open trap door, like a grave that hadn't been filled in yet.

Carter moved to the ladder and went down. It was only seven steps, and he reached the dirt. He had to crouch to move forward. He shone the light out ahead of him, expecting to find something terrible, expecting to see Vern waiting in the darkness.

He walked to where he thought he was under the kitchen. His light hit on something other than dirt. He pushed the light out in front of him. A mattress. It was stained nearly the same color as the dirt floor. He traced the shape of the small twin mattress pad until he reached the far wall. A thick pine log sat on a small concrete pad and held up the floor joist. Drilled into the log were two eye hooks, and drooling away from them were two short chains ending in clamps made of iron or deeply rusted and stained steel. Clamps made for wrists.

He tried to make sense of what he was seeing, and there was only one explanation. He had found where Vernon kept the girls.

4

"He'll be back soon." Veronica said it to Chester, but also to herself. She ran a hand down along the dog's skull and stopped to scratch at his ears to calm him. He kept sitting up and staring out in the direction Carter had gone, his breath fogging the window.

She hadn't yet figured out Carter McCoy. A man in his seventies, embarking on a second life as an assassin who wouldn't even take money for the job. He claimed he was dying, but didn't even know specifically from what. But something in that first time he'd shown up at her house made her see into him down to what she knew was a good soul.

She struggled with the contradiction in her own opinion. Her husband had done bad things and she now hated him for it. But Carter had killed and was planning to kill more, yet she thought of him as benevolent. That contradiction was what drove her away from the church after an upbringing by protestant parents who never questioned anything they heard spoken by a preacher in the pulpit. But even at a young age, Veronica wondered how a God who loved mankind could let such cruelty exist. Then it became obvious to her that light and dark, good and evil coexisted all around her and oftentimes inside each of us. How dark things got, you never knew until after it was too late.

She'd left her watch off, along with all her jewelry. It felt to her like he'd been gone ten minutes, but she knew waiting in silence probably made half that time seem like longer. She felt undressed when she came out of her room that morning, no makeup, no jewelry, this ridiculous camouflage outfit on. She didn't want to care what Carter thought of her, but she did.

He was a handsome enough man, and if they'd met decades earlier, well maybe…

But his love for his wife was obvious. Of course, as it always was, seeing a man's devotion to someone else only ever made them more attractive. That any man had the capacity to love completely made them a rare gem.

Chester let out a small grunt, and she wondered if he needed to get out to pee. She scratched his ears and decided to wait a little longer.

Any doubt took wing like a bird late for the southern migration. It felt good to know for certain. The mattress and chains didn't look recently used, but other than maybe blood stains on the cuffs, he wasn't sure what would indicate that they had been. No food plate or waste bucket. He had no way of knowing how long the girls would be kept under there. He didn't really want to know. The details didn't matter. One minute was too long, and it meant a bullet for Vernon Holliman.

Without proof of the other men, he didn't know what to do about them. He decided on innocent until proven guilty. The underground room was sufficiently hidden that they might not know about it. It was reasonable.

None of the women who accused Vernon of his crimes ever mentioned accomplices. To Carter, the men had made a poor judgment in the friends they kept but couldn't be assumed to be criminals.

Standing by him, even after the accusations, was probably some act of loyalty among men. Men tended to stand by each other in some lingering tribalism not yet lost to evolution. They trusted Vern and believed his denials. With crimes this horrifying, accepting them was a bigger leap than thinking it had to be untrue.

So Carter was left with isolating Vernon and killing him, but not the others. He needed to separate Vern from the herd.

Since it was Vern's cabin, he could assume he would be first through the door when they came back, but waiting inside left him no way out. The cabin had no back door. If he shot their friend, surely the other two would fight back, and being trapped inside wasn't a smart move to Carter.

If Vern had moved up here permanently, then a good bet would be to wait out the friends who eventually would have to go back to their lives and leave Vernon alone in the woods. But how long that would be, he had no idea. Not that he had anything to urgently get back to, but with Veronica and Chester along and with his numbered days, waiting on about anything became a dim prospect.

He did think how gratifying it would be to shoot Vernon, not fatally, but enough to incapacitate him, then shove him into the hole under the cabin and lock the door.

A chill ran through Carter. He didn't like having those thoughts. Didn't want to think he was capable of such sadistic images, or the satisfaction it would bring him to know Vernon Holliman was dying a slow death in total darkness inside a dungeon of his own design.

Were these new thoughts, only since he'd begun this new chapter of his life? Or had they always been there? Or were they inside all of us when pushed to it?

A boisterous laugh came through the trees. Carter snapped out of his thoughts and lifted the gun. He heard voices. He went to the small window over the sink and peered out. Three men were coming through the pines toward the cabin, two were dragging the eviscerated corpse of a deer behind them. Field dressed down to only a carcass and leaving a streak of pink along the snow.

Only from the news reports he read did Carter recognize Vernon Holliman from the trio. He was the tallest and widest of the group. His rifle was slung over his shoulder, and two hands gripped the front leg of the deer, a young-looking buck with a small rack of horns, but easily two to three hundred pounds, even after gutting.

The men were close, but approaching the cabin from the rear. If he moved fast, Carter could make it out the front and maybe reach cover in the woods without being seen. But Carter hadn't moved fast in many years.

Floorboards creaked, and his boots pounded as he crossed the tiny cabin as quickly as he could. He left the door open behind him, not caring if they knew someone had been there. He cut to the right and ran in between two of the cars parked out front; each one dusted with snow.

"Hey!"

He didn't know who had said it, but it caused him to pause. He crouched down between the cars and leaned on his knees. He could keep running, and they would chase him down. Even if they were only a few years younger, he doubted he could outrun three of them. And he didn't want to end up leading them to where Veronica was waiting.

"You, motherfucker."

Carter spun and put his back to the side of the one sedan. In the sharp, chill air, their voices carried clearly. He leaned out enough to see the men. They had dropped the deer carcass, and Vernon had unslung the rifle from his shoulder. Vernon was a solid man, thick in the belly and the chest. Carter didn't imagine many women having much of a chance against his bulk. The other two men were slightly smaller, but both round in the belly from years of beer and weekends spent parked in front of the TV watching Vikings or Twins games.

"Is he stealing our shit?"

"Fuck that, is he stealing my car?"

He could try to explain. Make up a lie, say he got lost. Abort the whole plan. Come back some other time, or apologize to Veronica that it didn't work out.

"You guys go inside."

"Vern, you know that guy?"

"I sure don't. Get in there, I said."

Vernon might be sending them away, but they'd be watching. Armed and waiting.

Carter heard feet on the steps, then the door closing. A light breeze rattled the pine needles like a million chattering teeth in the cold. He pressed his back into the passenger side door of the sedan, his only view the dense trees.

"You a cop?" came Vernon's voice. There was an edge of fear in it. He'd been waiting for someone to show up.

"No," Carter said.

"Why are you in my cabin?"

"Just lost."

"Bullshit."

Vernon's size twelve boots pressed into the snow with a sound that made Carter wonder how they ever got close enough to get a deer.

Carter peered around the front bumper of the car. The discarded carcass of the deer lay at the corner of the cabin. Vernon Holliman walked slowly in a crouch, his hunting rifle out ahead of him at hip height.

"You're Vernon?" Carter asked.

"Who the hell are you?"

"You know not guilty is not the same as innocent."

Carter set the gun across his knees. Got his right glove off by tugging at it with his teeth and then gripped the stock and laid his finger aside the trigger guard. Vern's rifle looked newer and more powerful, with a long scope the size of a mag light. But it would do him no good as the men were now only ten feet apart.

"You broke into my property. Anything that happens now is self-defense. Justifiable."

"You remember that phrase. Self-defense. Something those girls never had a chance for."

A second voice called out. "What's he talking about, Vern?"

"Shut up, Dave. Shut the goddamn door."

Carter heard the snow crunch under Vernon's feet again.

"You come onto my property," Vern said. "Armed and with ill intentions. Ain't no jury in the world would convict me."

"You ought to know."

Carter rolled to his right, came up flat on his stomach, and fired.

The shots came not like a thunderous boom, but as a sharp crack like a frozen branch snapping. Veronica sat up and leaned forward in the seat. Chester stiffened, aware of her anxiety. Two reports, then a third and a fourth.

She reached down and turned the key. The truck rumbled to life. She hadn't driven anything but her Volvo for years, but she pulled the shifter on the steering column down into drive and spun the tires for a moment before the truck shot forward.

Glass shattered as one of the windows in the sedan exploded. Each man had fired twice and nobody was hit. Vernon clomped up the porch steps and met Dave coming out, rifle in hand, but focused on his car and the shattered window. Carter ran for the trees, ducking his head between his shoulders. In ten steps, he was breathing hard and chugging out steam with each panting breath. He stopped behind a pine tree and turned back toward the cabin. The narrow tree didn't cover his whole body, so he turned to the side for more coverage. Vernon was looking in his direction and fired a wild shot into the woods.

The element of surprise was gone, and Carter was outgunned three to one. Retreat was his best option.

"You son of a bitch." Dave, angry about his car, fired a shot into the trees before Vern dragged him back inside.

"What the hell is going on out there?" Keith asked. He kept trying to look out the front window, but pulled back in fear of being seen by whoever had shown up and started shooting.

"It's nothing," Vern said.

"Bullshit, it's not nothing. You two were trading shots out there. Did you get him?"

"I don't think so."

"So who is he?"

Vernon waved a dismissive hand and gave a look out the window. "I don't know. Some asshole who wants to take the law into his own hands or something."

Dave said, "Is this about your trial?"

"Some people won't accept a not guilty and think they know best, God dammit. I can't help that."

"Vern, you said that shit was over and done."

"Well, I guess not."

"Jesus Christ."

Tires skidded to a stop on the sheen of snow. Vern looked out to see a pickup truck he didn't recognize.

"Fuck. The cavalry is here. Look, boys, this is an invasion of my property. Anything or anyone you shoot is self-defense." Vernon turned away from the stunned looks on his friend's faces. "They're looking to spill blood, so I say we get there first."

"This isn't the wild west, Vern," Keith said. "We can't just have a shootout."

"They brought this. It's them or us. You want to die here today?"

Vernon reached for the doorknob.

Carter saw his truck nearly slam into Vern's SUV. He broke from the trees and ran toward it. He saw Veronica behind the wheel, searching the front of the cabin, wondering what was happening.

Carter waved at her, tried to get her to back up and drive away.

"Get back. Go back!"

She saw him coming from the woods. She opened the door.

"No!" he said.

Chester stood on the seat, watching her and waiting to be eased down from the truck like always. She leaned forward and pushed on his chest to make sure he was back far enough when she shut the door.

The front door of the cabin opened, and from inside, two shots came quickly. Both hit the hood of the truck.

Carter lifted his rifle and fired as he ran. Two shots hit the wood side of the cabin, and then his trigger clicked on an empty chamber.

He heard shouting from inside, and all three guns erupted at once. The front of the truck was dotted with holes, and Carter slid to a stop behind

Vern's SUV. He heard Chester bark from inside the truck, then Veronica scream.

Carter leapt forward, his breath creating a cloud like a steam train leaving a station. He ran around the back of the truck and saw Veronica on her knees by the driver's door. He dropped and put his back to the rear tire, took out his box of shells, and thumbed four into the rifle, listening for more shots. He heard the men's voices arguing in words he could not make out. Chester let out a few more barks muffled by the glass.

He looked to his right and Veronica had curled herself into a ball and was worming her way under the truck.

"Stay down," he said. "Get under and stay there."

A spot of red stood out against the snow where she had fallen.

"Holy shit, holy shit." Dave held his rifle in one hand and faded back away from the door.

Vernon took up a spot behind the couch where he could see out the open door. "I think I got one of them."

"How many are there?" Keith asked.

"Not sure."

"It's a fucking ambush."

"Listen up," Vern said. Dave and Keith had no choice but to pay attention. "The best defense here is gonna be a good offense. Like I said, it's all justified because it's on my property, and they obviously came here to do us harm."

"Not us," Keith said. "You."

"Whatever. A bullet doesn't ask for I.D. We gotta get out there and make sure they don't box us in and breach the perimeter."

"What are you saying?"

"We take the fight to them."

Dave fell back farther toward the rear wall.

"It's that, or we die out here," Vern said.

Carter crouch-walked forward until he came even with Veronica. His eyes studied the front of the cabin.

"Are you hit bad?"

"I don't know. It hurts."

"Where is it?"

"My side."

"You stay under there, okay? Don't come out."

She'd brought a gun, but it was still inside the truck, behind the seat. Carter calculated how much effort it would be to get it out, if he ended up needing it. Then he remembered the handgun he'd taken from inside the cabin. In all the chaos he was surprised he remembered his own name. He reached for the gun and went to push it under the truck to Veronica, but dropped it when he heard a noise.

The front door to the cabin opened wide. Vernon was first out the door, firing as he came. Three shots all went into the hood of the truck, dicing the engine with .30-06 shots. He dodged left as the other two men came through the door and split up, one left and one right.

Carter leaned on one knee and fired twice. Keith fell with a pained grunt.

"Shit." Dave stopped and reversed course, headed back for the open door. Carter fired one at him, but missed and shattered the front window.

Vernon fired twice more, and one of the front tires on the truck popped and hissed. Out of bullets, Vern ran for the door as well. Carter leaned out to take a shot, but was too late. The door slammed as Vernon kicked at it with his boot as he ran past.

Keith's inert body lay on the wood plank porch, his rifle a few feet away where it fell.

Carter saw an opportunity.

"Let's go," he said.

He reached up and opened the door, stood, swinging the rifle over his shoulder on its strap, and lifted Chester down into the snow. He leaned back into the cab and reached behind the seat, his hand closing around the hardshell case for the revolver. He brought it out with him.

The truck was ruined, the flat tire the least of the issues. The engine block had been riddled with bullets, and he could smell fluid leaking from several holes. They couldn't drive away, but they had to go.

Chester was smelling Veronica as she crawled her way out from under the truck. Carter offered her a hand, and he pulled her the rest of the way out. Her jacket had a hole in it, low and near her hip. Blood soaked through the clothing.

"Can you stand?"

"I think so."

He helped her to her feet, keeping eyes on the cabin. Chester circled around them.

"Let's go."

"Where?" she said.

"Away from here."

He patted his leg to call Chester to follow, took Veronica's hand, and moved as quickly as the lopsided trio could go into the dense trees. They passed the discarded carcass of the deer, followed the path the men had returned on for a short while, then diverted into the woods.

"Is he dead?"

Dave hung back far from the broken window and the threat outside.

"I don't know," Vern said. "You want to go out and check his pulse?"

"Seriously, Vern, what the fuck is happening?"

Vernon crouched behind the couch and began reloading his rifle.

"I had a few threats after the trial. Didn't think any of them had the balls to do anything about it, though."

"That's what this is? About your trail? You said that was over."

"Well, not for them, I guess. Jesus, it's not my fault if some guy goes psycho over what happened to his daughter or something. This is as twisted as them seeking the death penalty, y'know? They wanted that for me. They wanted to kill me."

Dave had known Vernon for twenty-five years. When the trial hit, they would laugh at how absurd it all was. While Vernon was in custody, Dave came to visit, and they talked about the perversion of justice to keep an innocent man locked up and how the newspapers had already convicted him.

Did Dave have doubts? Sure. How could he not? They seemed to have some damning evidence. But Vernon was insistent on his innocence. And if he was kidnapping and torturing young girls, Dave would know about it, wouldn't he?

He spoke with Veronica outside the courthouse one day. She'd been convinced. She thought her own husband was guilty of these hideous crimes. Dave refused to believe it.

"Have faith," he said. In his church, his upbringing, he was taught not to question things that were too hard to think about. Have faith, they'd say. All will be explained when you become one with the eternal light.

He thought back to some times when Vernon would make a comment on a pretty girl. No big deal. Everyone did that. He tried to think of any time he saw something that should have made him suspicious, but he came up blank. He was that good, Veronica said. He fooled her all those years. Methodical. Fastidious in his planning. All the trademarks of a sociopath.

But Dave stuck by him because that's what friends do.

It's what Keith did, too.

Dave faced Vernon, held his gun down around his waist.

"Vern, I never wavered with you."

Vern snapped another cartridge in, and the gun was full. Six more shots, ready to rock.

"But if there's anything you need to tell me, now is the time to do it."

Vern looked up, saw the doubt on Dave's face. Saw the rifle in his hand. Vern took up his own rifle and pointed it at Dave.

"I don't like the way you're looking at me, Dave. I don't like the tone in your voice."

"I don't like that there are people here trying to kill us. Kill you, anyway. And Keith is…"

Dave went to the window and looked first toward the yard to see if he could spot the gunmen. Seeing no movement, he looked down at Keith, face-down on the porch. No movement there, either. A stain of red marred the back of his coat.

"He's not breathing," Dave reported.

"So they came here for a war," Vern said. "That's goddamn well what they're gonna get."

He went to his bedroom. In the closet was a second rifle in its case. He set it on the bed, grabbed two boxes of shells from the dresser top, and pulled a handgun from the top drawer.

Dave followed as far as the door and watched him.

"We have to call the cops."

"No," Vern said. "No cops. They tried to execute me. Did you not hear that part? The cops are fucking corrupted, and they just see what they want to see. They judge people and accuse them of things they never even did."

The pitch of Vernon's voice rose. His hands couldn't stay still.

"They try to say things that are totally normal are crimes. Totally normal things. They ruined my goddamn life. Fuck cops."

When he looked up, the doubt on Dave's face had gotten deeper, like lines etched by age.

"What?" Vern said. "You believe them now? You think I did those things?"

"I didn't say that."

"Well, you believe they're trying to kill me, right? They sent a fucking hit squad up here. They killed Keith. What more proof do you need?"

Dave held out both hands, pressing them down toward the floor in a motion meant to calm him. "I just think–"

"You think I fucking did it." Vernon fit a firm fist over the grip of the handgun, a .45 automatic. He took three steps across the room like a military march and held the gun under Dave's chin. "If I'm a killer, then why don't I kill you?"

Dave held his breath. The look in his friend's eyes was like nothing he'd seen before. They reminded him of a stray dog that had attacked him once while he was on his bicycle. It was thin, patches of hair missing, yellow teeth, but the eyes are what Dave remembered. Darting, unfocused, fear, and hunger in equal measure. It took ten minutes of fighting the dog, beating it with the bike, kicking it, and shouting before it ran off.

"Well, what then?" Dave asked. "What's the plan?"

"We fight back, God damn it. They're not locking me up again."

Vernon turned back into the room, slung the rifle case over his shoulder, shoved past Dave, and went back into the main room. Dave held tight to his gun, sweating under his layers of cold-weather gear. His faith had faltered. This man wasn't the same friend of two decades. He'd watch the eyes. He'd fight back against whoever he needed to. Against threats from the outside, or from inside the cabin.

Vernon tuned in to the hollow sounds under his feet. Empty for far too long. Much of the pleasure was knowing when someone was there. His pleasure, for as long as he decided.

He'd been without his hobby for so long his vision blurred. His skin itched. His tongue felt too large for his mouth. But this would provide some release. He had permission to kill. Invaders. Trespassers. A hit squad sent after him. He was impressed.

But they would pay.

The trees made a maze with no exit. No trails to follow, other than the one they were leaving in the snow and dead leaves. An easy path that would lead anyone looking directly at them.

Chester kept his nose to the ground, veering off between trees on some scent and then rejoining the slow progress forward. Two senior citizens and a dog with a gray muzzle would never make a quick escape, even before one of the trio had a gunshot wound.

Upon quick inspection, the bullet had gone in and out Veronica's left side, just above her hip. She held a hand on the wound, and the pressure, along with the cold, had stopped the bleeding for the most part. She felt lucky, for now. A bullet meant to take down a three hundred-pound buck had spared her.

"How are you doing?" Carter asked.

"Okay, I guess. I think. I don't know. It's shock, I think."

"Yeah, that would make sense. You let me know if you need to stop."

"I will."

Pine needles chattered above them as gusts of cold northern air pulsed through the woods like a fan on rotate. Their staggering footsteps scared off any wildlife within a quarter mile. No birdsong, no animal calls.

Carter kept one hand on Veronica's elbow, helping her along as best he could, but providing more moral support than physical. They'd taken off with no water or food, only two guns and thankfully warm clothes. The cold never seemed to bother Chester.

He knew he got one of them, but it hadn't been Vernon. He wasn't sure how it might have gone if she hadn't shown up. All he knew was it got worse. She was hit, and now they knew he was there and planned to kill Vern. It all would have gone better if Vern had shot Carter, and everything went black.

He started to feel a pain in his gut, like a cramp from all the exertion. It morphed quickly from muscle pain into the ice pick he'd become used to. He kept his feet moving, hunched over more until he was leaning out over his feet, but kept on moving. Carter grunted, but tried to hide it under the persistent thud of his boots landing on the hard ground.

The truck was useless, engine block pocked with holes. The area they were headed into spread over twenty-six square miles. More than sixteen thousand acres of land with only an occasional access road. They were walking vaguely in the direction of the lake, and there would be roads there. Means of getting to the cabins and small boat docks. He scanned the sky for a curl of smoke from a chimney, but all he saw were trees.

Carter stumbled. He felt as if the bullet had traveled through Veronica and now had punctured his abdomen, but he did his best to hide it from her.

"I think I need to stop a while," she said.

He slowed his pace and eased them against a wide tree trunk. He looked behind him, the rifle in his hands at the ready, though he was bent over as if the gun weighed him down. His eyes couldn't focus on the path they'd made. Blood rushed in his ears and made it hard to hear other footsteps in pursuit.

He whistled once for Chester, but it came out weak and airy.

Veronica leaned back on the tree bark, letting a low moan escape her.

"I'm sorry," she said.

"I should apologize to you."

"You told me to stay in the truck, and I didn't. But when I heard the shots…I didn't know what else to do."

"It's okay. Can't go back now."

She looked ahead, then behind them, to the left and right. Dense trees, a thick layer of dropped pine needles, and fallen leaves from the deciduous trees mingled in with the pines. Light dust of snow. Nothing to point the way to safety.

"So how do we get out of this?" she asked.

"I'm not sure I know," Carter said. "But by my math, you need a hospital. They're gonna be coming after us soon, if they're not on our trail already. If we don't get you out of these woods and get you treated, things are gonna get real bad, real soon."

"Don't worry about me."

"That's all I'm worried about."

He didn't say anything to her about it, but Carter knew what it was like to be shot. It happened at the start of summer as part of his first round of violence. He'd taken his bullet in the leg, and it still bothered him from time to time. A dull pain would remind him of the path the bullet had taken.

He had someone to take care of him. The girl, Bree, who he helped earlier in the year. She cleaned his wound, changed the dressing, made sure he didn't get infected. All of this from the comfort of his home, where he could rest, take pain pills, and stay warm. He offered none of this to Veronica.

A wave of pain made him drop to one knee. Veronica was in the throes of her own searing pain, so she didn't notice the distress Carter felt. Chester came to stop at his feet and looked up at him, wondering when they could go home.

"We need to find some sort of shelter. If they haven't caught up to us yet, I can circle back and if they're at the cabin, still, I can take them out. We'll use one of their cars to get out of here."

"You think you can do all that?"

"It's the only plan I've got. If we make it to the lake, we can circle the shore until we find a cabin and hope someone is in it. But I don't want to move you any farther than I have to."

She pushed herself off of the trunk. "I can make it."

"This isn't a time to be brave, okay? First step, the only step, is to get you safe. The rest we'll deal with."

Veronica slumped back against the bark. Carter felt the wave of his attack easing a little. He straightened his back.

"A little bit further, though," Carter said. "I don't want to make it easy for them."

He put a hand on her elbow again, and they resumed their slow and steady pace.

178

A morgue always has a chill to it. Winter, summer, doesn't matter: it is ten degrees colder at the morgue.

The reason is the refrigerated units housing the corpses, yes, but the morgue is also always underground on the basement level, away from anyone who might get lost and happen upon it. And since it's below ground, there are no windows. It has many of the hallmarks of the next stop—the grave.

Brian DeFore waited in the cool and thought about the tall man. A quick run of the plates on the Mercedes had turned up his name: Colin Conway. He worked in real estate. DeFore assumed they'd met on a job of hers, decorating a new home for a client of his or maybe staging a house before it sold. She did those on occasion, though she said they didn't pay very much.

Colin was younger than DeFore, drove a better car, which meant he made more money, and worked a job that Margot probably didn't mind hearing about. How could he compete? He sat thinking that his best bet was if Colin got slid into one of the wall-mounted drawers with the stainless steel doors, covered in a sheet with a tag on his toe that would probably stick out at the bottom since he was so damn tall.

So many ways to end up here. Some quiet and unspectacular, some violent and gruesome. Some due to health problems, some trauma. All ended up laid flat, lips slightly blue, still, and expressionless. All would grow stiff and experience that phenomena where it looked as if the hair and nails were growing, but it was actually just the skin around the fingernails contracting and pulling back.

Hearts stopped, brains ceased sending signals, lungs stopped inflating. A continuous cycle from the day we're born, and it just ends one day. The last contraction of that muscle in your chest and the blood stops.

"Detective?"

DeFore finally noticed George Knapp, the coroner, standing over him. He could tell it wasn't the first time he'd tried to get DeFore's attention.

"Yes. Hi. Hey. Thanks for meeting with me."

He stood and shook George's hand. They'd met a few times on other cases. George wasn't what DeFore wanted in a coroner, but that was determined by too many movies. He didn't have a funny quip about causes of death. He didn't blithely eat a sandwich throughout an autopsy. He was quiet, nerdy, and serious about his work, with a round belly and heavy glasses.

A native Minnesotan, his accent matched DeFore's for thick regionality. "I'm not really sure what all I can tell you. Guy was burnt up pretty bad. So, outside's a bust. No prints to pull or tissue to sample. Inside, though. Not consistent with death in a fire."

"No smoke inhalation, I heard."

"Nope. Lungs clear and pink. Not even a smoker." George held open the door to the storage room. "You wanna take a look?"

"Not if you're saying there's nothing to see." DeFore took no pleasure in looking at dead bodies, and he'd never seen one burned in a fire. If he didn't have to look, he'd just as soon pass.

"There was some head trauma on the back of the skull. Could have been a result of the fall. He was found on his back, so if he fell from a standing position that could account for it. Like I say, can't identify any bruising or surface marks on the skin since it's all pretty much burned black."

"Could be blunt force from an object of some kind?"

"Could be. But that won't get you far in court."

"Okay. I didn't figure I'd get anything, but I had to check."

"Tox scans should be back tomorrow, so if there are any poisons or something, I'll be able to let you know then."

"That'd be great. Thanks, George."

They shook hands again, and DeFore thought how much George's own hand felt like a corpse. Cold and pale from the environment he worked in.

This case was going to require looking into the wife, the ex-business partner and seeking a motivation. But even if he found a good one, without any solid evidence to make it a murder, this case would go unsolved. Another one. Too many.

Most days, it seemed damn easy to kill someone and get away with it.

The gun hadn't left Vernon's hand. He held it like a life preserver in a stormy ocean. Nobody had launched a second attack and he didn't see any movement outside when he dared a glance through the window. Definitely no movement on Keith.

They were sitting ducks. The attackers might have made it back to town by now and started raising an army to come back and get him for good. The police were probably on their way in black helicopters, or maybe waiting for nightfall when they'd don night-vision goggles and attack under cover of darkness.

"We should get out of here," he said.

Dave had been wondering how he could convince Vern to let him drive out of here alone. He wasn't sure he could, but he had to take a shot at it.

"I've been thinking I should take my car and head out. I'm just holding you back."

"You want to drive right into that wasp nest? There's probably a roadblock by now."

"A roadblock?"

"You don't think it was just those two, and that's it, do you?"

Dave turned his head toward the window. All was still and calm.

"I think maybe it was, Vern. Some guy who got a notion. Some sort of vigilante plan. But if I take the car and I can get Keith and drop him off, let them know someone's up here trying to cause havoc."

"That's what they want."

Dave had been watching Vernon's eyes. They still had that crazed panic of a hunted doe.

"If you want to get out of here, then you should, Vern," Dave said. "I think I'd just hold you back, though."

"No. We travel together. We split up. It's easier for them to pick us off." Vernon went to the door and flung it open. "They have all the license plates. They're running them now. Probably FBI or CIA, even."

He leveled his rifle at the sedan, Dave's car, and fired twice through the grille. The thick .30-.30 shells would penetrate deep into the engine block.

"Vern! What are you doing?"

"We stick together." He turned and fired on the two SUVs, blasting the hoods, the grilles, the tires until his clip had been emptied. "I have a plan."

"Jesus Christ, Vern."

Vern kicked the door shut with his heel. He came closer to Dave and set a hand on his shoulder. "I won't let them get you, Dave. You're safe with me."

Dave had never been less sure of anything in his life.

"First thing," Vern said. "We have to take care of Keith." Vern kicked the door open again, his hands still occupied by the rifle. "Get him inside," he commanded to Dave.

Dave hesitated. A small pause, but enough for Vernon to turn around and face him. The look in his eyes went from the worried prey to the hunter. A small change, but enough to make Dave hop into action. He leaned his gun against the back of the couch and squeezed past Vern through the doorway.

"Grab his feet," Vern said.

Dave held on to Keith's boots, making sure not to touch any part of his body. He pulled, and Keith slid a few inches. He was heavier than Dave expected. Deadweight, they called it. He knew why. He pulled harder, and he uncovered a wide smear of blood. It had already turned nearly black in the cold outdoor air. What hadn't already hardened spread across the porch boards like a giant brush had been dragged through, making a sweeping arc as the body turned toward the door.

Vern held his attention on the trees, scanning for movement. "Inside, c'mon, inside."

Keith's arms flopped over his head like he was calling a touchdown. Dave hadn't rolled him over, and he slid face-first across the rough wood planks of the cabin floor, driving splinters into the cold flesh. Once the corpse was fully inside, Vern kicked the door shut and marched toward the bathroom.

"In here."

Dave didn't question it, figuring they would stow him in the shower stall. The space was much too small for Keith if he wasn't standing up like usual, but if they folded him, they could do it. They could all go days out here without showering since the water never got much above tepid, and once you were around others for that long, you couldn't tell if you smelled worse or they did, then it didn't make much difference.

Vern went in first, kicked the faded rug out of the way, and bent to lift the latch. Dave watched as a hole opened in the floor.

"Inside," Vern said.

"What's that?"

"Storage."

"For what?"

"For whatever. Dump him in."

Dave pulled on the body and got him through the bathroom door. He had to straddle the hole and tug at Keith's heels. Once his backside had gone over the edge, the rest of him sank and nearly pulled Dave down with him. He let go of the boots, and the body fell hard and landed in a pile with Keith's face now turned upward, staring at Dave with a blank look and scrapes from the wood floors across his face like he'd been wrestling a raccoon. Dave turned away so fast he hurt his neck and stepped to the side, awkwardly tripping into the shower. Vern dropped the lid on the hole.

Dave stood straight, catching his breath.

"Vern, why is there a hole under the cabin?"

"Storage, I told you." He put a hand on Dave's arm and pulled him out of the bathroom. "Okay, we're going to pack all the ammunition we can carry and the warmest set of clothes you brought."

"Where are we going?"

"I know a place."

Progress had slowed to a shuffling walk. Even Chester looked ready for a break. All the good critters had gone underground. The woods turned out not to be the scent buffet he'd wanted it to be.

Overhead the sky was a flat gray sheet. No discernible shapes in the clouds, no movement overhead. The cloud cover was low, and Carter wondered if the geese would be flying above the dull cement-colored slab.

All around him were tree trunks and patches of brambles in thick clumps. There was no straight line to be walked. They turned and circuited around trees always with a mind to keep coming back to a center line, but he knew it was futile. He hadn't seen signs of a lake, or of any roads. No smoke on the horizon to welcome them to safety.

Ahead, he saw the first man-made structure he'd seen since they left the cabin. About ten to twelve feet off the ground was a platform with three walls of olive green tarp and two-by-four posts in the corners. A deer stand. Wooden blocks had been hammered into the tree trunk to make a ladder to the platform.

"Over there." He pointed for Veronica. She turned in that direction, and Chester followed.

At the base, it looked much higher.

"Think you can make it up there?" he asked her.

"I think so."

"At least we can rest and get a good view if anyone is coming or not. You can lay down."

"Any chance of a first aid kit up there?"

"Doubtful."

"I'll give it a try anyway."

Carter braced her as she started to climb. When her hand came away from her side, the palm was stiff with dried blood. He held her feet when she got high enough and then let her go when she moved out of his reach. He stood back, hoping she didn't fall. He could try to catch her, but she would just end up breaking bones on both of them.

With some effort and time, she made it to the platform.

"Oh, thank God," she said. "A blanket."

"Any supplies?"

"No. Two empty beer bottles."

He turned to Chester. "Let's try this, buddy."

Carter groaned when he lifted Chester. He hoisted him over onto his back and wore him like a backpack, two front paws slung over his shoulders. He gripped both front paws in one hand and grabbed the wood plank ladder with the other. With another grunt, he started climbing.

Veronica looked down over the edge. "Oh, be careful with him."

"I'm trying."

Chester made low whining sounds in his throat, but let Carter get on with his climb. Even ten feet off the ground the breeze was more intense, and while it cooled him, the chill burned where it nearly froze the sweat on his skin.

He pushed up and Chester's head came through the small square opening in the platform. One more step, and Veronica could grab Chester's front legs. The dog started crawling up Carter's back. Veronica pulled on his neck fur, then his back. Carter tried to hunch his back to give more of a surface to climb over. In a moment, Chester was in the deer stand, and Carter hauled himself up and through the opening. He sat and leaned against the tree, drawing deep breaths and puffing out clouds of steam.

Veronica stroked Chester's head and ears.

"Good boy. What a good boy."

Carter knew he should have a plan from there, but he needed rest above all else right then. They sat in the shelter, all three regaining their strength, for twenty minutes.

"So what now?" she asked. Exactly the question he'd been dreading. Logic pulled him in two directions. Get her to a hospital, that was paramount. But leave Vern and his compatriots, or try to finish the job he'd started? He hated to think of going after any man merely because he was a witness. Carter knew what he was doing was a crime. If he got caught, then justice would be served. But if Vern got away again, then what was it all for? One man dead already, a woman who had no business being out here shot through the gut.

"I'm not exactly sure, if I'm being honest."

"We made it this far," she said. "Not bad for two old folks."

Carter needed to think in the short term. Worry about her, not him. In recent months, he'd gotten quite good at ignoring anything beyond the horizon. No sense planning for a time beyond your time.

"You know what I decided is the moment you can consider yourself old?" she said. Her eyes were shut, silver hair leaning back against the tree trunk. She was trying to distract herself from the pain with thoughts larger than the hole in her side. "When it's too late to start over."

Carter felt that she needed him then. He sat beside her, cross-legged. Chester leaned into her on the other side like two support walls.

"There was a time when if I'd left Vernon when I should have, if I'd known any of this, then I could have started again. Found someone new, maybe moved. Maybe met someone like you."

Veronica opened her eyes for a moment and looked at Carter. He had to look away.

"But you get to an age when you are who you are and where you are, and the start line is behind you. You ever feel like that?"

"I guess so. After Ava passed, I wasn't looking to start over."

"I guess that's what I mean, too. The desire isn't there anymore."

Carter knew she was wrong. He'd learned a new skill. He'd begun a new type of life.

"This is the plan," he said. "You stay here. I'm going back to the cabin to see if I can get any supplies to help you. And if I can use one of the cars there to get back to town. Even if they took the two of theirs, the third car would still be there. I think it's better to bring help here to you rather than try to get you out on foot. I don't want to make anything worse than it is."

Veronica rolled half on her side. "It's not so bad. It's right on the edge. I can barely feel it anymore."

"That might be shock. Let me see."

She lifted her shirt. True, it was less blood than he expected. Part of him was thinking she would be leaking internal organs out her side, but it looked more like she'd taken a sharp branch to her side. He gently set a hand on her shoulder and urged her to roll more so he could see the exit wound. Same thing. A small hole, ringed in blood and bruise, but not open and leaking. Puckered and closed, but warm to the touch. The outside had gotten in where it didn't belong, and that brought infection. She wouldn't bleed out, but she needed more help than he could give her.

"Okay. I'm headed back. You stay here with Chester and rest. I'll be back as soon as I can."

"There's still two of them there."

"I know."

"And if you don't come back?"

"Follow his nose." He pointed at Chester. "He'll lead you somewhere."

Carter straightened his legs and grunted with the effort. He handed the handgun to her.

"You know how to use this?"

"Enough."

"Only if really necessary."

She took it from him and set it on the wood beside her. They both worked to cocoon the blanket around her. It was fleece with a soiled and faded Minnesota Vikings helmet logo on it.

He slung the rifle over his head and wore the strap across his chest so he could keep his hands free. He crawled to the opening and looked down for footing on the wood plank ladder. He seemed a hundred feet in the sky.

"You're a brave man, Carter McCoy."

"Brave and foolish are brothers."

She made a frustrated sound in her throat. "Just accept it. What you're doing isn't for me; it's for all those girls out there. The survivors and the ones who didn't. That's a noble cause."

"Yeah," he said. "My first one, the man I killed, I had justifiable reasons too. I told myself all the same things bouncing around your head right now. I already accepted it. I don't need to justify it."

"I'm sorry I got you into this. It's my fault."

"No, it's not. But I'll tell you, you're wrong about starting over. I know a thing or two about being out of time, and you've got plenty of it. While I'm gone, start thinking of what your next phase of life is going to be. Go ahead and think big, too. At our age, what comes next can really surprise you."

He dropped a leg down through the hole, found the first step with his boot, and climbed down to the forest floor as a light snow began to fall.

DeFore slid the gun into his glove box. All these tiny indiscretions had been so easy. Getting a gun out of evidence should be much harder. Getting it out twice should be impossible, but here he had done it. If Carter McCoy didn't want the damn thing, then he'd put it to good use.

His afternoon agenda included an interview with the ex-business partner of the late Jeremy Henault. A real estate venture that had turned sour. The transcript would go into the case jacket, but unless this partner magically confessed out of some overbearing guilt, DeFore had already decided the case would go unsolved. Whoever it was, the wife or the partner, had committed a perfect crime. They'd gotten away with murder.

See how easy it was?

The hard part, he knew, was facing down a man and pulling the trigger. He'd been through all the training when he first walked the beat. They prepared you for it like it was an inevitability. Treat it like one, and there was less chance of hesitation when the time came to shoot.

All those training scenarios were based in self-defense. Bad guys with guns intent on killing an officer were the ones you had to put down without remorse. They made no mention of men who had wronged you or women who had lied.

But if that damn old man could face down men and kill, then so could Brian DeFore.

He wondered if it was something missing or something extra in him that made it feel like something he could do. Was there some core empathy he hadn't been born with? Latent sociopathic tendencies? Or did he have some special chromosome that would let him shut off the emotions of it all and treat it like squashing a bug on the kitchen counter?

He arrived at the office of Alpha Asset Liquidations. A name dressing up what was essentially a foreclosure resale business that picked clean the carrion of failed businesses and flipped their assets and real estate for profit. Frank Saverio answered the door to the small office. No receptionist, and he seemed to be the only employee.

DeFore held out his badge. "Thanks for seeing me, Mr. Saverio."

"My pleasure." His face dropped like he'd spilled a secret. "Not a pleasure. Just something you say. But I'm happy to help with the investigation."

Frank pointed DeFore to a chair, and he went behind a desk. DeFore set his phone between them and hit record on the voice memo app.

"I'll be recording this conversation for my files."

"That's fine. Permission granted."

He almost reminded Frank that he hadn't asked for permission, but let it slide. Frank was nervous. Maybe he was on to something.

"So tell me about Jeremy Henault. I understand you two had a falling out over business."

"We wanted different things, detective. It was an amicable parting."

"Amicable? You went to court over the dividing of assets."

"Simply to get the legal bits right. Dot the I's, cross the T's as it were."

"Tell me how that went."

DeFore tuned out. He didn't need to remember the details, that was what the recording was for. His mind drifted to his next agenda item. Visiting Colin Conway.

As he watched Saverio's mouth move, DeFore wondered if this man was capable of murder. He tried to see if there was anything in this guy that he could relate to. Something that made them similar. A woman was involved, that was a shared detail. Maybe the wife and the business partner had a thing going. Whatever the motivation, there was some switch that got flipped, making someone who had never killed anyone suddenly become a murderer. DeFore wanted to see some indication that he could do the same. He wanted to know if a guy this normal could kill. And if so, then could he be just as normal and kill someone, too?

Maybe if he pushed this Saverio guy, he could get something. Maybe even a confession. But he wasn't going to do any pushing today. Do the interview, enter it into the file, move on. Much more important things to do today.

Snow clung to Carter's eyelashes. He moved quicker now that he was alone, but his version of quickness was still deliberate and less than fast. He retraced the path they'd made in the woods, marked clearly by two tracks in the snow and woven through like an errant stitch by Chester's wanderings.

Veronica could have been the type of woman he would have loved. He found it hard not to think about, especially after what she'd said. But she was right about it being too late. For him, anyway.

He'd been in love a few times. Before Ava, there were two other women he could honestly say he loved. None since Ava. He always enjoyed being in love. Giving yourself over to someone else, trusting them and knowing they trusted you. Then one day, trust disappears, and the relationship ends. He never had a bitter breakup, no hard feelings. A slow fade out like the end of a film. Then the lights come up and you start the search for a new partner to sit next to and watch the reels of your life turn and throw shadows on the wall.

And then the opposite of love: hate. That side of the page now had a longer list of names. Though the men he'd killed he didn't hate, necessarily. He didn't like that revelation. It seemed better to hate a man before you kill him. He hated their actions. The men, most of them, he didn't know well enough to hate. Like Vern. He didn't know the man. He'd only seen him for the first time when they traded gunshots. But he hated what he'd done. And what he'd done to Veronica.

She seemed to deserve more. A better life. He could help in his small way, but Vernon had stolen her best years, and no bullet could bring them back.

The sounds of his footsteps filled the gaps between trees. Wind through the pines made a steady wash, but his boots on the frozen ground made hammer strikes against the earth. Like he was building something out there. A coffin, most likely. But for who?

His own funeral arrangements had been on his to-do list. He didn't want to leave it to Ivana. What he wanted was simple. No gathering. No speeches. Lay him down next to his wife and daughter and let the grass grow over and bring them together again.

And get the cheapest casket he could find. The sooner he returned to the soil, the better.

He heard the buzz of a small plane moving above the clouds. A different world of sunlight up there. Down here, he was cut off and alone.

The trail bent and twined around trees, showed where they had stumbled, and stopped to rest. A light layer of snow had started filling in the footprints. Bullets rattled in his pockets.

He spotted the cabin through a break in the trees. He positioned himself behind a wide trunk and unslung the rifle from his shoulders. He kept his gloves and the safety on while he watched from a distance. He saw no movement.

Carter moved swiftly at a sharp angle and placed himself behind another tree. He could see the front more clearly and noticed the man he'd shot was no longer there. He might be inside right now nursing the same wounds as Veronica, the cabin a remote triage facility. The dead deer was still laid out where they'd dropped it. The empty carcass opened like a mouth in surprise, the head leaning on the rack of horns, tongue spilled out the side of its mouth, and the eyes gone milky white.

He watched the windows, but saw no signs of anyone inside.

He cut across to another tree with a better view of the side window. A simple tan curtain hung across the glass, closed, blocking him from seeing anything useful.

Carter eyed his truck. Good cover, close enough to hear anyone inside. Crouching as he ran, he moved toward the truck, waiting for a shot to ring out like a soldier crossing a field outside of Marseilles in 1943. He reached the truck and crouched below the windows, pressing his back against the driver's side door.

He listened but had to wait for his own breath to slow before he could hear much else. He knew his panting breath gave off steam that could be seen from inside.

Carter heard nothing but the light breeze in the trees and the slow drip of antifreeze from his wounded engine.

All three other cars were still there. They hadn't driven out of the woods. Perhaps they were waiting for some negotiation.

"I just want Vernon Holliman," he said, as loud as he could push his tired lungs. "Send him out, and nobody else has to get hurt."

Carter wondered what would work better, saying he was police or FBI. He felt no shame in lying to get Vernon separated from the others.

Nobody answered. He peered out around the front tire. Nothing moved. He looked at the other vehicles and saw bullet holes, flat tires. He didn't think it had happened during the firefight, but things were so hectic, he wouldn't discount it.

Carter convinced himself there was nobody there. He put one foot on the bottom porch step. It cried out like a doorbell chime. He could see now the dark stain on the porch moving in a swoop toward the door and vanishing underneath it. He climbed the next two steps and put his back to the side of the cabin between the door and the window.

"Come on out, Vern. You know what you did. Nobody else needs to get hurt."

Silence. He didn't expect Vernon to surrender quietly. Those first eager shots told him that. If they were inside, barricaded up, and all three rifles pointing at the door, waiting for Carter to come in, he had no chance.

That would leave Veronica and Chester alone in the deer stand. He wasn't really sure if Chester would lead her any place. He might walk in circles chasing scents until they both died of starvation. But he needed to tell her something. And whether or not he would come back depended on the next few seconds.

He put the glove of his right hand between his teeth and removed it. He clicked off the safety and held the rifle as steady as he could in one arm. Carter put his gloved hand on the doorknob and twisted.

196

The pile of viscera and organs from the deer still lay in a heap where they butchered the animal. In hotter weather the insects would be on it, crows filling their bellies, flies laying eggs. Vernon moved with purpose and a speed that was surprising for his bulk, Dave behind him like a leash had been tied around his neck. Vern held his gun in both hands, eyes vigilant on the breaks in the trees, looking for signs of their attackers.

"How much farther is it?" Dave asked.

"About a mile, maybe two."

"And then what?"

"We lay low."

Dave couldn't help but sound frustrated. "For how long, Vern?"

Vern stopped, the first time his feet had paused since they left the cabin. He spun on Dave and hoisted the gun a little higher. Not quite aiming at Dave, but letting his intentions be known.

"As long as it takes. You got a problem with that?"

Dave could smell the guts of the deer even with it fifty yards behind them. "No. No, that's okay, Vern."

"Good."

Vern turned and started moving his legs again in a steady march forward.

He'd thought about running many times during the trial. If he'd been paying closer attention, he could have run before the police arrested him. After that, he was held in custody for seven months. When the trial fell apart, and he got out, he swore never again to go back to jail. He'd heard stories of what they did to people in prisons if they found out you were sentenced to anything with a minor.

When Veronica told him he couldn't come back home, he was fine with it. She gave him a few hours to clear out his stuff, and after that, he knew the cabin would be his home for a while. He'd been trying to think of what came next, where he could go, and if he'd need to change his name.

Being retired, he didn't need to worry about being kept from a job because of his arrest. Even though the case was thrown out, he knew people would judge him. The case got enough coverage in the news that he knew he would likely have to leave Minnesota. Maybe the Midwest entirely.

Bigger than that, Vernon wasn't sure if he could use this scare to keep him from falling back into old habits no matter where he relocated. He'd been so preoccupied with the trial and the upheaval his life underwent he hadn't had many of the feelings that drove him to go out and do what he did for so many years. Usually, after he'd found his prey, it would satisfy him for up to a year. Then, he slowly felt the impulse creep back in.

Boredom, really. That's what it came down to. And if he moved to a new town where he didn't know anyone, he was sure to be bored. Maybe Canada. He didn't know the rules for changing citizenship after a mistrial, not an innocent verdict. But if they were sending kill squads for him, he knew he had to move on.

Then there was Dave like an anvil around his neck. Maybe he should have let him leave at the cabin. But he didn't trust that Dave would keep quiet and not ruin his chance at escape. He needed him close by for a while longer. But Dave wouldn't be coming along for what came after. He'd have to decide what to do with him on his long list of choices to make.

What he should have done, he realized now, was burn the cabin as they left. Maybe on his way out of town, that would be his last stop. A fitting end. Burn it all down before he could start again. Start it all again.

Chester leaned into her, curling his spine and tucking his nose near his tail.

Veronica lifted the blanket and draped it over him.

"You're good to stay with me," she said. "You learned from a good man, I suppose."

Vernon had never allowed pets in the house. Veronica had asked for a cat and a dog, even a bird once, but he refused.

"Oh, what a fool I was. I never should have driven that truck up to the cabin. Foolish, foolish of me. But what was I supposed to do, sit and listen while Carter was gunned down?"

She worked hard to lay perfectly still. Every movement ignited a fire of pain in her side. She was thirsty and starting to feel hungry, though the pain made her leery of eating anything for fear she would vomit it up. But she needed water.

She could see a thin layer of snow gathering on the wood planks by the open wall of the deer stand. To get there and scrape off enough snow to eat would mean twisting and bending her body in ways she wasn't prepared to do quite yet, so she tabled the idea. Let it accumulate more.

"If you asked me a million times what I thought I'd be doing at sixty-seven years of age, I'd have never come up with getting shot and hiding out in the wilderness with a dog I just met."

Chester grumbled and adjusted his position, nudging her to the side in order to get more blanket. Something about this dog just made her want to talk out loud to him.

"But I'll tell you what, I can't feel scared because I know those girls went through far worse at the hands of my husband. My husband! My God, I still don't want to believe it. It defies all logic to me. I must have been asleep all those years. If Carter had come to the house before the arrest, if he somehow knew what Vernon had been doing, then I suspect I would have been a target, too. An accomplice. That's what I am. What I feel like, anyhow. Standing by and doing nothing like a piece of furniture. Useless and helpless. I failed those girls. Failed them all."

She felt Chester's warmth, smelled his coat. Flat on her back, she could never see anyone coming. She'd be vulnerable, but she didn't care. Small gusts of wind rattled the branches above her. She felt the tree trunk sway slightly, like she was floating on the ocean on a calm day. She closed her eyes and imagined a sun-filled bay in the Caribbean. Dolphins nearby, sand as white as a sheet of new paper.

The cabin seemed to be talking to him. Each footstep came with a groan of floorboards or a high-pitched scrape of dry wood on dry wood. It didn't take long to pass through the whole place and see that he was alone. It worried Carter. It meant the men were out there, searching for him and Veronica.

He set down the rifle and got to work. He went to the fridge first. There were two six-packs of beer and several Dr. Peppers. He left the beer but got the cans of Dr. Pepper out and set them on the countertop. Not his favorite, but it would have to do.

Vernon was clearly not a cook, so everything he had was ready-made and easy to transport. Carter went to the bedroom and found a small suitcase. He upended the contents onto the floor and, took it to the kitchen, and filled it with the drinks, a half loaf of bread, jars of peanut butter and jelly, a bag of pistachios, and some dry cereal. In the freezer, he found several portioned-out venison steaks, and he took them for Chester. He hoped they would thaw in time, but he knew Chester would chew on them even if they were deer popsicles. In a cabinet, he found a half dozen small cans of Sterno for a cookfire and added those to his stash.

He went back through the bedrooms quickly. He came up with a knife in a sheath he could clip to his belt. He found a box of shells, but the wrong caliber. In the closet, he found a pair of binoculars that he put around his neck.

He wasn't sure how much he could carry, but he wanted enough to get back to Veronica and be prepared to spend the night if they needed.

Carter went into the bathroom. Behind the mirror over the sink, he found a tube of antiseptic, which he pocketed. Under the sink, he found a small first aid kit the size of a summer beach read novel. He opened it and counted gauze, adhesive bandages, a half dozen alcohol wipes, a pair of nitrile gloves, more antiseptic cream, ointment for bug bites and poison ivy, an eye patch, a pair of plastic tweezers, and small scissors.

He hoped it was enough to stave off infection from Veronica's wound until he could get her to someone who could properly help.

On the floor, the small rug he'd moved earlier was now bunched up against the side of the shower stall. Carter could see the thin gap in the floorboard where the hidden room lay below. He lifted the trap door. In a tangle of limbs, the man he'd shot lay on the dirt floor beneath him.

So he had indeed been killed. Only two men out there now, but both armed and both experienced gunmen. Against deer and wild turkeys, anyway. Carter wondered if he was the only one to have killed other men.

He let the door slam shut. He would have to call this in to DeFore when all this was over. The man had been killed by one of Vern's own rifles, so Carter had nothing to worry about linking him to the murder. If anything, the whole affair could be pinned on Vernon and a falling out with his friends, presumably after they learned the truth about his crimes.

But that outcome was still only a hope, not a guarantee. Miles yet to go.

He brought the first aid kit to the suitcase and threw it in. He hefted the case, and it wasn't too heavy. He decided against packing any plates or glasses. They'd have to do with their hands, though he did pack one knife for the peanut butter. He went back and put two of the beers inside; you never know.

Carter slung the rifle back over his shoulder and took one last look around the tiny cabin. He noticed a box of fireplace matches by the wood stove. He pocketed those in case he needed to start a fire. Carrying wood was a bit beyond him, though.

He stepped out onto the porch and saw that the snow had picked up. His tracks were nearly filled in. And if they were almost gone here where his newest footsteps were, then they surely were covered over back at the tree where he began. Where Veronica and Chester were waiting. His trail had been obliterated.

After three rings the call went to voicemail. The automated, pre-programmed message that came installed on the phone. DeFore wasn't at all surprised Carter McCoy didn't have the tech know-how or the desire to record his own outgoing message.

DeFore hung up before the message concluded. He didn't need proof of the call.

He had wanted to get the old man's advice. How the hell to do this thing. Not how to get away with it, but how to work up the courage to shoot another man in something other than self-defense.

What he decided on was to let his hate guide his hand. To never let the betrayal leave the forefront of his mind. He knew for certain that once he saw Colin Conway again, he wouldn't have a problem dredging up the hate.

He put his car in drive and aimed toward Colin's home.

Next, he had to decide what came after. Would she come running back to him? And would she admit the affair? Or would she come back quietly and never mention the tall man?

The shame of it was that it could be an opportunity to show her how valuable his job really was. And how good he could be at it. If DeFore solved the murder of her lover, she would have to be impressed.

But since it would be him pulling the trigger, the case would need to go unsolved.

He hadn't had time to think of someone to pin it on. That would take weeks or months of logistics and planning. He didn't keep a list of potential suckers fit for a frame job on his phone or anything. And ruining another man's life to cover his killing didn't sit well. If it were some criminal mastermind or drug lord or serial killer, perhaps, but central Minnesota was currently lacking in all three of those categories.

Maybe McCoy? The old man had given him the brush-off after the Landrum incident, he'd never been what DeFore could call friendly to him, and he also wasn't long for this world, so the impact on his life, or what remained of it, would be minimal. Maybe he was the perfect patsy. And he was a killer, after all. Not of this man, but others that he'd never paid for. Yes, maybe…

But that could come after. For now, this needed to be handled swiftly and efficiently and it needed to be wrapped up quietly and discreetly.

The bigger issue became, he didn't know if he wanted Margot back after this. He'd never be able to trust her again. He'd never be able to see her without seeing Colin between them. The image of them kissing and, soon, Colin's bloody body.

But he knew himself. If she came to him seeking comfort or solace, whether she admitted the truth about Colin or not, he would be there for her. Maybe not forever, but for a time. He could push her right back into his arms with the pulling of one trigger. Maybe that made him weak, but he didn't care. He knew he couldn't fight it. He was a romantic. He thought so, anyway.

Really, it was Margot who caused this. Her hand was over his, squeezing the trigger just as sure as he was. If she'd been honest, none of this would be necessary.

DeFore's hand slipped on the wheel as he turned, slick with sweat, but not from any heat. He felt his underarms were damp as well. He thought of the kiss. He pictured them together in the same bed he'd been in with her. Had she changed the sheets? He thought about the lies on the phone, the casual dismissal of his plans.

The hate came back, for both of them. It burrowed a spot behind his eyes, darkened the edges into a tunnel vision. He drove by memory to an address he'd only just learned. An address that would come across his desk shortly as a crime scene. A man shot. How many times, he wasn't sure yet. No clues, no evidence, not much to go on. DeFore would promise to get to work on it, but wouldn't act hopeful at the outcome. Then he'd get to work on the burned-up husband case. If he could solve that, it would take the pressure off the Colin Conway murder.

And then she would come to him. She would come back. She could be all his, forever this time.

Carter moved as if he had a limp. The suitcase of supplies weighed him down on one side, and he had to swing it forward with each step. He inhaled deep gulps of frigid air with each step and thought about slowing down, but then pictured Veronica with two men under the deer stand with rifles poised to shoot her and Chester out of the tree.

He knew he'd gone off course a bit. The trail of footsteps he'd left had been covered by snow. Ahead, he saw a mound of entrails and knew he'd come across where the men had field-dressed the deer. The pile of organs was nearly knee high in the middle; a light dusting of snow covered parts of the mound, but pink showed through where the heat of the organs had kept the snow at bay.

Carter was lost.

He felt he should have stuck to his instinct and never taken a job like this again. He'd been lucky before, narrowly avoiding disaster multiple times. It couldn't last. Almost no scenario he could think of right then ended with him surviving.

The suitcase had been in his right hand. With each step, he pulled to the right a little bit. With that unscientific calculation, he decided he had veered off course to the right. North or South, East or West, he had no idea. With no sun visible, he couldn't figure even the most basic of directions. He turned himself to his left and began marching again.

If he died out here, he would go with so many regrets. He'd be leaving Veronica alone and wondering about him. Without medical attention, she would likely die as well. That meant he was leaving Chester to the elements.

He could never get down out of the deer stand by himself, and Veronica could never lift him down in her condition.

He'd come into the woods to kill, but never those two.

He should have visited Ava and Audrey once more. Each time he went to the cemetery he had to contemplate it could be his last time. He tried to say the right things each time, to have the right last moment with them. Carter wasn't one to fool himself that he would be reunited with them in Heaven or some afterlife. He knew that was something people told themselves to stave off grief for a while. He'd never understood the impulse to lie to yourself better than in that moment of his lungs burning and his legs cramping.

Tree branches snapped under his feet like firecrackers going off. He thought about leaving the case behind to increase his speed and maneuverability, but it was the whole point of the trip. She needed the help inside the case, and if he ditched it out here he doubted he could find it again even after he found them.

His legs moved on. His very existence was a shock to many people by now. He had no earthly reason to be alive, still. What was one more afternoon of unlikely survival?

One thing he couldn't decide if he regretted or not was pulling that first trigger. Killing Justin Lyons had been the turning point, but he still didn't feel it was wrong. He'd been living his life out of balance, the same way he felt with the case weighing down half his body now. Nothing was straight, everything off course. Pulling that trigger helped counter the weight he carried, even if it meant that the weight of becoming a killer was added to balance the misery of losing a child. He hadn't unburdened himself—he'd added more burden to achieve a sort of symmetry.

If it were only him out here, he would sit down where he was, put the rifle in his mouth and be done with it. But he was not alone. Veronica needed him, and Chester needed him. It was enough to lift his boots one more time and once more after that.

He tilted his head down against the wind. The snow came in tiny, hard crystals. It wasn't gathering quickly at his feet, wasn't making his steps heavier with damp flakes, but it accumulated in gaps of tree bark, in old deer tracks on the ground, in the folds of his jacket. Carter hoped he had turned himself in the right direction. He hoped that Vernon and his friend had gone a different direction. Even if they were headed to town to report the crazed gunman who showed up at the cabin, he could hand over Veronica to the authorities who came to arrest him. He could live the rest of his days in a quiet cell with three meals a day.

He also knew that if he wasn't around his home, around Chester, able to go visit Ava and Audrey whenever he wanted, then he would not last long in this world. In the face of the disease, those were the things still keeping him above ground. Take them away, and he would succumb in days. He felt that in his bones.

He moved through the trees like a blind bear. He made noise, he tripped and stumbled, he bounced off tree trunks when he got off balance. Then, over the din of his tromp through the woods, he heard a beautiful sound. A familiar sound. Mournful and sad like a cry.

He heard Chester's howl and he turned toward it and picked up his pace.

The cold provided a welcome numbness. Veronica adjusted her position, careful not to twist her torso too much and re-open the now-clotted wound. Her whole body ached, though, not only where she'd been shot. She flexed her fingers, and they bloomed with a sharp soreness. She reached up and touched her nose but felt nothing at the tip, just pressure. She tucked her face into the blanket and let her breath heat her face.

Chester had been curled tightly to her, and where they touched was wonderfully warm. But something caught his attention. Down below, weaving in and out of the trees, were two rabbits. They moved quickly, darting in a stop-start progress and eager to get back to their den.

The motion had roused him, and he stared with a focus that didn't hint at his fading eyesight. Moving shapes and the scent of critters could still spark an ancient part of his brain. Chester let out the first bellow while he was still lying down. He soon stood up and started a string of howls, pausing only to take a breath.

Veronica grunted when he stood and pushed off her. A gust of cold air found its way under the blanket when he rose. She thought surely it was Vern down below, come to hunt her like an animal. She fumbled blindly for the gun, not wanting to turn fully on her side because of the pain.

Chester howled and mixed in a few barks. An alarm call, a warning bell.

Her hand found the gun. Cold on the plastic grip and more cold on the metal. She wondered if it was too cold for it to fire. She also knew from a lifetime in Minnesota that this wasn't all that cold. It was the not moving, slowing her blood flow, that made it feel colder than it really was. And she had lost some blood, too. That didn't help matters.

If Vern was down there, if he wanted her, then he was going to get a fight.

She pushed up to one elbow, Chester not slowing his alarm. She tried to look over the edge of the deer stand, but could not see down until at least fifty yards out. She needed to get closer to the edge if she were to have a clean shot.

She bent herself into a sitting position and felt a warm flow of blood on her side. She'd opened her wound again. She kept wrapped in the cocoon of blanket and shifted herself toward the edge. Chester took a break from his howling to watch where the rabbits had disappeared into the thick woods.

Veronica peered over the edge, expecting to see her husband stalking forward with a rifle in his arms. She saw only trees. Chester gave out one deep-throated bark. She looked left and right and saw no movement at all. With Chester now quiet, she closed her eyes and listened.

Feet shuffling and moving through the deadfall. Not very far away and closing in. She slid back from the edge and Chester looked at her, the spell broken between him and the now missing rabbits. If Vernon didn't know she was here, he might try to use the deer stand himself. To rest, to get a bird's eye view of the forest to look for her. She couldn't assume he knew this was her hiding spot.

He'd heard the dog, surely. But it could be someone's hunting dog. She didn't know if he'd seen Chester in the truck when she drove up.

If he wanted to, he could take random shots at the deer stand from below. The eight-foot by eight-foot platform wouldn't be hard to pepper with enough shots to get her no matter where she curled up. But if he came up the ladder...

She positioned herself facing the small trapdoor at the top of the ladder. Vernon couldn't use his rifle if he were climbing. She would wait until she heard him climbing the wood slat steps and then attack him from above when he was vulnerable.

The steps got closer. They made no attempt at stealth. He crashed through the trees, sounding like more than one man. Maybe Vern still had Dave with him. She heard the movement stop below her, heard panting breaths.

That would be Vern. Out of shape even though he liked to act like such an outdoorsman and athlete.

Chester tilted his head at the sound. Veronica set the gun in both hands, but struggled to hold it steady. She quietly removed her gloves while she felt the tree sway as the weight of a body pulled on the climbing blocks.

The metal of the revolver was slowly warming at her touch. She didn't know if it would be better to wait for him to pop his head up, or if she should look down and fire from above. If she attacked straight down, he might not even see her. And a bullet to the top of his skull would do the trick one hundred percent of the time.

He was struggling up the ladder, hauling all that extra weight that hadn't been there when they got married. She adjusted her grip on the gun, her fingertips losing feeling in the cold. She exhaled onto them and made small clouds.

Chester barked at the sound coming nearer. She almost told him to be quiet, but stopped herself to preserve the element of surprise. She leaned forward, deciding whether to aim the gun down into the hole without looking. Veronica wasn't sure she could deal with seeing a bullet enter a body, even if it was Vernon. But she needed to look. She needed to see that her shot landed, otherwise she was giving everything away and giving him time to get to her first.

She inched herself closer to the opening, the gun leading the way like a viper seeking its prey. Do it all in one motion, she told herself. Don't think too much, don't look directly. Fire at the shape, not the man. She inhaled a deep breath of cold air. Chester barked one more deep sound.

"Chester, quiet now."

It wasn't Vernon. It was Carter McCoy.

The top of his head crested the opening, and Chester began wagging his tail. Carter turned and found himself eye-to-eye with the barrel of Veronica's gun. He flinched and nearly dropped the suitcase.

"Jesus Christ!"

"Oh! Oh, I'm so sorry." She swung the gun away and set it on the wood plank.

He got one arm up through the hole and moved himself up two more steps, then sat himself on the edge of the hole, legs and one arm hanging through, then pulled up the suitcase through the gap and collapsed on his back, puffing white clouds from his mouth.

Chester came over and licked his face.

"Now, that's a more appropriate greeting.

He moved swiftly for a man of his size. Dave, on the other hand, was ready to drop. Through a break in the trees, they could see the lake, and Vernon stopped to eye some landmarks on the far shore, then turned a sharp right and picked up the pace. In two hundred yards, they came to a small shack on skis. The ice fishing shack was somewhere between the size of a garden shed and an outhouse. One square window on the back wall, a blackened pipe jutting out the top from the wood stove inside, and weather-beaten shingles coating the outside.

Finally, Vernon stopped his relentless march forward and took his water bottle from his pack. Dave came to a spot close by and sat in the mounting layer of snow.

The lake was flat and grey in the muted light under the clouds. In a few months, ice would form, and all around the lake, shacks like this would be towed onto the flat surface and holes drilled in the ice, fishing lines dropped in, and gallons of beer consumed on weekends where husbands would sit for hours in near silence watching for the end of a pole to twitch.

This was shelter, but only temporary. Vern knew that. They would stop here. He could clear his head and come up with a plan. He could decide whether that plan involved Dave or not.

"Jesus, I gotta rest," Dave said.

Vern looked at him sitting on the ground. "What the hell are you doing now, then?"

"I mean real rest. Inside. Can we go in?"

"Yeah. It's not five-star or anything."

Vern took off one glove and worked the dial on a combination lock. He opened the door and swung it open. Dave rushed inside.

There was a bench on one side, two stools, a hole cut in the center, the wood stove, and a small pile of cut wood from last season. A single shelf held a few cans of roast beef hash, baked beans, and tomato soup. On top of the stove was a single pot, its bottom blackened. There were still two cans of beer and three cans of Dr. Pepper. The beer was surely skunked from cycles of freezing and thawing since last season. But in a pinch, it would do.

Vernon set his backpack down, but kept the gun in his hands. Dave sat on the bench and leaned his back against the wall of the shack.

"We need a fire," Vernon said. He opened the iron door of the stove and peered inside. Only ash. He counted the cut wood. No kindling, no newspaper to spark to light. Might be tough with the snow outside, but they needed some kind of tinder to get it going.

Vern looked at Dave. "Get up. We need kindling. Something to start the fire."

"What?"

"I got logs, but no kindling."

Dave looked above him on the single shelf. He reached and brought down a small plastic bottle of lighter fluid. "What about this?"

"That's for emergencies."

"Well, what the fuck is this?"

"Would you just—"

An unfamiliar voice cut in. "Hi, neighbor!"

Vern's whole body jerked as if he'd stepped on a live wire. He spun, the gun rising to his shoulder.

Outside the open door were two men, unarmed. Both mid-thirties, dressed for the weather, one in a plaid overcoat, the other in a tan Carhart jacket. They lifted their hands in surrender.

"Who the fuck are you?" Vern said. "What are you doing here?"

"Hey, hey, hey." The man in the plaid coat spoke. "We're your neighbors. We live in the house around the bend, north of here."

Vern stepped outside, looked to his left and right, expecting to see others.

"Who sent you?"

"Nobody," the man said. "We were hiking around the lake. We live about a mile that way." He pointed with his raised hand. "We didn't mean to startle you."

Dave stepped out, leaving his rifle behind. "It's okay. We're sorry." He put a hand on Vern's shoulder. "Vern?"

Vern turned to him with that same vacant look in his eye. The disconnect. Wheels spinning too fast inside his skull.

"They're just passing by," Dave said.

Vern seemed to understand. He lowered the gun, slowly.

"Really sorry," the stranger said. He spoke quickly, words spewing out driven by nerves. "We've never seen anyone out here before. When we saw the door open, we just wanted to introduce ourselves. We just bought the place over the summer. It's...it's our first winter here."

"I've had this place twenty years," Vernon said. "Never seen you before."

"Yeah...like I said, we just bought."

Dave tried to be friendly. He raised a hand and waved. "Welcome. It's been a long day for us."

"Yeah. I can see that."

Vern's gaze flicked between the two men like a bird on the hunt. "You just happened along?"

"Yes. Can we...can we put our hands down now?"

"Yes, of course," Dave said.

Vern lifted the gun a foot higher. "Keep them where I can see them."

The man in the Carhart jacket tapped his partner on the shoulder. "Marco, let's just go and leave them alone."

Vern took two quick steps forward. "So you can go tell the others?"

"What others?" Marco said. "I don't know what you're talking about."

Dave tried to be calm. "Vern, they're just out hiking. Just let them be on their way."

"Please." The man in the Carhart jacket seemed on the verge of tears.

"I wanna know who the fuck sent you? The cops? FBI?"

"Vern, stop," Dave said.

Vernon spun to face Dave. He grabbed the front of his jacket in his fist. "I told you to go get some kindling."

"I will. Just let them get on their way. They're not here to harm anyone."

"No, sir. We're not."

Vern turned his attention back to the two men. "Then why are you here?"

"I told you. We were out hiking and–"

The man in the Carhart broke into a sprint. His heavy boots made him slow, and chunks of the newly fallen snow kicked up with every step.

"Hey, hey!" Vernon lifted the gun to his shoulder again.

Marco shrieked, "Andrew, no. Stop."

Vernon moved to follow, shouting, "Hey, hey," over and over.

"Vern, let him go," Dave said.

Andrew fell to one knee, then stood again and kept running. Vernon lowered the rifle.

"They're not cops," he said. "Cops wouldn't run like that."

Dave rushed to Marco and spoke quietly to him. "He forgot to renew his hunting license, so he's a little paranoid about getting busted. You can go. It's okay now. Sorry about this."

There would be a serious discussion back at their lake cabin between the two men, and Andrew would have some to do some explaining about why he ran away and left his partner behind, but Dave was happy if no shots were fired.

"Yeah. Go on." Vern waved a hand, and Marco took off running in the same direction.

Once both of their footsteps had faded away, Vernon turned to Dave. "You gotta be vigilant."

"Yeah. Sure." Dave let out a long exhale. "I gotta piss is what I gotta do."

"Go in the lake. That's what I do."

"Right. Okay."

Dave walked to the water's edge and unzipped.

"Quick thinking," Vern said. "That hunting license stuff."

"Yeah, thanks."

Maybe he was worth keeping around after all. Maybe.

Carter opened his second Dr. Pepper. They'd each had one already, but Veronica opted for a beer for her second drink. The poking and prodding of re-dressing her wound earned her something harder, but beer was all they had. The alcohol wipes had been the worst. When Carter cleaned around, and then inside, the two holes in her side, she cried out and cursed loudly. He apologized steadily, but kept up with disinfecting as well as he could. He covered each wound with two adhesive bandages, then gauze secured with tape. He found a flexible wrap for a sprained wrist in the kit and used it to wrap around her midsection to further cover the dressing.

"How is it?"

"Feels better already. At least the stinging is gone, finally."

"Sorry about that."

"Carter, you don't need to apologize for trying to save my life."

He didn't want to burden her with stories of what was on his mind: the day his wife died and how helpless he felt watching her suffer through a heart attack and not knowing what to do. Futile chest compressions were the best he could conjure, but they were too little and too late.

Wind made waves across the dark blue tarp that Carter had unhooked and let fall over the open side of the platform. Veronica felt foolish she hadn't done it earlier, but she hadn't been thinking her best and had been moving even less so.

He got out the peanut butter and made sandwiches. He unwrapped one of the venison steaks for Chester and gave it to him. He put it between his paws and gnawed on the frozen meat until the heat of his mouth began to thaw it.

Carter told her about his visit to the cabin. What he found and what he didn't.

"So they just took off?" she asked.

"All three cars were there. There's no place they could have been hiding inside. My guess is they went for the road, and they'll make it back to town that way. Or maybe hitch a ride."

"Then what happens? They go to the police?"

"I thought about that. If they do, they'd have to say why someone would come to try to kill him. He could lie, of course, but—"

"He's very good at that."

"Yes, I know. But going to the cops risks them looking deeper into that cabin, and with the whole area underneath and now a dead body in there, I have a feeling he's not keen on going to the police."

He handed over the sandwich and started making one for himself.

"So what then?"

"I have no idea. Right now my concern is getting you out of these woods and to a doctor. But we're losing the light. I fear we're going to have to stay the night up here."

He looked out the flap of tarp at the gently falling snow.

"I can climb down there and get some snow to melt so we can have water to drink. I don't think it would be a good idea to get drunk and try to get out of here with a hangover."

She lifted the nearly empty can. "This plus the Tylenol will be enough for me."

"I can find the cabin again, I'm pretty sure. If we can do that, then we can find the road, and it'll be a long haul, but we can walk out of here. And I bet someone would stop for us, being two old people limping along with a dog."

"You'd hope."

"I hope for a lot of things out of other people, and I'm usually disappointed."

She smiled around a mouth full of peanut butter sandwich. "Don't be cynical."

"You're telling me you got to this age in life, and you're not?"

She thought about it, swallowed, then sighed. "I think the last year and a half has maybe made me see the world a little darker than before."

"Most days, I feel like I'm seeing the world from the bottom of a well."

She laid a hand on his. "Look how high up you are now. Quite the opposite, I'd say."

"How can you be positive when you're shot?"

"Beer and Tylenol, I guess."

"You'd better get some sleep then."

She looked around the small platform. "Not much room."

"It'll do. Body heat will be our friend tonight anyway."

She nodded toward Chester. "He helps."

"He does indeed."

"It's going to be a long night, isn't it?"

"We can get moving at first light."

Carter dug through the suitcase for the pot and brought out a can of Sterno to melt the snow with. He crawled to the opening and prepared to climb down.

"Sorry you ever came to my door?" Veronica asked.

"No. Sorry you answered it?"

"No."

He nodded and began to climb.

DeFore couldn't hold it anymore. He'd been parked down the block from Colin's house for hours now, and he needed a piss. The street was tree-lined and exactly the kind of place a guy with real estate connections would live. Probably got the house before it ever went on the market. Several of the trees called out to him, just begging to be pissed on, but DeFore knew if he got busted for public urination, or even if a neighbor came out to yell at him, he was done for. You remember the description of the guy pissing against your tree when the cops come calling after the next-door neighbor gets gunned down. He drove a half mile away to a mom-and-pop coffee shop that looked like it had seen better days in a pre-Starbucks world. He bought a small black coffee and used the bathroom.

By the time he got back, the Mercedes was in the driveway. He kicked himself for not going earlier. He couldn't have been gone more than ten minutes, and of course, that's exactly when Colin comes home. Not that he planned to do it right when Colin got out of the car. He didn't know exactly when he might do it. It was harder to plan a murder than he thought.

In murder trials, they use the term premeditated a lot. He was there, in the middle of a premeditation, and he could attest, there wasn't a whole lot you could actually premeditate. The intention was premeditated, and that would be enough for a judge.

He reached for the glove box and took out his evidence locker gun. DeFore bet that all over America there were ten times as many guns in glove boxes than there were actual gloves.

Next, he put on gloves as well. It was chilly out there.

He walked straight to the house and around the side, away from prying eyes. Colin Conway didn't seem to like curtains, which was good for DeFore. Maybe Margot would help him pick out some good ones, or maybe this was her doing. A more modern aesthetic. Either way, it worked to his advantage since he could see through every window. No sign of Colin.

He tried the back door, but it was locked. He tried a few windows, also locked. Anticipating this, he reached into the inside pocket of his jacket and took out his lock-picking kit. He guessed there was some premeditation in there after all.

The kit had come into his possession after his first partner told him what a valuable skill it was to have. He coached DeFore in the subtle feelings of just the right resistance to know you have it. He hadn't used the skill much, but he considered it a necessary talent.

He found a set of French doors off the beautifully manicured back patio. A stone bench with a fire pit built in, grill surrounded by flagstone and planters that would be filled again next spring. He bent to one knee and got to work. In under five minutes, he had the lock undone. He entered.

Colin's home office. A desk with a computer, printouts of real estate listings scattered around. Photos of Colin on adventurous vacations river rafting, skydiving, skiing.

DeFore moved slowly and deliberately through the house, careful not to leave anything incriminating behind. His hat covered all of his hair, gloves meant no fingerprints, his shoes he already knew he would dispose of after. He'd seen the pitfalls and the tripping points of other would-be killers and knew what not to do far better than he knew what to do.

But God dammit, if that old man could do it, then so could he.

He briefly thought of calling Carter again and seeing if he had any last-minute advice. But no, he could do this and do it well.

He moved through a well-appointed kitchen. No dishes in the sink. He listened for a TV, some music, voices, or anything to tell him where Colin was in the house, but all was quiet.

A staircase led to the second floor with a ninety-degree turn halfway up the steps. After a quick glance into the darkened living room, he went for the steps. The house was well-built. No creaks on the stairs or in the floorboards. The quality construction unwittingly made the home more vulnerable to a killer moving about undetected.

A painting hung in the stairwell. Abstract with great splashes of blue and sea green. It looked expensive in a way that art you couldn't decide if you liked could be. Was there talent on display, or just a guy with a paint bucket and good PR? DeFore was obsessing over whether he thought the painting was worth real money that he didn't notice Colin Conway coming to the top of the stairs until too late.

"Who the hell are you?"

Colin's voice jolted DeFore from his focus on the painting. He'd made it to the landing midway up the steps. Colin stood with one hand on the banister, a confused and angry look on his face.

DeFore thought about answering the question for a split second, but the shock of seeing him there and the sudden panic about what he was about to do made him react without thinking. He pulled the trigger.

The shot hit Colin just below his sternum. He wore a Tom Petty t-shirt, and the shot hit Tom square between the eyes. Colin's look of confusion before was nothing compared to what came over him once he realized he'd been shot.

DeFore took two steps up the staircase and fired again. The second shot hit Colin's right shoulder. His left hand still gripped the banister, but he started to slump. DeFore took two more steps and fired a third time. That shot tore into Colin's neck, and he fell onto his back, his feet shooting out from under him and hanging over the top step.

DeFore was only two steps from the top now and stood looking down at Colin, gasping for air through the hole in his neck. He held the gun out in front of him like he might fire a fourth time, but seeing the blood pump from the neck wound made him certain the job was done. Blood had started to spread across the t-shirt, and a pool of red gathered under his head, soaking into the tan carpet that ran the length of the upstairs hallway.

The sound of the shots faded away, and the smoke from the gun dissipated as DeFore stood statue-still watching Colin Conway die. He realized he'd been holding his breath, and he exhaled, then drew in a deep lungful, and with it, the smell of the gunshots and fresh blood.

Colin's breathing slowed, and DeFore knew that he would wait until he saw the last breath leave his lungs.

A scream tore his attention away from Colin's doomed body. Peering out from the bedroom door, holding a sheet over her naked top, Margot stood open-mouthed and looking at Colin dying and at DeFore standing over him like he was posing for a paperback novel cover in the 1950s.

Carter woke up to Chester's cold nose in his face. His body was stiff and sore from the night out in the deer stand. More fearful than he wanted to admit, he reached for Veronica to see that she was still alive. At his touch, she made a noise and shifted her position. He removed his hand, trying not to wake her. Chester needed to get down from the stand in the tree and do his business. Carter did, too, for that matter. Getting the old dog up the wood plank ladder had been hard enough. Getting him down would be a dreadful way to start his day. They were ten feet in the air, too far for Chester to jump. Not with his old bones.

Carter pushed open the edge of the tarp and looked outside. The snow had stopped. First glimmers of light glowed in the east, but it was still before a proper sunrise. Clouds covered the sky again and it was likely the snow could start up again at any minute. Not too much had fallen in the night. Still an early winter snow, not the knee-deep, school-cancelling type of January and February snowfall.

"You need to get down, boy?" he asked in a whisper. For an answer, Chester nudged Carter again with his nose.

Carter scooted on his backside to the square opening in the wood plank and dropped his legs through, felt around for the first plank of wood, and got both his feet firmly situated. Chester came to him, and he scooped the dog up in his arms. It was all he could do to hold Chester, and he'd need at least one hand to climb with. He got himself standing on the top plank of the ladder and shifted Chester into one arm, resting on his shoulder.

Carter knew he had to move quickly. Chester squirmed a little at first, but then settled in. Carter felt blindly with his feet for the next wood plank, then the next. His left arm gripped the wood and kept them both from falling. With each step down, his anxiety faded a little, and with three to go, Carter jumped off and went to his knees in one motion, letting Chester off his shoulder to land in the snow. Without a thank you, Chester moved off with his nose to the ground.

It took a minute for Carter to stand up. His back hurt, his arms were sore already, and the day had only begun. He searched around him for any signs of visitors in the night, but saw no tracks in the snow, man or otherwise. He moved away to a tree out of sight of the deer stand and unzipped his pants. The cold on his exposed skin made him shiver.

When he got back to the tree with the stand, he knew he wasn't going to put Chester back up there. He climbed and got him another venison steak. Even being out of the freezer for the night, it wasn't thawed. Carter brought the steak and the pot and a can of Sterno down with him, careful not to nudge Veronica as he came and went. He pulled the blanket up around her and tucked it tightly to seal out any chill wind.

The thin layer of water still in the pot had frozen. He scooped more snow into it while Chester gnawed on the frozen venison steak. He lit the Sterno and held the pot over it, watching the snow melt to water.

Above him, Veronica's face appeared through the opening.

"I think I know where he is."

5

"An ice fishing shack?"

Veronica had climbed down mostly on her own steam and she leaned against the tree trunk now to catch her breath and evaluate whether she had reopened her wounds.

"Yes," she said. "I remembered it just this morning. As I was waking up, like the lingering part of a dream, you know? When you're not quite awake."

"And you think he might be there?"

"If they didn't take the cars and, like you said, if it's still dangerous for him to go to town, then it makes sense that he would go there, don't you think?"

"Maybe." Carter handed her the pot to drink from, the melted snow inside had some warmth to it to keep them from hypothermia.

"I've never been there," she said. "Ice fishing isn't my preference for a grand day out. But I know it sits on the shore until the lake freezes, and then everyone drags their shacks out, drills their holes, and sits in the cold trying to catch fish that didn't bite when it was warm. I'll never understand it."

"I guess it's worth a shot."

Whether they found the shack or not, if they made it to the lake, they could find help for Veronica. Though they were spread far apart from each other, small cabins dotted the lakeside, and someone would at least have a phone they could use to call a doctor.

The clouds overhead had gaps with edges like torn paper. Carter could see due East where the sun had crested over the horizon. From there he could turn and face West, the direction of the lake.

"You think you can make it?" he asked.

"I feel surprisingly able. You really patched me up."

"I don't want you to push yourself."

"And I slept better than I had a right to. You were right about the body heat."

Carter became suddenly shy and looked away from her. "It's saved many a person lost in the cold. Especially with a dog along."

"Yes, he was a godsend."

"Just so you know, the gas was him and not me."

"I assumed that."

He fixed them breakfast of more peanut butter sandwiches, the peanut butter so hard with the cold it tore the bread. They finished the Dr. Peppers, and Carter used another can of Sterno to heat more snow and fill his water bottle.

He pointed West. "That way."

"Okay."

Chester joined them when they started to slowly shuffle westward.

DeFore had a moment to think, to choose. Margot stared at him, doing the math to add up what she was seeing, but not believing the answer. Colin, bloody on the ground. DeFore standing over him with a gun. The smell of the blasting caps, the fresh blood, the fear in the air. As incongruous as it was, there was no mistaking what she was seeing. He could kill her. She had been the one to betray him, after all. He still never knew if Colin was aware he even existed or if she kept him secret. To Colin, DeFore would be the other man.

She wasn't coming back to him. Not after this.

For a moment, he even turned the gun her way, but he couldn't. He could never kill something he loved so much. So he turned and ran, her screams following him down the steps.

That had been eight hours ago now.

What a fool he'd been to not even think that she might be there. If he'd stuck it out, or just pissed against a tree, he would have seen them come back to his place, both get out of the car. He would have known to call it off.

Not so easy, after all, to kill a man cleanly. He owed Carter McCoy an apology.

She had to have gone to the police by now. He didn't go home. He drove around, fueled by adrenalin and doubt. He parked and thought and tried to sleep. He honestly had no idea what to do next.

Curious, he drove by Colin's place. From a block away, he could see the crime scene tape. He made a three-point turn and drove away. His crime was a part of the record now. A file had been created with his name as a suspect. A folder that would have been crossing his desk if the whole world hadn't turned upside down.

So his life was ruined. Not over, but ruined. He still had time, and he had options, but none of them good.

She had ruined his life. He knew then that he had chosen the wrong target. He meant to wound her by killing Colin. To prove to her that cheating and lying had their consequences. Even if she hadn't known it was him, she would have known that by her actions Colin was dead. She would have felt the pressure of guilt pressing down like a thousand feet of water overhead. Somehow, she would have known. Now, there was no doubt that she knew Colin's death was directly related to her lying. She would be feeling the weight right now. The blood would never wash off her hands.

But he should have gone to the source of the betrayal. He should have let go of the idea of winning her back. He should have taken her out instead. But he let his heart overrule his mind. Foolish.

At least it meant he wasn't a psychopath. A true psychotic would never have the empathy or the capacity to love enough to leave a witness alive like that. It only ended up putting his own neck in a noose. He'd sacrificed himself for her. Not that she would see it that way. Now, she would only see him as a killer.

Maybe now it wasn't too late to at least fix that mistake, a mistake that had brought down more than one killer: leaving the witness alive.

If he could get to her. But how?

She might still be at the station giving statements. Or they might have a man at her house, or watching from down the street. As if he couldn't spot a stakeout.

Going after her wouldn't get him out of trouble. That damage had been done. But it would mean she would have to know how her betrayal destroyed him. And how it needed to destroy her.

His car was a blinking red light for every patrol car on the street. He needed to ditch it or lay low until he could get to her. And maybe he would do the right thing and turn himself in before any more blood was spilled. But if he was going down for one killing, he might as well go down for two.

Dave woke up sore, his joints and muscles stiff. There had been barely enough space for both men to lay on the floor of the shack, head to toe, with Dave's neck at an awkward angle and his legs bent all night. Sleep was hard to come by. The only plus was the wood stove, keeping the tiny space warm enough all night, even though it meant getting up three times to add more wood to the fire.

He wanted to know the plan and to know when he could get the hell out of there and back to his life. Vern had slept with the rifle in his hands all night, cradled to him like a lover. Now, Vern hunched over the stove, waiting for the coffee to boil, and still had the gun in his hands.

"So what's the plan?" Dave asked.

Vern had been trying to work that out all night. He had no good options. All he wanted was his life back. His wife, his routine, his hobby. What he really needed to do was get out of Minnesota and start over far, far away. Maybe even Canada, if his arrest wasn't a hindrance.

"Coffee. That's the first thing," Vern said.

"Vern, I can't stay out here indefinitely. We need to get back to town and tell the authorities about Keith. I need to get back to my life."

Vern turned slowly, and if the coffee wasn't yet at a boil, his temper was.

"Don't you think that's what I want? Don't you think I want to be able to walk around anywhere I please without people recognizing me from that smear job the press did on me? Innocent until proven guilty? My ass. You saw how those people judged me."

"That's their problem. What do you care as long as you're innocent?"

Vern turned back to the coffee. He curled his shoulders until he looked more like a boulder than a man.

"Vern...?"

"We all got urges, Dave. Every man on earth. I don't care who you are. We all got urges."

"What are you saying?"

Vern lifted the pot off the stove and poured two cups, black. He handed one to Dave.

"I'm saying we're staying put for now. I can't go into town just yet. I'll think of something."

Dave let the tin mug burn his hand and he looked deep into Vern's face to search out the truth.

"I...I need to know what we're dealing with here. Were those people cops? Are there more coming? Do they think I'm involved in this somehow?"

"I told you, it was probably some do-gooder citizen trying to be judge and jury themselves. It's persecution is what it is. And I can't trust the goddamn cops, either. Dave, you're all I got."

Dave set down his coffee. "I don't want any part of this, Vern. I need to go."

"I can't let you go, Dave. Like you said, they'll treat you the same as me if they see you. They think all kinds of crazy things. They tried to kill us. You saw it. They killed Keith. It's not safe out there for either of us."

"God dammit, Vern, what did you get me into?"

"Drink your coffee."

Vern sipped. In the confines of the shack, he seemed like a bear looming over a meal. Dave could imagine a young girl cowering under that cold stare. He could see it all now. Everything he never wanted to believe was true.

They moved at a steady pace. Veronica never complained about any pain or discomfort, even when Carter saw her wince after an awkward step, or lean against a tree for balance. Chester would veer off into the trees, chasing some scent, then wind his way back to them, never out of sight.

"You doing okay?" he asked.

"Yes. Now, please stop asking me that. If I need to stop, I'll say so."

"Sorry. You don't need to act tough, though. You're injured."

"I know that. I'm the one who was shot. Let's just keep moving."

A gust of wind knocked snow from the branches of a nearby tree, and a flurry of wet clumps fell in front of them.

"I curse the day I ever met that man," she said. "I'm supposed to be walking on the beach in Florida, or someplace we retired to. I'm supposed to be bouncing grandkids on my knee. I'm supposed to be anywhere but here trying to kill a monster in the woods."

"Sounds like you curse the day you met me. You wouldn't be here otherwise."

"If it wasn't for you, I'd still be pouting at home, wishing I could do something about him. At least now I'm finally doing something."

Carter thought, *if only what you're doing isn't dying out here.*

He knew what she meant, that feeling. When he decided to kill for the first time, it was for the need to be doing something. Something that had been left undone.

"What we need is to find somebody who can help you and get us out of these woods. I don't know about you, but I'd like to eat something besides peanut butter."

"I can wait. But Vernon, that can't wait any longer. It's long overdue."

A break in the trees slowly came into view. A hundred yards out, it became clear they had reached the lake. When they finally broke from the trees and stood on the muddy shore, the wide, flat surface of the lake nearly made Carter dizzy after the dense tangle of the trees. It felt as if he could get a deep breath at last.

He looked left and then right up the shore, but saw no structures. No cabins, no fishing shacks, no boat docks.

"The going will be easier, at least," he said. "We just need to pick a direction."

"I know Vernon used to talk about the deeper end of the lake being to the North. That's where the best fishing was."

Chester walked to the water's edge, stepped in with his front paws, and then retreated quickly away from the cold water.

Carter faced North, to his right. "Okay, let's try that."

Carter led and the moving was definitely faster along the shoreline. They moved off the muddy edge and into the first row of trees, but having the open expanse on their left made everything feel easier. In the center of the lake was a small island and Carter could see how this was an idyllic spot for weekend getaways and fishing trips. Nothing like what they were bringing to the lake. They were making crystal clear waters muddy and fetid with death.

They moved ahead quietly, each of them feeling the weight of getting closer and what that meant if they found the shack and if Vern was hiding out there. In any hunt, the moment of anticipation shifted over to the moment of pulling the trigger, and that shift was enough to give a man pause when he was faced with actually making that choice to kill. Many men hesitated, found that they lacked the desire any longer or had to admit they never fully had the desire. Carter thought of the women and the families he saw at the group meeting. He thought of the dug-out pit under the cabin. The dirty mattress and the chains. He thought of the blood on Veronica, a bullet from her own husband. The monster lurking in the woods. The monster that had been living in her house all those years.

The smell of a fire hit his nose at the same moment he noticed a curl of smoke rising above the trees. He called Chester to him, and the dog obeyed. Veronica stopped and watched Carter's face as he zeroed in on the sight and the smell.

"Up ahead. There."

He pointed, and they both looked. Through the dense trees, they could see a small structure. A pipe chugged smoke through the roof.

"That's got to be it," she said.

"You stay here. Keep Chester with you. I'm going to check it out."

DeFore parked behind a grocery store, then took a bus followed by a ten block walk to arrive outside Margot's house. Ditching the car felt like an act of finality. Like he knew he might not return to it. Her car was nicer than his, anyway. It would easily carry him over state lines into a new life.

Now began the waiting, his least favorite part of the job. And this was all part of the job, according to DeFore. Colin had been a liar and had stolen from him. Stole the woman he cared most about in the world. That's a crime worthy of punishment.

And Margot, she lied, she cheated. She broke his heart. Crimes, all of it. And his job is to punish criminals.

He had the clothes on his back, the gun in his pocket, and nothing else, least of all a plan. He only knew he had to see her one last time. What happened then, he would figure out when he saw her.

Her car wasn't in the driveway, no signs of movement behind the windows. Probably still in for questioning. They'd have to let her out eventually.

He brought out his cell phone. One sign-off from a judge and they could use it to track him, if they hadn't already. He dialed Chief Winters.

"DeFore? That you?"

"I don't know what she's telling you, chief, but I bet it's not everything."

There was a pause. No doubt Winters telling someone to trace the call.

"Why don't you come in, and we can discuss it. I'll get your side of it. Where are you?"

"Did she say she was a cheater and a liar?"

"We have her statement. I want yours. I know you, Brian. I know this isn't you."

DeFore watched the house. The house where he slept over. Where he made her breakfast.

"You never know who you are until it's too late, I guess. And it's too late. Damn it, I know I fucked up. But I'm leaving. I won't be any more trouble. And hey, this one goes down as solved, right? No arrest, no conviction, but you know who did it, at least. That's better than most."

"DeFore, come in, and let's talk about it. It's not too late to save this thing."

"Oh, chief, it's way too late."

He ended the call, dropped the phone on the ground, and stepped on it. He twisted his heel on the screen until it cracked, then stomped until the phone broke in two. He took the pieces and threw them down a storm drain, then took up his spot, leaning against a tree halfway up the block.

She had to come home soon.

A trio of fishing poles leaned in the corner of the shack. Vern picked one out.

"I'm hungry."

Dave hugged the back wall of the shack, his rifle in one hand, barrel pointed at the floor. He thought of shooting Vern, getting away while he was injured or dead. But he couldn't bring himself to shoot another man. He wasn't convinced he could get off a shot without Vern shooting first.

"I got a few lures, but we could use some bait," Vern said. "Why don't you dig us some worms?"

"Worms? The ground's near frozen."

"Yeah, shit. Lures it is, I guess. Grab a pole."

"I kinda gotta use the men's room."

Vern laughed. "Men's room? Hell, we're in nature. The world is your men's room."

"Not just a piss, you know what I mean?"

Vern nodded. "Don't do it too close to the shack. And bury it. And while you're digging, look for some worms. You might get lucky, catch some hibernating."

"Yeah, okay." Dave walked out the door, waiting to see if Vern was going to follow him. Vern stepped out, rifle in one hand, fishing pole in the other, and walked toward the lakeshore.

Dave took his opportunity. He walked slowly so as not to spook Vern or tip his hand, but he thought about the route they took to get here. He wasn't sure he could retrace his steps. The two men who had come by ran North along the shore, presumably back to their shack. But he couldn't walk along the shore without Vern seeing him. He needed to head into the woods a little, then cut North. If he could find the other cabin, those men could help, and they wouldn't need much explanation.

"Don't be long," Vern said.

"Yeah. Jesus, though. My guts are churning. You're not feeling it? Maybe something we ate?"

"Tough it out. We'll get some fresh fish. Better than any canned stuff."

Out in the cold, Dave realized how warm the shack had been. The stove did well to heat the tiny square of wood planks, necessary when you're out on the ice.

He gave a few tentative looks over his shoulder, but Vern was focused on the water. Dave had to tell himself not to run. His boots crashing through the woods would alert Vern, and he'd be trying to outrun bullets. Get a hundred yards away from the shack, Dave told himself. Fifty, even, but get away and then turn toward other cabins. Find somebody to help him get out of here and back to real life, not this surreal "guy's weekend" from hell.

It hit him again, the fact that Keith was sitting crumpled under the floorboards of Vern's cabin and that Vern just dumped him there like he was bagging up the trash. He'd been arrested for a reason. They had to have evidence if they brought it to trial. Some anomaly, some loophole the defense found, let Vernon free, but they were right all along. Vern was a predator and a killer, and Dave ate with him, drank with him, fished with him.

He looked back toward the shack, already hard to make out through the trees. He counted his steps, a little further now. He gripped the rifle in both hands, listening behind him for footsteps. He couldn't focus the way he did when he was hunting deer. For the first time, he felt like he knew what the deer experienced. Always so skittish, always on the lookout. Paranoid, to Dave, but now he understood. No place was safe in this world.

The snow had a top layer of crusted ice, and each step came down loud and sharp, but he picked up his pace, not concerned about the noise. Dave was so focused on what was behind him he didn't notice what was in front of him until he stepped into a small open space between two clusters of trees and found himself looking at a woman with a dog. She was bent down, petting the dog on his head, and hadn't seen Dave. For a moment, he thought he should call out to her, get her to lead him to safety away from Vern, but then he realized he was looking at Veronica, Vern's wife, as if this weekend could get any stranger. He ducked behind a tree.

The memory of gunfire and the sound of the reports came back to him, and he recognized the jacket she wore from the cabin. This was the woman who had pulled up in the truck. She was one of the shooters.

He had no idea why or how she was out here in the woods, but it couldn't be good. Dave turned and ran back toward the cabin.

Carter poked his head up from his hiding spot. He'd gotten close enough to hear voices, but not to hear what they said. He ducked out of sight and waited. It had gone quiet for a half minute now. He'd circled to the north side of the shack, about fifty feet in from the shoreline. He could see the structure and the curl of smoke leaking from the roof.

He moved from one tree to another, ten paces closer. He waited. No more voices. He chanced another move, this time closer to shore. Through a break he could see the water, then movement. He crouched down.

A figure stepped to the edge of the water, then climbed on a log that jutted out a few feet into the lake. A bear of a man, Carter knew it was Vernon. He didn't see the other one and assumed he was still inside.

Vern cast a fishing pole out into the lake and stood on the log, watching the water.

Carter was no sharpshooter, but he wondered if he could make the shot from where he was. He lifted the rifle to his eye and struggled to find Vern through the scope. Once he did, there were two trees in his way that he didn't think he could shoot around.

He would have surprise on his side, but only for a moment. Missing wasn't an option, or he could have another sloppy volley of gunfire, like out at the cabin. He needed to be sure he could hit him with the first shot and not give Vern a chance to turn and fire back. He needed to take the shot, eliminate

Vern, then deal with the other one when he came out. *If* he came out. If not, then leave him. He'd be smart to stay put.

Carter picked a tree closer and moved slowly toward it. He went for stealth, not speed, with Vern's attention on the lake. He could smell the wood from the fire and hear the gentle lapping of water on shore.

He reached his intended cover tree and leaned into it. He brought the rifle to his eye again and sighted on Vern's back. Vern, who had his more powerful rifle slung over one shoulder, waiting to fire back at Carter. Vern shifted a few shuffling steps down the log, farther out over the water, and Carter's angle was lost.

He took a few tentative steps to the side, then stopped to see if he'd been heard. He kept his eyes shifting back to the shack to check and make sure there were no surprises. He took three more steps and found cover behind a thinner tree. It wasn't as wide as his body, but would protect most of him from any shots fired his way.

He felt like this would be the one. It offered a clear enough vantage point, and he'd closed the gap by fifty feet. He could hear it when Vernon belched and then spit into the water.

Carter tightened his grip on the rifle, took up the slack on the strap, and raised it to his shoulder. Closer to his target now, it became harder to sight through the scope. Every minute movement shook like an earthquake through the lens. But he found Vernon's back, the wide olive green of his parka like a boulder covered in lichen.

With his thumb, Carter switched off the safety. Then he heard Chester barking.

Veronica fell backward when Chester barked. The dog took three bounding steps away from her, then turned back when she cried out in pain. She looked vulnerable on the ground, her face twisted in agony. Chester walked back to her.

She saw a figure moving away through the trees. A man had been there. Too small to be Vern, she thought, but he was hard to see from so low on the ground and through the pines.

Chester came and licked her hand.

"I'm all right, boy," she said. "You gave me a fright, though."

She didn't try to get up right away. She put a hand to her side, but there was nothing she could tell through her layers of clothing. Her wound had jolted with a sharp sting of pain, but it was to be expected with a fall like that. She didn't think she was bleeding again, but she couldn't be sure.

Chester's head spun quickly back toward the trees, and a moment later, she heard footsteps quickly approaching. She scrambled to reach down to her waist and draw her gun, but it was buried under the layers of her coat, her shirt, and her undershirt. A growl started in Chester's throat, and it erupted into a bark as the footsteps got closer.

"It's okay, Chester. It's me."

Carter came out of the trees, moving as quick as Veronica had ever seen him. Chester's ears dropped from their alert, and his tail began to wag.

Carter rushed to Veronica and bent to one knee.

"Are you okay?"

"Yes, yes, I'm all right."

"That wasn't his regular 'I saw a squirrel' bark."

"There was a man here."

Carter scanned the woods. "Here?"

"He ran off when Chester barked."

"Which way?"

Veronica pointed toward the lake.

"The other guy," he said.

"Dave. I don't think it was Vernon."

Carter knew it wasn't since he'd been holding him in his sights when Chester barked. *And if it had been, you'd probably be dead*, Carter thought. "He's going to warn him." Carter cursed himself for not taking the shot when he had it, but the barking had caught Vern's attention, too, and he had turned around toward the sound, nearly dropping the fishing pole and tumbling into the water. Carter had narrowly ducked away without being spotted, and only because Vern's attention was focused on Chester's warning calls.

"Do you think?"

"Of course. I have to go after him."

"Help me up."

"You're staying here." He took her arm and helped her to her feet. "I found the shack. I know where to find them."

"Is it safe for you to go?"

"All I know is it isn't safe for you. Keep Chester here. I need to try to catch him."

Carter took off in the same direction Dave went, again moving quickly, his breath creating clouds around his head.

Dave wasn't sure what came next. Of all the people to see, she was one he didn't feel he could trust. She and her partner had shot at them, after all. Killed Keith. He could go back to the fishing shack and warn Vern. Maybe see what his take on it was. But he could trust Vern even less. He turned North, aimed for the cabin belonging to Marco and Andrew. He wasn't entirely sure he would ever trust anyone fully ever again, but he had to trust those two for a little while to help him get off this lake and to safety.

Branches whisked past him at eye level, scratching at his skin. He ducked and wove in and out of the trees in a serpentine pattern.

He stepped and heard a branch snap. The bitter cold turned the dead wood brittle, and it cracked like a firecracker. His ankle cried out in pain and twisted, sending Dave to the ground. His rifle leapt from his hands and skidded out in front of him.

Something was definitely wrong with his leg.

A second branch snapped, the sound echoing through the woods. But Dave was on the ground, not moving or stepping anywhere. When a sharp sting of pain dug into his leg higher up on his thigh, he realized it hadn't been a branch. Those were gunshots. The pains he felt were bullets.

Dave rolled onto his back and searched the trees for the shooter. Could it be Veronica? He doubted it, but nothing would surprise him anymore. There was the other man out there, the other shooter.

He realized he didn't have his gun. Hot blood seeped down his leg, and the initial shock rolled away, leaving burning embers of pain in his thigh and down near his ankle.

The sound of footsteps coming closer, not too fast. A deliberate stalking pace.

Dave rolled onto his stomach and began to army crawl toward his rifle. Snow got down his collar and into his shirt, stinging his skin with the cold.

A third shot rang out, more distinct this time. Closer, and unmistakable. He felt the round slam into his back. He went face-first into the snow. He knew then the moment of fear after a deer has been hit, but before it dies. The pain and shock and confusion all wrapped in an inevitable understanding that this is where and how it ends and it was always going to be this way.

Dave managed to lift his head enough to see his rifle still a good ten feet away, harmless as a fallen branch on the forest floor. The footsteps marched closer until they were next to his head. He felt a boot under his shoulder lift him and turn him over on his back.

"God dammit."

Dave cracked his eyes open and saw Vern standing over him.

"God dammit, I thought you were him. What the hell are you doing running like that out here?"

Dave moved his jaw, opening and closing his mouth as if there were words to be said, but nothing came out.

Veronica heard the shots. She'd been here before. No truck this time, but the same explicit instructions to stay put. Then came another shot. Then another. The same rifle. A one-sided fight.

Chester tensed next to her, anxious about the noises and how her attention was focused far into the woods beyond where they could see.

She felt as inanimate and helpless as the trees around her.

"Well, shit."

For the second time, she disobeyed and followed the sound of bullets.

Vern watched the last breath cloud from Dave's mouth. The air cleared, and Dave went still.

He'd heard a dog bark. A dog? Made no sense other than a manhunt. Bloodhounds on his trail. He damn well wasn't going to stand by and let them ambush him. He was going to bring the fight to them. He'd heard the sound of Dave running and saw a flash of movement, and fired without thinking of anything but his own survival.

Only after he flipped him over did he realize he'd shot his last remaining friend.

Look what they made him do. Just like the girls. Whatever black magic they held that made him do the things he did to them. The way they smelled, the way they walked, the way they screamed when he touched them. They liked to tease him. To pretend they didn't like it, but he knew. He knew they wanted everything he did to them.

But he was the predator, not the prey. He wasn't about to stand around in the woods and let them hunt him. He was the hunter.

Vern reloaded his rifle from the loose shells in his pocket, then turned back toward the fishing shack.

A nervous shudder ran through his body when Margot's car pulled into the driveway. This was different than at Colin's house. More doubt, more fear. She got out looking tired. She shut the door and leaned back on the car, put her face in her hands and, drew in a deep breath, then let it out. Her hair had been up in a ponytail and had come partly undone. She held her purse in front of her like an armload of firewood. After her moment of respite, she pushed off of the car and walked to her front door.

DeFore knew the pause, and the exhale were her way of acknowledging the end of one trauma. She'd given her statement, told the police all she knew, and had left it in their hands to catch him. He knew they would have assured her it was a foregone conclusion, and they'd probably have him in custody by the time she got home. Chief Winters likely spoke to her himself to reassure her that it was over and Colin's killer would be found and arrested, cop or no cop.

He waited until she shut the door and then crossed the street to her place. He'd asked her for a key when he thought things were going well. She'd denied him. Looking back, it was one of the first signs that their relationship was unbalanced. He didn't let it deter him, and one morning after he'd slept over, he took her car to go out and get coffee and croissants, and while he was out, he had a copy of her key made. She might have seen it as a violation, but he knew she could trust him. After all, he was a sworn officer of the law.

He waited at the door. He knew her routine. She'd set her things down in a disorganized pile, then head straight for the shower. If she'd been up all night at the station, she'd be dying for one. She showered first thing in the morning, after the gym, after a long day, after sex, after being out of the house at all for more than a few hours.

He gave her a few minutes, then opened the door. It should have felt like coming home, like falling into welcoming arms. Instead, it felt like a stranger's home. A place trying to look comforting and cozy, but actually hiding a cold façade haunted by ghosts.

He could hear the water running as soon as he stepped in. Her purse lay in a pile, half spilled, by the bottom step next to her shoes which she had kicked off, the laces still tied. Too tired to put anything away properly.

DeFore took the gun from his pocket. He climbed the stairs.

The first time he'd set foot on these steps it was to follow Margot up to her bedroom for the first time they made love. His heart pounded then a few beats slower than it did now. In both cases, he knew what came next. He'd experienced both sensations. Sex and death merged in his mind.

Her bedroom door was open, and by the sound of the shower, so was the bathroom door. Still, he walked quietly over her carpeted hallway. Everything in her house had its place. All of it meticulously designed as a showcase for her work as well as a comfortable living space. She never liked being at DeFore's place. He could tell she wanted to give him decorating advice, mostly consisting of, "You should throw that out." He thought it was a sign of how much she liked him that she let him keep his decor, but now he saw it as her not wanting to be bothered with a project she knew she would never finish. He hadn't seen much of Colin's place in the dark and the only memory that stuck in his brain was him recoiling from the shots at the top of the steps and then Margot appearing with her mouth agape.

He knew he could burst into the shower and catch her by surprise, end this all quickly, and the sound of the running water would mask some of the shot, the blood would all wash down the drain. But he couldn't do it. Not yet.

Looking at the bed, a flood of memories filled his head. Even the sound of the shower reminded him of the way she would jump up and rinse off after. She went out of her way to reassure him that it wasn't her "washing off" the sex, but it was just what she did. Always had. He thought it was cute.

Once he'd joined her and tried to get things going again, but she begged off, saying she had things to do.

The water turned off and he felt another nervous tremor through his body. He waited in the hallway until he heard her step out into the bedroom. He turned himself into the doorway.

"Margot."

She froze. She didn't scream, just stood still like an animal caught and confused.

"I had to see you," he said.

Her hair dripped water onto her shoulders. He could see her shiver.

"Brian…"

He couldn't do it. He knew he could never kill her. He loved her too much.

"I'm sorry," he said.

The words made her tense up. A tear fell from one eye and mixed with the drops coming from her hair.

"I just…" he said, "I got crazy when I found out about him. I don't…I mean, why? Why didn't you tell me? Why did you have to sneak around like that?"

Margot still hadn't moved beyond the twitching of her muscles beneath the skin. "Why are you here?"

"Just that. Why? Answer me that, and I'll go. I'll leave forever. I swear."

"I…I don't know."

"That's not an answer."

She sniffed, the tears moving quietly down her cheeks, her nose running. Fear behind her eyes. The air was damp from the shower. She always turned the heat to scalding.

"I don't know, Brian. I was figuring it out."

"You should have told me."

"Okay." She kept her eyes moving to the gun still at his side.

DeFore took a step into the room. Margot backed up. She stood between the bed and her dresser.

"I know I did a bad thing. A wrong thing. I just…I went crazy, I guess. I don't know." He laughed for a moment. "I just said that's not an answer and now listen to me."

She swallowed, then squeaked out the words, "What do you want?"

"I came here to maybe kill you." He saw her flinch, and he quickly explained. "But I'm not going to. I promise. I can't. I love you." He turned the gun toward the ceiling, neutralizing the threat. She still focused on it in his hand, black as the shadow of death.

A single sob caught in her throat. She choked on it, and it set off a flow of tears.

"I'm leaving. I need to, obviously. I want you to know you can come with me."

The fan in the bathroom hummed. She wiped her nose with the back of her hand and then dried it on the towel.

"Come with you?"

"Yes. I don't know where yet."

Her face hardened. The tears stopped.

"Yes. Okay. I will."

He smiled a broken half smile. "You will?"

"What's my life here now? How can it ever be the same?" She looked down at herself. "Can I get dressed?"

"Yes, of course."

When it became clear he wasn't going to leave or turn his back, she dropped the towel and opened the top drawer of her dresser.

DeFore admired her body all over again. They were both middle-aged, past their prime, but she was still sexy as hell. He let the gun drop to his side, his grip loose.

"You made me realize a lot of things, Brian. How the world really is." She snapped on a bra. "You taught me a lot about how people really are deep down."

"You didn't like hearing it."

"But you were right," she said. She pulled on a pair of panties, opened the second drawer down, and started picking through t-shirts. "It really changed my perspective on a lot of things."

"I'm glad. I know they're hard lessons."

"Important ones, though. Did you know you even convinced me to buy a gun?"

Her hand came out of the drawer, and she turned, a brand new, never-fired Sig Sauer in her hand. She squeezed the trigger with a deadly calm. Three rapid shots. They clustered in DeFore's chest on the right side. He fell to the carpet.

Margot dropped the gun, screamed, and ran.

Carter reached the shack and slowed his pace. He panted for breath like Chester on a summer day. He'd heard shots off to the North. Which rifle had fired them, he couldn't know. They were far from where Veronica was, though, and he held some comfort in that.

A pain in his gut that started while he ran grew in intensity.

Not now, not now.

The adrenaline, the fear, like cold air around him, gave him something else to focus on. He turned his mind away from the pain, ignored it until it admitted defeat, and retreated to its hiding place to wait for another opportunity to attack.

He crept to the side of the shack, seeing no one and hearing nothing. The door was shut, and smoke continued to curl from the chimney pipe. On the shore, only twenty feet from the shack, he saw a fishing pole abandoned and resting against the log that jutted out into the water.

Vern was nowhere around.

Carter had choices. He could go after Vern and hope to find him in the trees, or he could wait here and try to ambush him if, or when, he came back. Or perhaps Vern was inside right now, waiting to ambush Carter.

He turned and faced the door. He held the rifle in one hand and reached out for the handle with the other. It was hard to balance the gun in one hand and the length of it almost kept the door out of reach, but he twisted to one side and put a hand on the wooden latch that held the door in place. He tensed his muscles, prepared to fling the door open and dodge to one side in case Vernon came out shooting. In his head, he counted down from three.

A rifle shot sounded, and the wall of the shack splintered, but not from inside.

He jumped, and the rifle fell from his tenuous grasp. A second shot punched the side of the shack, and Carter could tell it came from just North. Vern was so close he could hear the footsteps.

With nowhere else to go, Carter opened the door and fell inside the shack.

He rolled on his back and kicked the door shut. Inside, it was warm and a little bigger than the back of his pickup truck. Carter feared he'd just cornered himself and made an easy target. Two fishing poles leaned in the corner, and with nothing else to grab onto, he picked one up and held it in front of him.

Two bullet holes shone light into the shack, like eyes watching his final moments.

Vern's heavy footfalls sounded outside, slowed, and stopped in front of the shack. Carter knew he didn't have any defense. He put his body flat against the wall beside the door. He swore he could hear Vern's labored breathing outside.

The door handle turned. Carter lifted the fishing pole like a baseball bat.

In a swift motion, Vernon kicked in the door and had the rifle down around his hips, ready to fire. From the side, unseen and unexpected by Vern, Carter swung the fishing pole, and the narrow tip cracked like a whip against his forehead. Vernon leapt back, a red welt of blood opened over his eyes.

Vern nearly tripped over Carter's fallen gun, but he stayed up, both hands tight on his own rifle. Carter had no choice but to charge and swing the fishing pole again, lashing Vern across the arms, hoping he would drop the gun, but he held firm.

Vernon squared up, raised the rifle to his shoulder, the black barrel pointing between Carter's eyes. Vern was beyond the reach of the fishing pole now. Carter had failed. He'd lost the battle and would die not at home, not in a hospital bed, but at the edge of a dark lake with water waiting to freeze.

"Vernon, stop!"

Only one voice in the world could make him heed that command. Vern turned to see his wife, arms extended and a gun aiming at him. And a dog by her side.

"What in the hell?"

"I should have done this the moment I learned the truth about you."

Carter cried out, "No! Don't, Veronica. Don't shoot."

She hesitated. The gun shook at the end of her outstretched arms. Vern held the rifle on Carter, letting it dip to aim at his heart.

"You don't want to do it," Carter said. "Once you do, there's no going back. I don't want that for you. You don't need to carry that with you. You have a lot longer than I do for a burden that heavy."

"Put the gun down," she said.

"I never treated you badly," Vern said "I never lied to you, just never told you about it. I thought you'd hate me."

"You were right."

Carter pleaded with her, "Please. Don't do it. You don't want to be a killer."

"There's never been a man on this earth who deserved it more."

Vernon was close to crying. "She's right." He kept the gun on Carter, but he spoke to his wife. "I'm sorry. For everything I did. I'm sorry. I couldn't help it. It's a sickness. A disease. I know that. I know it was wrong, but I just couldn't…" He trailed off into tears.

Carter ignored the gun pointed at his chest. "Please," he said to Veronica. "Please don't."

At her feet, Chester let out a small whine. He took a few steps toward Carter.

"Stay," he commanded. Chester stopped.

"You stood by me," Vernon said. "All those years."

"I didn't know what you were."

"I'm your husband."

"You're a sick monster. A demon. A devil."

"No, no, no. I never wanted to see you look at me like that. I didn't want to see your judgment for the things I…" He was sobbing now.

"You should be sent back to hell."

Veronica spread her feet shoulders wide, adjusted her grip on the gun.

"Don't do it," Carter said, more of a helpful prayer than a command.

A high-pitched whine came from the edge of the water. All attention went there as the fishing rod spun out the line rapidly, the bait in the mouth of some fast-swimming fish. When the line ran out, the pole leapt from the log and splashed into the water, disappearing quickly.

Carter saw a chance and struck out with the pole in his hands, slashing it down across Vernon's arms again. He charged forward, putting himself inside the range of the rifle, and he bear-hugged Vernon.

Vern cried out, but Carter gripped harder. Vern managed to get the rifle into one hand, firm grip around the stock, and bring it up under Carter's chin. He turned to face Veronica with Carter between them now, a shield against any bullets she would send his way.

Veronica's eyes went wide. The gun wavered and swung to the side, then back again. Anywhere she aimed, she was pointing at Carter.

"I never meant to hurt you. I love you."

Carter said, "Veronica, put down the gun. Just walk away. Take Chester with you. Just go."

"I'm not going to leave you."

"Just don't shoot. You don't want to become a killer. You need to trust me. It will change who you are. Don't let him do that to you."

Veronica trembled in the cold. Tears rolled from each eye and burned cold down her cheeks. Chester barked once. Veronica dropped the gun.

"Good job," Carter said.

"I really never meant to hurt you," Vernon said.

He pushed at Carter and shoved him away. Carter stumbled and went down to one knee. Vernon now had a clear shot at Veronica. There would be no way she could retrieve the gun before he fired. And Carter was still ten feet away. He couldn't stop Vern from firing, but he could try to block it. He pushed up and stood straight, like a tree had suddenly taken root and sprouted up between Vern and Veronica. Any shot would have to make it through Carter first.

Instead, Vernon turned and walked into the shack. He closed the door behind him.

Carter and Veronica stared at each other across the distance, wondering what he had planned for them, when a single shot rang out, muffled by the wood planks of the fishing shack.

Carter exhaled and fell to the snow, first to his knees, then onto his chest. Chester ran to him, licking his face and making small whining noises in his throat.

"It's okay, boy. It's okay now."

6

They made their way North along the shore of the lake. They left the cabin door closed. No need to look inside.

It was slow-moving. After all the exertion and the finality of what had happened, Veronica's body surrendered to her injuries in a way she wouldn't let herself before. She leaned on Carter as they walked, and Carter held on to her, ignoring the shooting pain in his own gut. He didn't dare tell her about it. With each step, it felt like a sharp stick driven deeper into his abdomen, but he held her up anyway.

Chester veered off into the trees, following a scent, and they found Dave face down in the snow. They stood over him for a moment, unsure what to say, so nobody said anything. After what felt like a respectful amount of time, they walked on.

An hour later, a trip that should have taken a third as long, they came to a cabin. Marco answered and let them in. Carter explained that she had suffered an accident and they needed help. He didn't mention Vernon or the gunshots.

After an ambulance was called, Carter called a tow truck and gave them directions to Vern's cabin, told them which truck to tow out. Leave the others. Don't go inside.

The ambulance took her away, but wouldn't take the dog inside. Marco and Andrew gave Carter a ride to the hospital. They seemed anxious to end their time in the woods and return to Minneapolis. Carter thanked them when they dropped him, and he could see a thousand questions in their eyes, but they would have to go unanswered.

Carter fell asleep on a bench outside the entrance to the hospital until an orderly came outside to check on him. He said he didn't think they would allow Chester inside, but the man said he wasn't going to let someone sleep in the cold and that Chester was okay to be in the waiting area.

They brought Carter a bottle of water and put out a bowl for Chester. Both were asleep again within minutes.

Margot spent another night at the police station. She'd run out her front door and into the arms of a policeman who was supposed to be there to watch the house until DeFore was caught. He'd been late for his shift.

She gave her statement, and her home was designated a crime scene, so when they finally released her, she went to a hotel. The department officially apologized and then braced for a lawsuit when she finally got over the shock. Margot wanted to put it behind her, if she ever could.

All the dangers Brian DeFore warned her were lurking out in the world, and the biggest danger of all she invited into her bed.

She felt guilt for how she handled dating two men at once. She hadn't told Colin, either. She wanted to figure some things out. She didn't want jealousy or pettiness. She hadn't counted on murder.

Margot had felt like a fool when she bought the gun. She knew Brian would be proud of her, but she hadn't confessed it to him because she didn't want to see the smug I-told-you-so look on his face.

The gun had been taken into evidence. She told them she didn't want it back.

Captain Winters looked at his roster and tried to think of who he could promote to homicide. No rush. The two latest bodies, everyone knew exactly who the killers were.

Carter spent two nights sleeping on chairs in the hospital waiting area. He went out for cheap food and to get Chester something to eat. His truck was fixed, and the mechanic called it a "minor miracle" that there wasn't more damage. It still cost him eleven hundred dollars.

Carter left Chester in the familiar confines of the truck cab and went upstairs to see Veronica.

"I'll be back. Then we can get home." He petted Chester and scratched his ears. "I know I promised you a cushy life from here on out, and I'm sorry if I misled you. I never meant to put you at risk. You did well, though, old boy. You did well."

Through the lobby and up to the second floor, he moved slowly, his feet shuffling a little. He felt his age more than he ever had before. He knocked gently on her door. The color was back on her face. Her silver hair was spread out around her on the pillow. A set of monitors silently watched.

She smiled when she saw him come inside. "I worried you left me."

"Just giving you space. How are you?"

"Better. Much better. Maybe that's the morphine talking, though." She smiled and gave a glance to her IV line.

"I'm glad we got you some real care."

"The doctors said the wound looked good, given the circumstances. You cleaned it well."

"I'm glad."

"Have a seat."

He sat next to the bed, and she never lost the grin when she looked at him.

He smoothed his hair and crossed one leg over the other.

"Have they…did they find everything?"

"They got an anonymous phone call," he said. "Told them where to find everything. As best as I could remember, anyway. I haven't heard anything about it, but it's not my problem anymore."

"What if they call me and I'm not home? They'll have a record of me being up here in the area."

"No law against getting away from things for a few days. Especially given what you've been through."

"But they'll put two and two together."

He held out a calming hand. "You have an alibi."

She nodded slowly, understanding. They needed each other. Each held a secret now, shared only between them.

"Will I see you again?" she asked.

"I'm not sure. Probably not. I think the best thing is if you forget all of this. Vern moved out and that's the last you ever saw of him."

"And good riddance."

Carter stood. He laid a hand over hers. Both their hands were thin, sharp bones showing, their skin fragile, worn down by time and experience. But they held each other tight.

Veronica kept her grin pasted on, but tears welled in her eyes.

"Thank you, Carter. For stopping me."

"You would have seen it again every time you closed your eyes."

"Thanks for everything. I'm glad you came to my door."

"Put it behind you. Shut the light off on that part of your life. I know what you think, but it's not too late to start over again. Trust me."

She nodded, her hair shifting against the pillow.

"You feel better," he said.

"You give that dog the biggest steak you can find," she said. "And tell him it's from me."

Carter smiled and nodded, then passed through the door.

His house was as cold as a deep freezer. A small pile of snow had gathered inside the open window.

The bird was still inside. Scattered droppings littered the path from the window to the kitchen as if it had made a migration route out of his home.

Carter closed the window and scooped up the snow in a dust pan and threw it in the sink.

"Well, I guess we have a bird now," he said to Chester. He turned on the heat and lit a fire. The bird he found in the kitchen, perched on top of the fridge. It looked at him like he was invading the bird's home, as if all birds lived in a three-bedroom farmhouse on an acre and a half of land.

Carter set out a shallow dish with water on the counter.

"If we're gonna live together, might as well be comfortable."

When he had arrived home there was a slightly wilted bouquet of flowers on his porch. The card was a hand-written string of thank yous from the Barnes family, the man who he saved from a vehicle rollover. Ruben was home now and on the mend, all thanks to Carter, so they said. The flowers were stiff and frozen and half dead. They fit in perfectly, he thought.

He fed Chester and then sat down on the couch. He let out such a sigh of satisfaction at the familiar contours of the couch that Chester looked up from his dinner to see if Carter was all right.

"Just happy to be home, bud."

The fire warmed the house slowly. Carter added another log and sat back down. Chester joined him, still licking his jowls and getting any last morsel of food he missed. The bird came into the living room and chirped once, then settled on top of the bookshelf.

Carter fell asleep to the mix of birdsong and the crackling fire.

The next day, Deena, the nurse from Ken's assisted living home, came by the house.

"I wasn't sure I had the right address," she said when he answered the door.

"You found me," he said. He opened the door and invited her inside. Chester came to greet her, and she petted him on the head.

"What can I do for you? Here to try to recruit me for one of those empty rooms?"

"No. You seem like you have a pretty sweet setup here."

He hoped she didn't take notice of the bird shit. "We get by."

"No," she said, then reached into the deep pocket of her parka. "I was wrong. Ken did leave a book unfinished."

She held out a thin book with a green bookmark jutting up like a shark's fin from the pages. It was a small paperback with a pastoral scene on the cover called *Montana, 1948* by Larry Watson. Carter hadn't heard of it.

"I figured you might want it," she said. "I don't know, it just kind of made me sad sitting there unfinished."

He took it from her. "Thanks."

He flipped to the end. Only a hundred and seventy-five pages. He could manage that. The bookmark sat on page one-twenty-eight. Pretty close.

"I'll start it tonight," he told Deena.

"If you like it, let me know. Maybe I'll read it too. In his memory."

"I'll do that." He looked at the redhead, someone who had done a kindness with nothing to gain from it. A truly selfless act. "Hey, do you like Mexican food?"

They entered Mesa Grande, and Deena immediately said, "Oh, it smells good." Only one other table was occupied since it was early for dinner, but too late for lunch.

"Want to sit at the counter?" he asked.

"Sure."

Ivana saw Carter from the kitchen, and she came rushing out. He was used to her enthusiastic greetings, but this time, she wore a mask of worry. He stopped as he was about to introduce Deena and let Ivana speak what she seemed desperate to get out.

"Carter, did she write you too?"

"Did who write what?"

Ivana wiped her hands on a towel tucked in her waistband. She took a letter from her pocket and held it out for him.

"I was going to come by after closing tonight. I got this in the mail today, just before lunch. I should have closed. I should have come right to see you."

"What is it?"

He took the letter, postmarked in California. No return address.

"It's from Katherine," she said. "It's about Breanna."

Hearing that name for the first time in months, Carter took on the same look of concern. He studied Ivana's face for what kind of bad news he should brace for.

"Katherine says she's in trouble," Ivana said. "She needs our help."

About the Author

Eric Beetner is the author of more than 30 books of crime fiction, thrillers and westerns. He has been a nominee for the ITW award, Shamus Award, Derringer and a 3-time Anthony Award nominee. He's also written over 100 published short stories, screenplays and TV scripts. A former musician he currently works in the TV industry and has received 8 Emmy nominations.

AUTHOR WEBSITE (live link):
www.ericbeetner.com

SOCIAL MEDIA HANDLES (live links):
IG: @ericbeetner
Threads: @ericbeetner
Bluesky: @ericbeetner
Facebook: https://www.facebook.com/eric.beetner

Also by Eric Beetner

There & Back

All The Way Down

Two In The Head

The Year I Died 7 Times

Criminal Economics

Rumrunners

Leadfoot

Sideswipe

The Devil Doesn't Want Me

When The Devil Comes To Call

The Devil At Your Door

Dig Two Graves

Nine Toes In The Grave

White Hot Pistol

Blood On Their Hands

Stripper Pole at The End of The World

Split Decision

A Mouth Full Of Blood

A Grifter's Song: The Sound of Breaking Bones

Guns & Tacos: Burritos & Bullets

With Frank Zafiro:
The Backlist
The Short List
The Getaway List

With JB Kohl:
One Too Many Blows To The Head
Borrowed Trouble
Over Their Heads

www.ingramcontent.com/pod-product-compliance
Lightning Source LLC
Chambersburg PA
CBHW020607110726
47899CB00002B/416